ROBBY

YA LIL BASTARD

Look at me, Mom; I'm on top of the world.

MartyR.

Copyright © 2022 Marty R.

All rights reserved

First Edition

ISBN: 979-8-218-01963-1

Printed in the United States of America

DEDICATION

This book is dedicated to George (Robby) who by his incisive reading and quest for self-education taught me that knowledge was indeed the key.

Gwendolyn, for the caring stability she so lovingly provided. Rita, Theresa and Ray, Georgette, Grace, George Jr., John, Senior and Junior, Oriel, Matthew, Marc, Flora, and Bill (Ace)

To my loving wife and best friend, Marie.

My sincere and humble thanks and appreciation to all the special souls who passed through my life as theirs unfolded, whose advice, stories, experiences, strengths, sadness, and humor, inspired this book.

TABLE OF CONTENT

PROLOGUE		IX
CHAPTER 1	YA LIL BASTARD	11
CHAPTER 2	GHETTO-VER	31
CHAPTER 3	GIT A JAB	43
CHAPTER 4	AM-BITCH-ION	73
CHAPTER 5	THE BROTHER SOLD	85
CHAPTER 6	STREET SMARTS	111
CHAPTER 7	CLIMBING DOWN	125
CHAPTER 8	GROWING NOT GOING THROUGH LIFE	171
CHAPTER 9	MR. PATROLMAN-ME-VERSUS-ME	185
CHAPTER 10	FALL FROM "HIIIIIIIIIGH GRACE"	217
EPILOGUE		265

PROLOGUE

This is a story about a boy's evolution into manhood, from street smarts to intelligence. His street smarts helped guide him out of the ghetto. His intense quest for knowledge and education made his path unique. His accidentally acquired business skills helped shape and make him comfortable.

It is also the story of an organization which became so powerful no one dared to cross them. When they got together, they both grew and learned that sometimes when you get everything you want in life, it may not have been worth the cost.

Experience the journey of being rich and poor, tempted by good and evil. This story is told with wit, masterful insight, humor, and precise analogies. Both were willing to work hard for the success they achieved except when the path to success was suddenly paved with golden opportunities and shortcuts.

They both became ruthless and cunning, but the boy, still deep inside the heart of the man he became, listened to the voices from deep within which kept trying to remind the man of the teachings of all those who tried to steer him toward the good he was exposed to.

Much of what you are about to read was inspired by true events.

CHAPTER 1

YA LIL BASTARD

There stands one sweaty, sloppy, and very stupid twelve-year-old kid, me. Twenty stories above the city of New York on the top of my projects, high above this Harlem ghetto, home of the famous soul-food restaurants, nightclubs, hardworking people, junkies, drug dealers, and beautiful cars. I live on one of the meanest streets in Harlem. I am standing on the top edge of my project roof, standing with my big toe touching the concrete, right through my worn-out sneakers. Not even Converse, these are Condemned All Stars; they were brought at a cheap shoe sale, if you buy the laces, the sneakers were free. At this point I am one with this building. My wits are keen, I am consciously aware of my being. I am feeling an array of emotions, and I am high on adrenaline. I am also excited, exhilarated, and acutely aware of my path, my enviable destiny, yes destiny. I will not exploit the suspense any longer; this is not about suicide. In my mind's eye I can picture the neighborhood crowd later giving me a ghetto ticket-tape parade. That's when everyone throws their losing lottery tickets or number receipts out the window. I would be the first twelve-year-old given such an honor. I have been divinely puppeteered from the collective experiences in my life, to this moment, to be here now, at this time, at this place. I was born to be here; all paths, thoughts, and decisions brought me here to ride this moment's momentum into greatness. On this day I will carve my name in both the minds and hearts of my peers, my neighbors, as well as my enemies. I peer out to take a good look around me; I now summon each of my senses to this precise dimension of reality. My entire body is now on heightened alert, Defcon 5.

I begin to scan the pavement below. Put in the simplest of terms, it is ground zero below me. It is the playground of the Harlem Cultural Projects, I see children playing below. I am too high up to hear exactly what they are saying, and who cares. The girls are jumping double dutch, and the boys are just walking around the playground, most are limping from the money they have to hide in their shoes. In the ghetto most kids had to hide their money in their shoes in order to keep it when the tougher kids search you. When they would approach you they would never say, "Give me your money," they would always say lend me some money. I guess that was the conditioning for the inevitable bad-credit syndrome because they never had any intention of paying it back.

Looking down they seemed like little ants, little black ants, and a few red ones. They are playing games, laughing and having fun, never realizing that they are about to be witnesses to the greatest twentieth story ever told. There are three painted barrels below. Watching the children run in and out of them I say to myself with a certain level of authority, "Ants, definitely ants."

While scanning below, I again take inventory with my newly acquired heightened senses for the last time. I can smell the water from the East River across the street from the building; it has a faint salt smell, with a scant scent of ghetto pepper. The smell was kind of like having an aquarium in a Goodwill store. As I turn my head facing the river, I see the sightseeing boat coming down the East

Marty R.

River. This boat would pass our neighborhood at least three times a day. I could barely see the faces of the people on the deck but heightened from this position. I can see some of the river hawkers standing up on the boat to get a closer look at our project; yes many of the sightseers would stand up when they got to Harlem, as if they were on some kind of Amazon cruise passing a rare native village, with full-grown pygmies. The older folks in my neighborhood referred to this boat as the *Immigrant Love Boat*. Oh yea, back to my mission. All of my senses were now approaching Optimal Readiness Gazing for an Abundantly Swollen Man— (O-R-G-A-S-M)— whichever you prefer. I am immediately jolted back to this plain of reality by a voice behind me. The voice was saying, "Do you see him, is he there? Go ahead. Just do it, man, just do it." I immediately turned my head back around and glanced at the person lying on his belly right next to me. It was my friend Davey. Davey was the person who co-in-spired this moment; we shared this feeling of retribution against our enemy. Davey was on his belly in a much-safer spot on the top of the roof than this fool standing up; he too was watching the ants at play. I could detect the anticipation in his voice, as it went from co-conspirator to cheerleader. Next to Davey was a dirty brown box; it contained some of the materials for my weapon of ass destruction. In the box was the paraphernalia of the instrument, which was to be used to help carve my name in the ghetto legend book of greatness. Inside the box was a big red balloon in case the one I was holding in my hand suffered a service breakdown, from premature anticipation. I was holding its brother in my hand. He was also red and already overfilled with water. It took both Davey and me a half of an hour to fill it with water. It was like being in an operating room with a fickle doctor. It couldn't be too hot or too cold. We filled it up downstairs in my apartment, then we had to lug it up the stairs to the roof. We handled it as if it were a newborn baby that we had both just assisted with its delivery. Once born we tied its umbilical cord to ensure a long, carefree life. We then created a smaller twin just in case. OK, back to this moment.

Robby

I stepped back and knelt down gently, while carefully holding the red child, my child, carefully, and oh so gently. I brought it to my chest where I just cradled it. I then repositioned myself back to my position of advantage, standing up straight again. I could feel the temperature of the water inside my child; except for the sound of the water gushing back and forth hitting the red walls inside, there is silence. I again allowed my toes to scan my position, to the edge of the roof, in anticipation of the coming event. One misguided, hardy sneeze or breeze would have caused me to falloff this roof. I thought that I would probably laugh at my dumb ass on the way down. I could not see our intended target so I broke the silence by asking Davey, "Do you see him?" Davey was now on his knees right next to me. This would have made one beautiful ghetto family portrait, both of us glaring around top to bottom at the ground below us, while I held our child in my arms. Just then Davey screamed, "I see him, he's coming." I quickly zeroed in on the target. There it was, the manifestation of my greatness; it was the housing policeman, who we affectionately called Officer Dumpling, aka Flub a Dub. He was making his usual rounds. Officer Dumpling was sort of a robust fellow, much like Friar Tuck in the *Robin Hood* novel. Dumplings was a big man, five by five, whose uniform never quite fit him. He had these very large legs, which were not quite set right, they were awkward. The sides of his inner thighs would always rub together whenever he walked. Whenever he entered your space you would hear his thighs rubbing together. On a hot or humid day one could actually smell his garment cloth burning between his thighs by friction. I've never seen him from twenty stories high before. He still looked big from up here. It was like looking at a walking target with a black bull's-eye. He was waddling and swaying from side to side. Just a head on a body with the mannerism of a penguin tilting from side to side, walking in his usual slow pokey manner. It was like watching a wave in the ocean. I could see his large head looking in every direction, watching everything in his path, observing everything going on, as he waddled like a bowlegged penguin straight to our direction.

Marty R.

I now became severely aware of the red child in my arms. We now shared the same body temperature. My child was heavy and somewhat wet. I glanced down and looked at it in my arms. I nearly lost my balance for a second, but the pending inevitability of great-ness helped me stay straight and level; it was as if tiny gyroscopes were divinely inserted in the bottom of my worn, torn sneakers through one of its many holes which kept me grounded. Officer Dumpling waddled closer toward our direction, very confident of his standing in our community. He was in charge and knew it; he was saluting old ladies with his nightstick, bowing his large head to the hardworking men getting home from work, putting the evil eye on the children playing, as if he was trying to implant his divinity in their minds. I bet you're wondering the reason for this caper, or as I like to call it, going after "fat on this hot tin roof." What drove me and Davey to this moment, you wonder.

Well, just two days prior to this, Dumpling was solely responsible for another friend of ours to be placed in a juvenile detention center for something so trivial, so stupid, it hurts my heart to even think about it. Tooths was our friend, our partner, one of the boys. He got his name by having one really extra-large front tooth that he would gladly show. One day we were hanging out with the gang all sitting in the staircase listening to each other's belly rumble from hunger, whenever there was a lull in the stories we used to tell each other, which were lies about our misadventures. Tooths, whose belly was always blessed with a hearty meal nightly, because his father had a profession. His father was a man who created with his hands daily, a person of standing in our community, a person we saw when we had to give a boost to our self-esteem. Tooths's dad was a barber.

Tooths was the one telling us a story, and as he spoke, he could hear our stomachs talking back to him. It was as if he spoke hunger pangs fluently.

He stopped his story and said, "Give me whatever pennies you have and follow me friends, I'll get everyone something to eat." Tooths then shared with us his plan to feed the masses; with some hot dog, the plan was brilliant. In our neighborhood there was a short Italian man who had a hot dog cart on the corner every Friday and Saturday afternoon. Fridays were usually payday in the ghetto. For those who worked, this hot dog cart was the closest thing to going out to dinner that was available in our neighborhood. Well, this being a Friday, Tooths went up to this ghetto entrepreneur, jingling some loose beer bottle caps in his pocket; it was mixed with the few of the pennies that he had just collected. So, along with the soda bottle caps and an arrogant attitude, he gave the sound and appearance of a man of means. He strutted over to the cart, as if he was going to partake in this culinary fixture. Nunzio was the name of this fine establishment. Nunzio was known for never giving out a free sample. No matter how many times we would beg for a hot dog on credit, he would refuse. We could stand in front of him crying for one hot dog to share with ten others, our bellies could be rumbling in unison, and he would not give us one piece of stale roll. He would only issue one swipe of mustard per dog, and if someone would ask for more he would just spread the same swipe out. He wasn't prejudiced or anything like that. He was what white America would call a shrewd businessman who looked at his bottom line. Nuzio would exploit his Italian heritage when it was to his advantage. If you asked for something free or even more of something, all of a sudden he couldn't understand English. Nunzio made a good living selling to the cab and bus drivers on First Avenue. For a slight fee he would also keep the beer cold for the Dominicans who use to have a full-time job playing dominoes on that corner. If Nunzio gave a piece of the leftover stale bread to the pigeons the piece had to be so rotten you could best believe that he was vaccinating them against polio. Nunzio made enough money from Dumpling alone on his paydays to support his ghetto investment. Whenever it was Dumplings pay-day Nunzio made sure he was well stocked, The adults referred to it as the law of supply, and da man.

Crime peaked when it was lunchtime and payday, during Dumpling's patrol shift. You could have snatched a woman's pocket-book and got away with it, unless you were stupid enough to take it to Nunzio's and make an order while Dumpling was eating. Anyway, Tooths stood before Nunzio on this day with the smile that earned him his nickname. He confidently said, "Friend give me your finest, with everything on it" as he rattled the caps and pennies in his pocket. Nunzio bought it hook, line, and sinker. Nunzio's creation was spectacular, even from our vantage point in the bushes across the street. Yes I am here to tell you it was stupendous, magnificent, a virtual feast on a bun. Nunzio even took his time and seemed to cut and groom the sauerkraut. As it neared completion one could clearly see that this was a symbolic tribute to Tooth's father, Nunzio applied the mustard like a great painter spreading the finishing touches in hieroglyphics design. Tooths slowly reached in his pocket just when the fruit of Nunzio's labor was being pushed directly in front of him and like a Lizard's tongue on a fly he quickly snatched the creation out of Nunzio's hand. He then ran like a gazelle, without dropping a strand of kraut. Nunzio being the businessman he was, and not wanting to lose one dime to thievery, he abandoned his cart and took off after him. You may ask why a shepherd would leave his flock to chase one runaway sheep. I guess he figured that it was still daylight and that the older adult domino players, and shopkeepers would watch his cart. *Wrong.* Things being as they were no logic or loyalty in the game of ghetto poker. We then pushed the cart into the nearest buildings hallway. I see a lobby of the nearest building hallway right into the lobby. I see your friendship, and I raise you ghetto culture. The shopkeepers took it as a sign that they could now sell more food; they were mostly the same nationality as the domino players, and cultural obligation exceeds friendship. The other adults just laughed and watched as we pushed the cart into the hallway of the nearest building behind us. Yes we immediately gave the beer keeping cold in the cooler back to the Dominicans; we paid them the homage to ensure their silence. We all feasted on Nunzio's food until the only thing that was left was frankfurter-colored water. Even some of the adults that Nunzio thought would cover his back came inside for a snack. It was like watching piranha devour a hot dog cow, a virtual eating frenzy. This was my first encounter with the term *cultural obligation.* Everyone kept their mouths shut if we shared. We were all very full on franks rolls and soda, and after our most splendid meal, someone belched and said, "Hey let's go and find Tooths to thank him." No, we did not save him any of our meal; we knew that he got away with the hot dog he snatched. There was no money on the cart. Nunzio, being the businessman that he was, kept his cash in his pocket. We all figured that Tooths being part ghetto jackrabbit simply gave Nunzio the slip and was probably at home thoroughly enjoying his meal. Later that evening we heard the news that Tooths was indeed fast, he just wasn't lucky. As Nunzio chased him, yelling "Stop, thief," they ran right past Dumpling and close enough for Dumpling to get a good look at both Tooths and the hot dog he was holding. Dumpling wasn't concerned about chasing anyone; that could have given him third degree burns on his thighs. That evening Dumpling and Nunzio paid Tooths's mother and father a visit. Nunzio made a positive ID. I heard that the dollar amount that Nunzio placed on his entire inventory of hot dogs and soda was more money than he made all year. It was because Tooths's father was employed and a Muslim, and he would have done anything to save his son from jail. He would have agreed to pay back double the amount. Even if they were pork franks.

Although Tooths's father put it in writing that he would pay back every cent Dumpling still issued him a Juvenile Delinquent (JD) card, the following day Tooths lost his famous grin. He was taken to court, and the judge told his parents to bring him the following day to the juvenile detention center where he was to spend six months. Nunzio was at the trial hoping they threw the book at Tooths, and he was mouthing the words in Italian: "Hang him, burn him, give him some gas, let the electricity flow through his ass." Before Tooths was taken away he managed to give a revolutionary speech in the stairwell of our building. It sounded much like a cross between Marcus Garvey, Martin Luther King and Malcolm X. He said, "Don't remember me as a man who stole hot dogs, remember me as a man who tried to feed the hungry." It was simply moving. That night we all held a kangaroo court. Dumpling was charged with contributory negligence for being able

Marty R.

to ID Tooths. He was given a fair and just trial and was found guilty. He was sentenced to six hours in a stuck elevator. We would call in an emergency from the top floor and then wait for dumpling to respond. When he entered the old, dilapidated elevator a group of us would then run out of the stairwell and kick the elevators door after it closed. This caused the car to become disabled. As the alarm sounded we would pry open the alarm box located above the door and disconnect the wires. Dumpling only yelled for help for a minute or two before he became tired and went to sleep. Escaping through the hatch at the ceiling of the elevator was not even a dismissed option. Even if he could jump up to reach the trap door and made it, he would have needed a shoe-horn and a gallon of pork fat to fit his bloated butt out of it, and if he missed the trap door the impact of him coming down may have caused the elevator car to fall. Justice was served in the gang's mind, but not for me, being the defense attorney for Tooths in our mock kangaroo court, I thought that he got off too damn easy. I used to go to Tooths's house on Sundays after his family returned from the mosque and fill up on bean pie and ice cream, no pork whatsoever. Tooths wasn't even allowed to watch Porky Pig on television. So as far as I was concerned, Dumpling's punishment did not fit the crime. He just went to sleep in the elevator, and by the time he woke up someone called the office to fix the broken elevator. So in legal terms, hence, therefore, subsequently that was how we wound up here on the roof.

The young men in our group were just like the kids anywhere in the world. We had our good times and bad times, we had seasons for all the different things we would all do. Our group had kite season, spinning-top season, roller-skate season, and so on. Officer Dumpling was now approaching ground zero. As he got closer I couldn't see his legs; from this angle looking down, if he only had a red hat on, he would have looked like a giant bull's-eye floating toward its target. The waddle was still present, but without any lower-body movement he now looked like he was floating on water, you couldn't see his legs or feet. I remember thinking, what a

Robby

funny-looking sight. It looked like a slow-motion scuffle-board game. When he got to where the janitors were sweeping the walkway, it looked like an aerial view of a curling tournament. Once again Davey positioned himself on his stomach; we were now communicating telepathically. It was time to let go of all of my earthly consciousness, let go of all that I knew to be true. It was time to become one with my big wet red son. I leaned my head back slightly and positioned my eyes looking up out of the top of my head. I was now as close to the edge as one could be without falling off. I heard Davey say, "Be careful, man," but I wasn't sure if it was words or heavenly thoughts that I was picking up. I looked like a little black gargoyle, like the kind I would see on the buildings down-town. Yes a Harlem-styled gargoyle holding a red child in his arms, with holes in his sneakers. All powerful, and all knowing. Dumpling is now floating in the perimeter of ground zero. For a brief moment I stopped to daydream. I am being carried on the shoulders of my friends, and the crowd is cheering me. I am being carried above the crowd and some are laughing at the holes in my sneakers. They were all celebrating; it was Harlem's equivalent of pitching a perfect game. It is time; Dumpling is floating practically beneath me. He is now on the walkway, which leads to the building's entrance. He is tip-ping his hat, greeting the elderly people whose job it was to occupy the benches in the neighborhood daily. I now begin to position my rubber red son; it is now away from the safety of my chest and into the palms of my hands, which are cupped. I feel a slight twinge of guilt over the pending loss of my son, but I also fully understand that this is the reason for whence he came into this world. I can feel my heart beating through the water. I hear my son speaking to me. I can now speak and understand balloon fluently. He is whispering, "I will make you proud dad, I will do you proud." I place my right wide-open hand on its behind. I gently lift it near to my face and gently kiss it. Dumpling is now a few steps from being directly underneath me. I take one last look at his position. I half close my eyes and take one last look at my red boy. I remember thinking, "Behold, my son, for who I am well pleased." I gently push my son away from my face and drop my arms. The motion was like a three-year-old throwing a basketball for the first time. It was a reverse rowing motion. I heard the water inside my son bid me a fond farewell. I then heard Davey sigh. I was immediately filled with a strange sensation of guilt during the first few seconds of its descent, as it floated away from me. I felt a pang of panic at that precise moment as I thought for a second, my baby, my child, what have I done, but I knew that I had to eventually let it go, it had its own purpose in this life to for fill and for a brief moment I understood what most parents understood and that was that too much love is hate, I had to let go. I stepped back from the edge and watched it. I looked in Davey's direction, we made brief eye contact, and then quickly looked back at our red kamikazee. There was only silence. I got kind of dizzy looking down at it but was occupied with anticipation, so I dropped to my knees next to Davey looking down. Reality started coming back; this was the first time I realistically thought to myself with conviction, damn I really could have fallen off and killed my dumb ass self.

The red boy just dropped, no it soared, I suppose it could have been the heartfelt emotions I had but I could swear that it glided as it descended. I felt an overwhelming feeling of pride. I was totally convinced that the only thing that my red child wanted to do was to please me and have the world know that I was the father. I muttered with a feeling of pride and admiration, "That's my boy." We watched it for what seemed like hours in a still silence, both of us engaged in the moment. Again we caught each other eyes and smiled but only for an instant. We had that look of two proud parents watching their child at the Olympics going for the gold. From my position it looked like I was off target by a few feet. I kept changing the position of my head to make it look like a hit. You know, like people in a bowling alley who tilt their heads to make it look like they threw a strike, when they really know the ball is off course and headed for the gutter. I was on my knees, and Davey was still on his stomach. Then suddenly it happened: the world was back at regular speed, and Dumpling had reached ground zero a few steps from the front door. He was about to extend his arm for the door, and the baby locked right on him. My heart started beating fast, it was like the red boy had a homing device, I mean homely device in it. Now I had a bird's eye view, and it looked like a real possible bulls eye. From my vantage point I saw a big fat round blue target, with a tiny red dot in the middle. The red dot grew smaller and smaller. A smile broke out on my face; I knew that this would either be a direct hit or one hell of a glancing blow. I began counting backwards: 3 ... 2 ... 1 ... SPLAT! a direct hit, a one in a million shot. The last thing I saw was dumplings hat fly off while his head snapped back, the water around him seemed to glisten. For a brief moment I could have sworn I saw the water cause a small rainbow around him. All of the people on the benches turned to his direction, and I could hear the faint sound of old people laughing. I looked at Davey who was already looking at me with a crocodile's smile on his face. I immediately saw in his eyes a light gleaming something that I immediately recognized: respect, admiration, and pride.

    I fell straight backward while Davey rolled over on to his back. The world belonged to us for that brief moment, laughter bellowed throughout the entire neighborhood. We were both on our backs looking up at the heavens, I was laughing as if a feather infiltrated one of the many holes in my sneakers. A bright beam from the sun seemed to shine directly on the two of us, we just couldn't stop laughing. Soon we realized that it was now approaching the time to get up and run the hell away from here. Our entire getaway was planned and rehearsed. We planned to open the roof's door and haul our now serious asses away; we just couldn't stop laughing long enough to execute it, the moment was too perfect. Who wanted this moment to end? Every time we would try to get up, we would think of Dumpling waddling sideways after he got hit, and we would fall back down howling. I was the first one able to get out a spoken coherent word; it was "Come on, Davey, we better get out of here."

    Even though we were assured that the elevators in our building were as slow as molasses in the winter, I still felt that it was time to scat. I again began saying

"Let's get out of— " but no sooner than the word here had left my mouth, the metal doors to the staircase flew open as if they had been blown apart. BANG! This was the only entrance or exit to the roof. Behind it stood a wet, panting, extremely angry Officer Dumpling. He had no hat on his head but had his nightstick in his hand. This large, robust, flub-a-dud, jovial round fellow managed to get his oversized carcass to run up twenty flights of stairs in about thirty seconds. I can just imagine the sound that his pants made. The clothes near his inner thigh were smoldering; he was breathing like a fish out of water, trying to swallow air and gasping for breath. His eyes were full of hatred glaring at us, and hate was even radiating from his nightstick. Needless to say, our laughing suddenly, abruptly, stopped. Davey and I again locked eyes and in falsetto harmonic unison mumbled the words "OOOOOOOH CRAP." I heard my mother's voice, repeating her favorite saying, "Son, there are three things that you must always remember in life: there is *do*, *don't do*, and *overdo*." We relished our moment a little too long. We went from *don't do* to *overdo*.

Dumpling still couldn't speak. I prayed that he would be stricken with a heart attack. I suddenly felt no kindred to any damn red balloon. I looked at Davey; he looked like a person alone on a deserted island for twenty years who was suddenly awakened by a damn surprise party. We were both sure that we would both soon travel the path of that damn, no-good, bastard balloon. A tear that was in my eye wanted to get a better look at Dumpling but had no need, want, desire nor ambition to travel the long trip downward to the pavement below, so it quickly jumped out my eye and ran down my cheek. Davey's tears had already acquired ringside seats. We were now both crying as Dumpling began to stagger toward us, I was trying desperately to reconnect to my earlier state of consciousness and telepathically communicate with Dumpling's heart to please stop beating. But all of my acute awareness and power of concentration were gone. I was like Samson with a damn crew cut. This once magnificent gargoyle was now reduced to a sobbing black fool who was about to be thrown off the roof.

Dumpling reached out his tree-trunk arms and grabbed us both, placing his hands with his fat fingers behind our necks, squeezing the hell out of us. He then pulled our shirts by the neck as if he wanted to snap our necks, both the buttons on our shirts popped, and our shirts were now opened at the neck, the few buttons still holding on were pulled up to our shoulders and were now choking us. I looked at Davey one last time to say goodbye but his eyes were closed. Mine were wide open as we both realized that this might well be our final moments on this planet. But wait, just then I could see people looking out of their windows at us, in the building across from us. They were looking directly at us. Yes the benevolent lord and savior had given us just what we needed at that moment, the second best thing to Dumpling having a heart attack. Witnesses.

I still couldn't breathe well with his choking me with my shirt, but at least I was feeling pretty confident that he wasn't going to kill us by throwing us off the roof. Yet I wasn't entirely sure that he wasn't trying to choke us to death. I suddenly heard a tiny faint voice inside of my head, it sounded like Dumpling's inner voice requesting my heart to stop beating. Dumpling began to violently shake us. He was coughing like crazy, but now he was coherent. He began to yell, "Ya lil bastards! Ya lil bastards!" Davey's eyes were still shut; I could see that we were still standing very close to the edge. Suddenly it was much too close now for my comfort. I tried backing up away from him just in case temptation had gotten the best of Flub-a-Dub, who was still shaking us on every syllable he spoke. He was still shaking us while uttering the phrases "Ya lil bastards, ya lil bastards!" Man he was angry. For a moment I thought that I was hallucinating. He began to look like the damn crazed Black Santa Claus who got stuck in the chimney and thought he caught the kids who blocked his access to the house, and the cookies left on the table. Dumpling was big, black, red, and sweating. There was a big vein sticking out from the middle of his forehead. It looked like a cross, a wrinkled, crooked cross. I now took his anger to mean that he wasn't going to kill us, but I thought, *Man, us two boys got one*

Marty R.

sincere ass whipping coming up.

He was still shaking, still reciting, and now spraying us with Dumpling sauce flying out his mouth, as he better pronounced the *b* in *bastards*. I looked down and the last button on my shirt looked up at me and said, "What the hell, you got my ass at John's Bargain Store, I never signed up for this crap." POP! Now I began to wonder how long was he going to shake and choke us. I remembered *do, don't do,* and *overdo.* Mind you I then thought, *If this is some macabre way of relieving stress and anger, then by all means choke me, man, choke on.* The tears on Davey's face were now having a relay race. I was trying to get his attention to assure him in my expression that it's all right, he's not going to kill us, because if he was we would have died already. I wanted Davey to look at the buildings and see the witnesses. But Davey's eyes remained tightly shut. I think that he was deep in prayer. Suddenly I was made aware of a highly curious occurrence. As Dumpling yelled, "You li'l bastards," Davey's mouth began to lip sync the words with him. Holy crap I thought, Davey was totally under Dumpling's spell. It was like watching a crazed puppeteer and his slave puppet. Dumpling was in total control of Davey's will, as if they were now both calling me a li'l bastard in unison. I wasn't really caring what they were saying. I was still alive, and by all indications I was going to stay that way. Survival was the only thought in my mind. Who the hell cared what words were being said at this time? I was just thankful that I was able to hear them.

Dumpling was now getting back in control of his breathing. I'm not saying breathing normally because he always sounded as if he had a stuffed-up nose to me. I could still hear him wheezing. Dumpling looked me directly in my eyes; I was still looking at the cross on his forehead. He said very forcibly and with complete authority, "Where do you live, boy? What's your name? You li'l bastard." My mind was now racing one hundred thoughts per second. I couldn't believe that he didn't recognize me. He had chased me out of the stairwell in this building at least a thousand times in the past. Either he must be really pissed off, or my fear of being killed must have really transformed me into someone else. I was thinking now that if I lied about who I was, I would get an ass whipping from Dumpling. If I told the truth, I would get an ass whipping from my mother.

I was instructed time and time again to never go up on the roof of this building, let alone to stand on the edge to throw something off it. My mother was at home, and she saw me breath liquid life into that damn red bastard balloon. When she asked what I was going to do with it, I said that I was going to the playground. At this point all of my illusions of greatness were now gone. I now was in the survival instinct mode, and I realized that an ass whipping from Dumpling was my best shot, because after he was finished, it would be done and over. Old girl's anger would linger. So with tears in my eyes and the saddest face I could muster, I replied Brown, John Brown. I heard about him in school and what he did for the black people. If he could get me out of this crap, he would be my hero for life. I looked into Dumpling's eyes. He was still not recognizing me; he shifted his eyes to Davey. I took a deep breath and thought he bought it, and I breathed a sigh of relief. He then shifted his eyes back to me as if he forgot something; he then again asked where I lived, and I suddenly remembered that the Nugents who lived on the thirteenth floor of my building always worked and were never home. Between the two of them, they had about seven jobs.

I replied, "The thirteenth floor." He brought that too. It was now up to Davey to lead him astray. I prayed to the Lord to please give Davey the strength and the will to lie. When you're afraid you will ask the Lord for anything. Dumpling's attention now turned to Davey. He was still choking Davey, and his eyes were still shut, when dumpling asked him the same questions. He loosened his grip from Davey's shirts to give him a chance to respond. "What's your name, and where do you live?" To my sheer amazement, once again in unison with Dumpling, Davey mouthed the words that Dumpling said without even looking at him, when he added "You li'l bastard." Now I was worried. Davey was seriously under Dumpling's spell. I tried telepathically to talk to Davey. I was saying,

"Davey, my brother, we're halfway home. Now I know you can lie, just think of a good one now just open your eyes and look at me, Davey. Please, friend, just think half the crap was now brought and bagged. Just give him the rest and close the sale."

Now the truth was that I lived on the tenth floor, and Davey lived directly above me on the eleventh. I prayed again even harder this time. "Oh Heavenly Father, creator of heaven and earth, please give my friend the strength to tell a lie in this, his hour of need."

Just then, Dumpling gave Davey a violent shake, as if he had telepathically intercepted my prayer before reaching Davey, and wanted to mix up the words before they entered Davey's head. He repeated his questions. "Your name ya lil bastard." Davey slowly opened his eyes like a newborn baby taking his first look and breath of life. I was still praying silently, and mentally, praying for Davey to look at me. His eyes looked like blood in the snow. My eyes wanted Davey to know that I had asked for and received special divine permission for him to lie, which would not go against him come Judgment Day. But Officer Dumpling, skilled in the art of interrogation, and sensing that Davey was taking entirely too long to answer, he released Davey's collar completely then grabbed the front of his shirt. He pulled Davey directly toward his face until they were face to face, nose to nose. He looked in the eyes of his hypnotized puppet and repeated a third time with finality in his voice, "I'm talking to you, boy."

Davey never even glanced my way he was looking at Dumplings bottom lip which was now quivering. Davey slowly began to speak. "My name is George, George Robinson," Davey answered. Davey did it, he lied as I did, but I could not rejoice. I was not able to share the joy of the moment with him. Davey then shut his eyes and dropped his head. You see, my partner in crime did close the sale; my friend and my ace boon coon did indeed lie. But the truth was that it was my name he gave Dumpling, and in the next sentence the address he gave was mine also. Life lesson number one: never ask the Lord for permission to sin. Yes, my prayers were answered, but the karma associated with it was a bitch.

Davey then proceeded to give Dumpling my apartment number. Oh the severe price one pays in the quest for that elusive thing known to common men as "glory," the trials and tribulations one must suffer in fleeting, hopes of achieving it. Dumpling walked us down to the twentieth floor to catch the elevator. He was again holding us around the collar. I mean, where the hell could we have run to in the damn elevator? I was now very confused and afraid. I wanted someone on the outside to kick the damn elevator door so it got stuck, but the thought of being stuck in here with the anger of the balloon-wet Dumpling and his crazed turncoat puppet quickly passed.

During our brief ride downstairs, Davey finally opened his eyes to look at me for a second. He had a severe crap-eating look on his face. He slightly lifted his shoulders, and a wave ran down both arms to his hands, with a look on his face that said, "Hey, take a picture with me looking beyond stupid, for the *Asshole of the Year Magazine.*" I mumbled and looked back with a facial expression that said, "Shut the hell up." The elevator doors slowly opened on the thirteenth floor.   Just as I planned, no one was home, but I didn't feel lucky. We then walked down the stairs to the tenth floor, with those swollen nubs still around our necks. When the staircase door opened, I could hear the sounds of the tenth-floor hallway. I could hear my mother's voice on the telephone. I also heard the rustle of Dumpling's pants rubbing together. At that moment, I couldn't imagine why I didn't want to get thrown off the roof. As we got closer to the door, flying down to the pavement wasn't such a bad idea.

I could hear mothers voice was laughing loudly; the phone was in the kitchen right by the front door. I turned around to look at Davey who was on the other side of Dumpling but slightly behind me, but all I could see was Dumpling's belly. I couldn't even see the hallway. As we reached the door, my body was drowning in an array of emotions: betrayal, fear, disappointment. I was a one-man's Shakespeare play. As we reached the door, Davey now appeared right next to me. One thing was now abundantly clear to me, and you didn't have to have been clairvoyant to see it. I was standing on the threshold of catching holy hell. Dumpling now stood behind me and mother in front of me behind the door. Dumpling took his night-stick and banged on the door. My mother's laughter now became a voice of major concern. "Who's that?" she yelled. She now had the sound of startled curiosity in her voice. I could hear the other apartment doors on the floor open in response to that horrific knock.

Officer Johnson, aka Dumpling, replied, "The police." I turned to look to see how many other people were watching, but all I could see again was protruding belly, plenty plenty belly. When my Old Girl opened the door, she stood frozen; she looked at me and then straight at Dumpling. Flub a dub told her the story. She just stood there looking at him, but when the word roof was mentioned, she started staring at me. I borrow

ed the look I saw Davey flash in the elevator. When he was finished telling the story, he offered her Davey. She screamed, "He isn't mine, this one here is mine!" That was followed by a slap in my head that made the bells at the Vatican chime. I literally felt a wad of wax fly out my other ear, I remember hoping that it hit Davey. I could faintly hear the neighbors who were looking out their doors laughing, like the idiot Romans watching the gladiators die in the arena.

Dumpling, who may have been mad that I lied, smiled when he knew that Old Girl was on an ass-kicking roll, so he said, "I'll come back later and explain what will happen to him next." He asked her where Davey lived and what was his name. She gave up everything. She looked down at me as she was talking and gave me one of her world-famous "take-off punches," as if her hand was a plane and my head was the damn airport runway. Dumpling then said, "You two need to finish your business," interpreted, that meant "Kick the crap out of him, lady." I then felt another plane land on my head. When he walked away, the door closed, and I was bracing for a slew of emergency landings, I thought I was about to get a north, east, west, and south ass whipping, just as sure as a pigs private parts were still pork.

Robby

When the door closed, just the opposite occurred. Old girl grabbed me, held me tight, and cried like a baby she said, "boy, why? what's wrong with you? Don't you know you could have gotten killed if you had fallen off that roof?" She just held me and rocked back and forth as she cried like a baby. I felt really bad that I caused her so much pain and really lucky to be in her arms at this point. My mind finally went blank. I didn't care about the next happening or anyone's reaction to this mess. I just basked in the moment, lovingly tucked in her arms.

CHAPTER 2

GHETTO-VER

Although he didn't take us down to the station since Dumpling assumed that justice was handed down by Davey's parents and my mother. I later heard that Dumpling stood outside Davey's door laughing at Davey, yelling as his parents went after him like master dealing with a runaway slave. One lady down the hall from Davey said that from where she was standing he looked like a ton of licorice Jell-O in an earthquake; we both did get juvenile-delinquent cards. This was just another curve ball in a long list of strikes about to come my way. I was getting in trouble on a daily basis, not for really bad things, just stupid mischievous crap.

Davey and I were demanded to appear in court. Somehow, in spite of all the trouble it caused me, the lasting memory of seeing Dumpling at the door on the roof, soaking wet and panting for air, was getting funnier and funnier by the minute. I may have thought it was funny, but I put my poor mother through holy hell. My mother, who I called Old Girl, was always in my corner. She was a mulatto, raised by her two parents who emigrated here from Barbados. She had a powerful sense of family instilled in her. Whenever she was inspired by sincere emotions, which beckoned her to say "I love you," she would sing the words, wrapped in a copyrighted melody straight from heaven to her. "I love you" was the greatest thing she had to give, and I heard her sing her song constantly. Her love was sincere and unconditional. To Old Girl, love was a reward within itself.

She adored her family and thought that her father was God's mold for the perfect man. To Old Girl love was what it was its soul was manifested in three words. "I love you" shot straight from her heart, and her heart would ring when inspired, which reflected the essence of her soul. Yeah, my Old Girl was the best, but as many women who try to see the best in life, Old Girl was vulnerable. I later developed my philosophy that some women in our society are stigmatically conditioned for emotional failure. How, you ask? Well, it's the damn dolls, the ones given to little girls, and all those stupid fairy tales young girls grows up with. Phrases like "they lived happily ever after." Bull. This helped create an illusion that can never become real for many women, not in this fairy castle called "ghetto land." One has to know how to truly love one's self before one can bestow that kind of love on someone else.

I am not saying that there aren't those kind of women in the ghetto who won't put up with any crap in their life and won't allow anyone to mistreat them, but they are rare especially in young people. As for that damn doll young women are given, it conditions a young female to give love no matter how raggedy the doll gets, no matter how dirty or torn up it becomes, and it gives back nothing in return. Yes, a doll was man's greatest creation. It conditions a girl to just give and not to get, a doll just takes no matter what and it conditions the female child not to expect anything in return. A doll doesn't bring anything to the damn party. I rest my case. Old girl wanted to marry a man who could be a strong, positive, loving male figure for her children, like her father, which sometimes caused her great pain looking into the souls of some of the shady characters in the ghetto. In the ghetto, and I guess on this planet, there are many male chameleons who become what the moment calls for; its evolution in its rawest form. Good men are especially hard to find for one as pure, open, and honest as my Old Girl was; she was conditioned for the pickings by immigrants who saw the best in people and the inventor of the doll. You know how some women will try to be the psychiatrist when they should be the hypnotist. A psychiatrist tries to understand the cause of one's actions, what makes a person do the things they do. They ask a smoker, "Why do you want to smoke? What caused this need."

Yeah most women want to be the psychiatrists and try to under-stand the man's faults, to try to help to change them, when they would save themselves a lot of unnecessary heartache by being the hypnotist. The hypnotist doesn't care why the hell you do what you do, they simply command you to stop it, and I mean now. The bot-tom line is that these slick kind of people quickly become the kind of person that the sincere lover believes that they are, at least for a little while. The damn doll-conditioned girl then endows them with all of the attributes that the illusion of true love can create. My mother was a woman of strong family values, instilled by my grandparents. My grandmother Nanny was a strong black woman full of pride and dignity. The kind of person whose very natural appearance was her makeup. She was endowed with what God thought was important to endow true believers with. She was short, dark skinned, with her hair cut short to the scalp, and chubby, not fat— chubby. She had full lips, perfectly curved, as if heaven's most gifted artist designed them. She had huge hands for a woman. Her feet were wide and hard: fat, flat feet that could crush broken glass to sand. She was adored by my grandfather. She couldn't talk about her husband without rocking, clutching her hands in her lap, and smiling. They were both from the Island of Barbados. They left when they were both fifteen years old in search of a better life. She left with one small bag of clothes and a head full of folk songs, stories, and traditions. My grandfather adored her.

I would get to hear my grandmother's stories and songs over and over until I knew each one backwards, they were therapeutic for both of us. They relayed a sense of tranquility and better times in Barbados. Life in America was much harder, and more demanding. She often talked about her journey here and how the anticipation of a productive life in America was the greatest joy a foreigner could have. This was before she actually arrived here, before her dreams began to unfold into American reality. My grandfather was an average-height, dark-skinned, good-looking man with striking features. He was a God-fearing man who instinctly understood what universities were trying to teach about human nature. He resembled the actor Tyrone Power with round cheeks. He had black curly hair, a muscular build, and a handshake like a vice grip. His smile was dis-arming, and his diction was that of the Queen's English. Can you imagine two fifteen-year-old kids totally committed to each other seeking a better life? All the fifteen-year-old kids I knew were getting kicked out of school or were dropping out.

Nanny told me that the first time she and Grandpop saw snow, they put some in a bucket so that they could send it home to show their families. It was another time in America for black people from other countries. Hope overshadowed all barriers; they had nothing to compare America to, except their conditions at home. America had paved streets instead of dirt roads. America was the best place to be, not just because of the opportunities, the promises, and the dreams of a better life. In spite of the barriers that lined the path of dreams and opportunity, which were interwoven in the overall fabric of this land. It was hope and the manifestation of dreams at its finest for some, and a better life for many others, but the fine print was a price that no one really knew they would have to pay until they got here. The cover charge in America was astronomical. Now I ain't saying that life didn't have its share of fun and games, or that life here com-pared to where many of immigrants came from wasn't a lot better. You just experience that the lesser of two evils is still evil.

Soon after arriving here, my grandfather landed a job as a sign hanger on the railroad. He was part Horatio Algabra, part Marcus Garvey. He believed hard work had as much to do with destiny as being kind and good gathered positive karma. He believed being a hard worker was the only way up the ladder. They settled in New York's Harlem, where many of America's uninvited blacks lived. They soon were the proud parents of a daughter. My mother was a beautiful little girl. She was fair skinned— don't ask me where that gene came from— with full black features, full lips, a pudgy nose, and dark eyes. Shortly after her arrival she was given a sister, Sadie, who was the total opposite of Old Girl. A dark skinned girl, with full white features. A pointy nose, thin lips, and light eyes. She came complete with wavy hair. My grandparents firmly believed in education and knowledge as the second steps up the ladder, which could lead one out of the ghetto into mainstream society. Yet they wanted their children to become educated, not indoctrinated, by never forgetting their Barbadian heritage.

One winter's day while coming home from school, my mother, sixteen years old, was with my aunt who was fourteen. My aunt Sadie took my mother to a restaurant to treat her to a meal with her first paycheck from her first job as a coat-check girl in the neighborhood hotel. As they waited to get served, enter the man to be my father. He was a real street player, very hip, which is the street equivalent to wise and slick. You know what *slick* means, that's what white America calls a person who they label as someone who could not be trusted or who isn't sincere but is probably a lot smarter than they are. My father was the epitome of ghetto educated; he was proud to be a "career nigger." You talk about opposites attract, in walked this tall, slender, light-skinned man, who walked like a king. He was self-assured and had the way about him. My mother was awestruck. In her eyes he was the most handsome young man she had ever seen, probably because I wasn't born yet. He walked as if he just knew it, remember she was only sixteen, very naïve; she was dressed like a schoolgirl. He was about twenty-four years old, and let's just say … coool. His family was from the island of Jamaica.

Love at first sight is a funny thing, and when you are pure at heart, the qualities that extract any emotions from you make you sincerely think that they must also be pure of heart, or so you think. My future father spotted my mother and gallantly walked up to her. He looked her over as if she was a slave in the market, then stared into her eyes, then whispered into her ear from his six-foot-three-inch frame: "Excuse me, but I have no choice in this moment. Because of your beauty my heart has taken over my mind and body. You may feel that this is a forward action. Not at all, darling, this is an awkward reaction. You see, from this moment on we are to travel down one road through life together, and that road will inevitability lead us to eternal happiness. You are going to be the mother of my children. You will be my reason to be the best me that I could be. I don't know what brought you here today, but I sincerely thank whatever it was for us." Interjected into the meaning of his words just spoken was, "Can we have sex?"

My mother was both frightened and enthused. Now under-stand how one set of words could have such a variety of different meanings. Old girl immediately thought and projected because of the high moral values instilled in her, that family and marriage went hand in hand with the word "children." Dad coming from a bro-ken home, his father having never married his mother meant exactly what he said "You're going to be the mother of my children," period. It was "love meeting lust" at first sight. Oh yeah, he was attracted to this beautiful child, but it was as I said before, it was because he could recreate himself in her naïve eyes and be what she imagined him to be, and by making her believe this was what he was, allowed him to experience the fantasy of being that person for a while.

After their initial meeting he would later meet her at the school and walk her home. My Aunt Sadie hated him. There were many other younger men in the neighborhood enchanted by my mother's beauty and innocence, but Old Girl was hit right between the eyes by Cupid's cousin, Stupid. That little arrow-shooting sniper bastard who arbitrarily hits his targets with no regard for compatibility or eternal happiness. He sees the opportunity to shoot the damn arrow, and he shoots. Make no mistake, on Cupid's job description he was not to perpetuate love, his job was merely to make sure the male and female species survives. Come judgment day, he better be armed with that damn bow because many angry people are going to want to kick his butt. As time progressed, my mother couldn't wait to introduce Dad-to-Be to her father, and Dad-to-Be wanted to do whatever it took to be able to spend time with her so he could continue to have his way with her. While she thought in terms of everlasting bliss, he was only thinking about fattening frogs to feed snakes. He had girls all over Harlem, some women too. Well, the day arrived when the two worlds would finally meet. Old girl set it up so her beau could meet her family at their house. She got dressed in her Sunday best. Aunt Sadie wanted a front-row seat and Old Girl was like a child on Christmas morning.

Finally, two loves of Old Girl's life were meeting, talking, exchanging ideas. I have heard that the most underrated day or event in a woman's life was when her two favorite male loves meet for the first time. It is also one of the most revealing days in a father's life as to exactly understand what did he raise. Yeah, I heard this story a couple of hundred times already, except that it never quite came out in song. Grandpa was sitting in the kitchen while Grandma faithfully served him dinner. Grandma was beaming with joyful anticipation of the arrival of her daughter's potential intended. She had heard about him many times and also endowed him with the qualities Old Girl gave to him. He had already passed two of my grandmother's conditions for marriage. 1. He was light-skinned and 2. He had good hair. He had all the things that a person has nothing to do with. If you don't think black people aren't racist to other black people, you're from another planet. It has gotten a lot better, but man, to some people being dark-skinned in those days was a double whammy. On the other hand, my grandfather expected a great deal more in a potential suitor for his little girl. He expected things such as honesty, openness, responsibility, and dedication to one's job, allegiance to family, all the things my dad lacked, but remember Old Girl described him with angelic qualities. She knew he was rough around the edges compared to Grandpa's expectations, but as all women naively believe when they choose this sort of man, all he needs is a good woman to give him the inspiration to want to achieve, to have a happy family life. It's usually not until much later when the image is chipped away by time and reality sets in that a woman begins to finally realize their love is not what they thought they were or hoped they could be.

    Then comes the hard dose of truth and the realization that I cannot change anything about this person. The only thing that I have the power to change is my attitude toward him. For most women, that is the day of their rite of passage into womanhood. Yeah, although she thought he was nearly perfect, he was still beer in a champagne bottle. He looked good on the outside, light, full-bodied, expensive. Inside he was dull, with a big head, but the man could jive; the man could talk. Unfortunately for my dad he never learned that one of the most important lessons a man learns in life is when to shut up and listen.

Marty R.

He had lived by his wits and instincts, which were fine-tuned by the ghetto, and he wanted to dominate Old Girl, so in order to tighten his grip on her he had to confront and hopefully loosen the one who had the tightest grip on her at present, her father. Why else would he agree to come? To Dad, all people were stupid, but he was hip enough to know that although all people were stupid, you still had to deal with them. When he knocked on the door one could feel the energy in the house. It was like being at a revival meeting. He was greeted by Old Girl and was immediately led to the kitchen, where the tribal chief sat. All he had to have done was maintain direct eye contact, give a strong handshake, and listen more than he spoke, and he would have been fine. Grand pop was a traditionalist who knew what he expected in a man, but my future fathers bull crap had no plan, it just reacted. A wise man can play a fool, but a fool can never play a wise man. My dad entered and tried to be amusing and witty. The light, loose handshake was delivered along with the eloquent greeting of "Hey, Pop." My grandmother still saw only the champagne and all the small glasses of champagne inside the bottle just waiting to get poured out at future births. She was already light-headed and approving due the possibilities of being a grandmother. To my future dad, Grandpop was just another hurdle he needed to ghettover on. Not jump over just get over any way he could. An arrogant mind has no regard for anything. If you were to con an arrogant mind out of their money in a brilliant way that they could turn around and use that same con to get rich, they would never make a dime. They would only want get revenge on you for conning them. An arrogant mind does not soak anything in, it only shoots out.

Grandpa's attitude had always been a reflection of his mind; he knew no pretense, just protocol. He was a here-and-now man, long before Jean Paul Sartre's here-and-now philosophy. Old Girl couldn't care less about a hearty handshake; she believed that family love would tighten his grip and lock his eyes front and direct; to Old Girl love was capable of anything.

She stood outside the kitchen with Grandma as the men stayed inside the kitchen and spoke. On the table was a bottle of rye with two shot glasses, and like a fool Dad drank most of it, while his mind kept repeating to his brain, "Try this con, no, how about this one. OK, this will get him."

When the kitchen door finally opened two hours later, Grandpop walked out, and slowly, he put on his hat and coat and went directly to the front door. He went for one of his infamous long walks. They say that as he left the house, he never made eye contact of any kind with anyone, he even held his head down so that no one could read his mind. Dad remained in the kitchen still sitting in the chair at the table with a half-empty bottle of rye in front of him. Old girl stormed in immediately, searching Dad's eyes for a sign that all had gone well, although she instinctively felt Grandpop's sudden departure wasn't good at all. Dad looked into her searching eyes and simply said, "I got to get." Old girl timidly asked, "Well, how did it go?" to which Dad replied in his usual descriptive manner, "Cool. I had him eating out of the palm of my hand." Grandma, who stood at the door, just put her head down as the mental champagne glasses began to look empty. Aunt Sadie was too concerned with her sister's emotion to revel in the moment.

Dad said, "I'll see you later" and staggered out of the door. Old girl sat at the window of the kitchen watching him as he made his way down the street. She began to cry, not really knowing why she was crying, but suddenly realizing that she should be crying. She sat at the window until she spotted Grandpop. She ran down and opened the front door for him. He still made no eye contact with her as he walked up the steps, and his head was still down as he reached the top step. That was when he stopped and looked up at her. His eyes were red, and he softly said, "Nanny Noochie [his pet name for her] I've been walking and thinking." Mom knew the red eyes were a bad sign and they were not from the rye. Although he drank rye most of the time, it never showed any effect on him. He went on to say, "I have been walking, thinking about you. You see, I know you, and I know exactly how you feel about that young man. I can see the love you have in you, and I can feel it in you. I can see it in your face and realize how much a part of your being he has become. He is part of your reason to smile and laugh out loud. The sheer mention of his name opens your eyes and parts your mouth in much the way the eyes and mouths around Moses opened as he parted the Red Sea, as they the former slaves of Egypt looked in front of them for a more fulfilling life. I would look at your face as you spoke of your beau, and I would feel happy for you, for on your face was a young woman's completion, a completion, which demanded attention. It was as complete as a smile could be, leading those around you who love you to smile along with you, just knowing how completely happy you are. Noochie, I spoke with this young man for a while, or should I say listened. I had not prejudged him on anything by what you told me about him. I had no misconceptions, nor allowed any false hopes to interfere. I met him with a blank mind once he walked into the kitchen, and I allowed him to draw upon it a picture of his heart, his soul, and his character, so that I could understand the quality of the man. Any blank parts not filled in by him, I would have gladly filled it in with a picture of your smile. Noochie, I cannot give my blessings for he is a man with no reason, and any man you cannot reason with is not worthy of one's love because they will always feel they deserve to be loved, not because of who they are, but in spite of who they are. They feel as if they never have to earn anything in life, it will come to them because they deserve it. His sense of entitlement surpasses his sense of responsibility. In other words, your beau's picture is fine, it's the X-ray that shows disease. He is not the man for you."

With that, he grabbed Old Girl and hugged and kissed her as she cried.

Robby

She later told me that in her daddy's arms, secure in his true love, and respectful of his opinion, the only voice she heard over and over in her mind was "You're going to be the mother of my children." So soon, yes very soon indeed, was my entrance into this dimension of reality, and two years later my sister appeared.

CHAPTER 3

GIT A JAB

Dad did marry her and his words came true; she became the mother of his children. They didn't set up house as married people do; she stayed in Grandpa's house and Dad stayed on the street. Grandpa retired and went back to Barbados to build a house so he could send for Grandma. I was told that I was one beautiful baby; my grandma did get the glass of champagne she wanted. The next few years after my arrival were somewhat uneventful. I spent most of the time simply getting much taller and even better looking. Each time I would run into my parents' friends, they would all say, "Boy, look how tall you've gotten, you sure grew some." I thought that they really meant to say *gruesome*, it was totally confusing. My grandmother used to sing a song from Barbados about a tomboy who was also a thief named Bratty. There's a part in the song that goes, "She is the cleverest thief I know." At an early age I wanted someone to sing my praises and to immortalize me in lyrics. I didn't know this Bratty, but I constantly thought what could make me the kind of thief people would sing about. I mean, what was there to steal back then in Barbados? I patterned myself after my father. He was always dressed nice, and whenever I was with him and someone would ask me what I wanted to be when I grew up, I was told to say "a pimp." A little boy looking up to his father makes no judgment calls when they are young. As I got older, just like my father, I could steal the stink out of craps with-out my fingers smelling. My grandmother's values dictated to drag me to church every Sunday where I would be literally threatened with everlasting damnation; yet in spite of this, I knew that I liked to steal. I needed to steal; it pleased my father. I just never knew that the word *thou* in the Ten Commandments before the words "shall not steal" referred to me also.

It's utterly amazing how one's true nature coupled with a severe sense of never-ending entitlement can exceed ones family's values. But the fact of the matter was, my father's instilled shortcomings lapped those pokey church instilled values tenfold. Another factor at work during my childhood was the call of the wild; it was the ghetto's mentality as well as Social Darwinism. Survival of the physically and mentally fittest. I was now in school and really enjoying it. Yes, contrary to the social stereotype that you may have already endowed me with, I actually enjoyed school. I wanted to learn as much as I could, for two reasons: first to frustrate my teachers to no end who felt that if inspired and shown the right direction, I would be capable of great accomplishments. It's a shame that my street mentality far exceeded all their ambition as well as my own. And secondly, I instinctively knew that only with a well informed mind can someone compose a great lie or to put it in the most common terms and explain the lie in great detail.

My only ambition was to be more than my father was, and in the hood he was a legend. People with sense hated him, but to the average brothers he was a king. I was sure I could surpass that. School was fun for me; I was the class clown, every class had one. I would wisecrack all day; I was sort of like a heckler taunting a comedian teacher, only the teachers were serious and rarely laughed. I would also invent elaborate ways to frustrate my teachers. I remember one English teacher who had just broken up a fight that I had with another student. As she separated us by pulling us apart when we reached a safe distance from the crowd, she softly whispered in my ear, "I should make your mother come in tomorrow, with your imaginary father."

Boy that hurt. At first I was stunned. I had no idea that anyone thought that, but I guess when a child attends school and a parent is called in for a conference as much as my mother was and she shows up alone always, one may get that impression. My dad had absolutely no interest in my schooling; for that part she was right but she believed he didn't even exist. Never the less, it hurt. Not just because of what she said, which was cruel; it was also her not believing that I really had a father that I actually knew. But because of the realization that my father, would not even care enough to come here and prove his existence, no matter how much it may have meant to me. It was because of that insult rendered to me that I went home that evening obsessed with revenge; it was that inspiration that made me the unique inventor of the "Fart in the Bottle."

That night while in the bathtub thinking of ways for revenge, cheerfully passing gas, and laughing at the smell. I got an inspirational brainstorm. I noticed that my fart after inception would immediately rise to the top of water and then dissipate into the air as the bubble popped. I felt like I had just understood the thesis of gravity for the first time.

I then wondered if I were to have an open jar, strategically placed on top of the water at the time of the fart's exposure, could I then harness the full blast of a fart, inside of the jar? Dare I try this experiment? I got an empty mayonnaise jar and tore the label off. All things had to be perfect to test my hypothesis. I placed the top tip of the jar right below that water line. I then sent out a fart scout to see exactly where it would greet the surface. Once I determined the exact location I placed the jar into position, like all men of science, I soon became alarmed when I could no longer beckon a fart to appear. I know how Benjamin Franklin must have felt waiting there for the damn lightning. He also had a great idea but he could not control the lightning. I pictured him standing there flying a kite just waiting. As any great inventor would tell you, "patience is a virtue." I sat in that tub, still as a rock, until bath water turned uncomfortably cold. I was about to give up and get out when suddenly inspiration called again. I felt a slight rumbling in my stomach. It felt like Ben hearing the thunder rumble. At first I wasn't exactly sure if this was an all-ghost fart, and not its solid counterpart, until a tiny fart scout popped out to see where it was, and was there a toilet bowl under me? Once convinced that it was entirely gas, I repositioned the jar and yelled, "torpedo one away."

It was a direct hit, all net, right inside the jar; no rim, all net. I then placed the lid on the jar while it was still submerged to harness the full effect of my achievement. Yes, I now was the only person who I have ever known with an actual fart in a bottle. Now what to do with it? I felt like a sadistic Aladdin with a portable crap-smelling genie. What were the ramifications of this invention? How do I derive the maximum uses out of my achievement? I could drop it in the classroom like a bomb. NOOOOOOOOOOOO, I had a better idea, but it would entail making a new bomb. I suddenly remembered that I had caught a glance of some artificial flowers, roses to be exact, on my grandmother's table. I thought that I could dispute Shakespeare's line that a "Rose by any other name would still smell like a Rose." I ran to the kitchen and began drinking a gallon of milk. I ate some leftover broccoli in the icebox, and I began to shake and dance like a spastic hula dancer. I needed more gas and fast.

I grabbed one of the roses, and I ran to the tub. I filled the tub with enough warm water to get comfortable and harness the power to make it bearable. When I opened the first jar the bathroom smelled like a fertilizer truck just exploded. This time I placed the artificial rose in the bottle and did everything that I had done before, all over again. Only this time, in no time at all, an all-volunteer platoon of volunteer scout farts appeared. I let loose so many that at one point I feared that the bottle would crack from the entry of farts crowding its space. I was touched by the fact that so many had so unselfishly volunteered to partake in this first-of-its-kind venture. When I placed the lid on underwater, I felt a tear come into my eye. You see, my so-called imaginary father was pretty much like the farts in the bottle. You may not be able to see it, but you will be damn sure that it does exist. I held the artificial flower in place with my finger. I repeated the gestures and had my final creation ready and able.

When I presented my creation to the English teacher the following day she blushed. I guessed that she took it as a peace offering, and it was a piece of my body that I was offering. When she opened it to smell the rose, I blushed. She took one snotful, sneezed, and dropped the bottle. It was then I said, "Oh yeah, excuse me." I laughed all the way to the principal's office. I was not your average child in school. As I said, not really bad, just mischievous. So now you have some understanding how this lost soul wound up on the roof of the projects to rain on the cop. It was now time to pay the piper for my deed to Dumpling.

I had to miss school to appear in court on a Wednesday. I clearly remember standing before Judge Archie Bama. He looked like he took no crap or prisoners. He quickly began to flambé my dumb ass. "You are an uncouth youth with severe emotional problems and abundantly too much free time on your hands. What do you do after school besides cause trouble?"

I replied, "Homework, sir." The court-appointed lawyer I had just shook his head in agreement with the judge. I looked at him and thought, *Why don't you just give him a stick to beat me with?*

The judge then said, "Didn't you know that you could have killed that officer?"

With a water balloon? I thought; this being my first offense I was placed on probation and ordered to stay out of trouble for 2 yrs. He also ordered me to get a part-time job after school and appear back before him in a month. *Get a job,* I thought. There were grownups in my neighborhood who couldn't get a part-time job, and no one in our group had a job. *How could I get one?* As I turned I saw my mother and grandmother sitting and crying in unison.

Upon reaching home I was given the welcome by my chums as if I were returning as a conquering hero. When they asked me what happened, I whispered "That judge didn't want any of my crap. He seemed scared of me." When I got upstairs my mother still cried. My grandmother called me into the room and also cried. It was now her turn to hold me tight, as she rocked back and forth. It was only then that I got a glimmer of how screwed up what I did was. I really hurt the people who really loved me. My grandmother went over to her shelf and got the Bible she brought with her when she entered this country and said to me, "Boy all of life's answers are in this book. When you get hungry and thirsty and need to fill your body and soul, just open this book. Just don't do stupid things again."

I couldn't take her crying and rocking, so I took the Bible from her and held it to my chest. She fell on her bed and cried. I realized that in her hopes as she left her home land, she never imagined this kind of experience in America. I went to bed and even said a prayer, I asked God that I quickly find a job. I had no skills, just a lot of stupid imagination. I thought maybe I could be a freelance Supreme Court justice or something important to make my family proud again. I was inspired to find a part-time job after school tomorrow and finally straighten out my life. Not that I really thought that anything was wrong with my life. I just knew that I hurt the people around me, all except my dad. When he was told what happened, he said, "I'm disappointed in you, boy."

I thought he would be just another voice in the family's dis-honor. He then said, "If you would have told me you were going after that fat fake cop, I would have given you a used condom with some quarters in it."

I kept on the straight for a time after that, for me only a righteous existence. Every morning I would repeat my mantra for my family: there was going to be a renaissance in my life. I would get up and ready myself for school and leave the house with a whole new outlook on life. All I knew was that I had to show my family the extent of my newly found conscience, and I was prepared to do so, even if deep down inside I didn't believe it.

The next week in school there were no jokes, no talking out loud, no playing around. I was as serious as diarrhea. I was thinking *job*. So every day after school I hit the pavement with the enthusiasm of a prostitute. I just knew someone would want me to work for them, anyone. After about the 529th no, it was apparent that this wasn't going to be easy. Now in America at this time you had your racism, the ones who would just look at you and say no job for you, as if they were experiencing an orgasm when they said it. And then there are your closet racism variety; they would treat you in a nice way, and you would leave feeling better but you still had no job. Their spiel was young man, you have terrible timing. I just hired someone" or "Try again next year Tuesday."

After about three weeks of rejection, my plea of "Can I please have a job?" started to sound like a metaphysical question. Time was running out for me, and now every time someone would say no, I imagined the judge throwing everything at me including his shoe. It was beginning to get hopeless. I went from my thoughts of being a freelance Supreme Court justice to settling for a job as someone who fixed the blown-out light bulbs on a Ferris wheel. Although my mother still never said a word, I sensed that she was at the end of her rope with me and was about to just let go and pray for God to watch over me.

My grandmother on the other hand was an incurable optimist. She kept saying "tomorrow, tomorrow," and each day she prayed harder and harder. It's amazing when you see a person with that much faith, no matter what frown the face of disaster is wearing. She sincerely believed that I would be saved in the eleventh hour. I had no such faith, no job, and not even any hope to take with me on the bus. It was now Wednesday of the last week before my court appearance. I was now conditioned to hear the word *no* after my asking for a job. If only I could have just gone into an establishment and said, "I bet you a quarter I can make you say 'no,'" that could have been my job and I would have made good money from doing it. I was down-town in desperation, going into any store now, even women's clothing stores. I was now willing to suck farts out of restaurant chairs and blow them out the window just to be working.

It was a dark, dreary day as I stomped the pavement in search of the elusive job, when I noticed a crowd in front of me. As I approached the scene, I saw a man lying on the pavement in front of a cheap restaurant. He was an older Spanish man, and he was holding his stomach. I could see that there were bloodstains on his apron and on the ground around him, he had just been stabbed. Now living in my neighborhood I witnessed stabbings, beatings, and shooting victims constantly. I was somewhat immune to the carnage, but on this day I saw something more, much more. I saw a man with an apron on lying in a pool of blood in front of a restaurant. I saw a sign that his blood wrote, which spelled "HELP WANTED." This meant *Job* inside, vacancy, position immediately available. Open for business, come in and work.

Marty R.

I stepped over the old man who I now referred to as the answer to my prayers. My grandmother's prayers were probably responsible for his present condition. Oh yeah, the Lord does work in mysterious ways. Can I get an amen? The crowd parted as I walked into the restaurant. I took my last look at the bleeding man who was now being attended to by some passerby nurse, and I thought, *Go, my son, and sin no more.* Now I knew that they had an opening. I just didn't know what the stabbed man did, nor did I care. He didn't strike me as valedictorian of restaurant school, I felt I was able to do whatever he did. Once I got inside I heard the lowdown. He was a dishwasher who had an argument with another employee over a woman who apparently didn't want either one of them, and the old man laying outside, as my grandmother would say, got a knife run up his rass. There was total confusion going on inside as some people were trying to go on with business as usual, even with the damn appetite spoiler directly outside. I found the person in charge, and by the end of that day, case dismissed. He said that I looked too young to be a dishwasher; I told him that if given the chance I would do him proud and do whatever he asked. My case was later thrown out because I got this job, yet I was warned in no uncertain terms that if I ever so much as have a fly come to court and say that I threatened to rape, it with a toothpick, I would not pass go, not get a paycheck, and go directly to jail.

I began work at my new job as dishwasher, making about sixty-five cents an hour and all the food I could scrape. I quickly developed a taste for having some change in my pocket. School soon became a thing of the past; I mean, why not? I was self-proclaimed smarter than the other children. I knew that I already knew it all. I was sure that I was put on this planet to play the lead role, and everyone else was merely an extra, stand-in figures in my play of life, who were only here to animate my life, placed here by the Almighty

Robby

merely for decoration, whose only function was to breathe the left-over air I didn't use. Don't misunderstand me, all was not heaven at Joe's Diner. Remember that in all of the confusion on the day that I applied for the job it never struck me as curious that I was never asked my name, my age, nor for any identification, or if I was in school or not. I .got an affirmative "yes" without one "no" to every question that I asked. My only thought at that time was that life was going to be good now, that I had just gotten off the go round and landed on easy street, or so I thought.

You would think that a young man as smart as I only thought that I finally found this fantastic job. I was now just going to make money and live the straight and righteous road. I would now live happily ever after. Well, let me tell you something. I later found out about life. With all his great imagination, Walt Disney wasn't completely truthful with us. Unless you're a real prince or a princess, no one lives happily ever after, and not all stories start at the beginning nor end at the end. Life goes in cycles: when it's good, enjoy it for that moment because the moment won't last that long being it's just a moment.

You see, the manager of Joe's Diner was Joe himself, he was also the owner. As the song by Nat King Cole goes, "Joe was a boy, a very strange enchanted boy." His laugh lasted a little too long for any joke told to him; he always walked fast and would sing songs that no one else knew. He was young, about 24 years old, white, tall, slender, and well shaven. He smelled better than any woman ever smelled. He was the only white man I had ever met who could dance like a black and keep a beat. Whenever he came into the eating area, he would dance for the customers. You see, my friends, although I didn't realize it at the time, Joe played for the other team. When he would walk into the kitchen where all the workers used to meet to laugh and joke, it always became quiet. Although Joe would say, "Why is it so quiet in here?" as soon as he entered, you could hear a rat piss on a cotton ball.

Marty R.

I didn't know, or cared, nor completely understood, anyone's sexual politics at that time. We had people in my neighborhood who danced better and dressed nicer that the rest of us, who wore much brighter clothes, but we never paid them any mind. As far as I was concerned, I had found this highly respectable profession, and I was making money. I may have been the youngest one at Joe's, but as far as I was concerned that only meant that I was the most ambitious. I was not only washing the dishes but once in a while I would walk over and watch the cooks do their thing. I would get to eat all the scraps that I could eat; even the cooks wouldn't throw out the good parts of the discarded meals. They all kept bags to take the food home in, what a country. Most of the other workers would look out for me; they liked my smartass attitude, and no one was threatened by me taking their job away from them or messing with their woman and having me wind up as my dishwashing predecessor. There was absolutely no competition with me.

I was now spending more and more time working than going to school. I quickly deduced that time was money, and money was needed. My mother thought that all was well, and that I was in school and working only part-time after it. She was actually happy with the change in me, which she deemed was *responsibility*, as far as she and the family was concerned. I was now in a whole new sphere of my life; instead of stealing the things that I wanted I would actually pay for them. I was actually living the high life and having the time of my life, but as I stated earlier Walt Disney wasn't totally honest. I could have envisioned working there for the rest of my life washing dishes. I took pride in my work. I liked the other professionals, and they liked me. Now the only problem was this in a nutshell. The owner liked me a little too much. He started off this attraction in a very subtle manner. One day for no apparent reason he began calling me "Sunshine." "Sunshine," the other workers would laugh under their breath, but no one thought that it was really very funny.

"Why Sunshine?" I would ask the other workers. "What does it mean?" They would look me in the eye and say, "Because Joe can't wait until he gets the son down." I understood perfectly. In my neighborhood I didn't know somebody, who knew somebody, who had known somebody else, who they called "Sunshine." The more I understood, the more nervous I became around him. He would prance into work in the afternoon and say, "Where's my Sunshine?"

This was not the kind of situation that any young man should have to be in. Although I loved my job and liked my life at this point, the attention of another man who wasn't related to me, or related to anything that I could relate to, really racked my nerves. Now every time Joe would dazzle into the kitchen, he would just stand behind me and watch me do the dishes. I knew just by the way that the other workers would look at him looking at me that I was in deep trouble. They all would laugh and joke and ask me if I ever tried generic vagina. This was a sad, ironic twist of fate; I was saved from a detention center because of this job, but at either place if I dropped the soap I was in trouble. There were benefits to this unconformable situation. As time went by I really got used to having steady money and the time just flew by really fast; this would have been a dream come true had it not been for my not-so-secret admirer. I was about thirteen when I started and was approaching sixteen now. I got to work at 8:00 a.m. and stayed until we closed at 11:00 p.m., seven days a week.

I learned so much from my coworkers and the customers. I still looked young for my age, but was not a kid. Joe was constantly trying to tan in my sunshine. Joe would sometimes make up a table and serve me lunch, and I do mean lunch, not the scraps from the kitchen. I mean top-of-the-line lunches: steak, pork chops, chicken, and vegetables, including dessert. The workers would joke that I was being fattened for the thrill. He was also fattening frogs to feed snakes. I didn't think it was funny, but the meals were excellent and the service exquisite. I really enjoyed having this job at first. I would make it to work be it rain, flood, crap, or mud. Had I only known in advance what the damn bill would be, I would have refused the meals, mainly because of the unwritten, expected tip. But all in all, I really had gotten used to this.

There was this one time when Joe had the cook prepare a steak that you could cut with a feather. There was no such steak on the menu; Joe brought it in to be prepared especially for me, and he had the chef personally prepare it just for me. I tell you, while eating a meal such as that, Joe and the situation he presented didn't seem so bad. One day I was asked to do a delivery, which was rare. When I got back in the kitchen I was suddenly awakened to the reality of this situation. I was warned, and rewarned, and told in no uncertain terms by my coworkers that I must confront the situation head on, no pun intended. I was told by the cooks to tell Joe that although I enjoyed working here, and loved the special meals, that I did not play with anything but girls.

I wasn't a worldly fellow, but my sexual hormones were calibrated, awakened, and activated at the age of twelve, by a close friend of my sister. Her name was Marsha. She was a woman in a young girl's body. She was my first understanding of the beauty of a woman. Marsha was oh so very beautiful; she had long slender legs, big thighs, and full shapely lips. I remember that the first time that I saw her in shorts I immediately fell in love with her. Marsha had a smile that could melt a snowman. All of the older boys in my neighborhood used to talk about sex, and some would tell of their experiences. Most would lie, but at my age, a bona fide boner questioned no sources. Marsha use to come over to play with my sister. Sometimes she would stay over the weekend. Many times she would sneak into my room and just sit next to me and smile. I couldn't understand why she was smiling, but I always gave her my best smile right back.

Robby

During the summer when it got really hot, the rich white people whom my grandmother worked for would allow my grandmother to bring her grandchildren to their house to swim in their backyard pool. They had a huge inground pool that I could not believe was just for them. I was used to going to the public pool, where everyone in the neighborhood would go. The water at the white folks' house would always be dark blue. At public pool the water was aqua blue in the morning when we arrived and then turned light green by the time we would leave. I used to think that the color had something to do with the sunlight. One day I heard a pool maintenance worker explain this phenomena to the owner in scientific terms. He was an old white dude who would put the chemicals in the water. One day I overheard him tell the owner that the change in the water's color were from all the ghetto kids pissing in the pool.

After hearing that I learned to hold my breath for minutes at a time, and I never opened my eyes underwater, but I did keep pissing in the pool. This employer family lived in Valley Stream Long Island. One time, one summer we were allowed to come to their house when they were away on vacation and use their pool. It was because they liked and trusted my grandmother, and they didn't have a dog, so we got to swim while they got their house checked on. Whatever the reason was, it was good to get away to the clean, open, fresh country setting. The pool was theirs and theirs alone. On this visit my sister had asked if she could bring Marsha. The four of us went up one Saturday afternoon on the bus; my mother came also. The house was fantastic. I couldn't even imagine having a place like this to call home and experiencing the privilege of living there.

We would bring sandwiches and juice and enjoy the day swimming and having fun. I would sometimes sneak around the house and look in each room in amazement. My grandmother would always get upset if I ventured too far and would yell, "Now, boy, don't touch or break anything." and as usual she would put things in the worst possible light. My grandmother would use the worst analogies to make her point.

"Boy, if ya break a vase, ya gonna have to work for forty years to pay for it, and no good woman is gonna want ta marry ya with forty years of vase to support." I got the message. My grandmother once told me a story about a party her employer, Missy, was having. Missy felt there was too much work for my grandmother to do alone, so she hired another worker to assist. The other worker was related to the house worker across the street. My grandmother described her as a two-dimensional slave, the kind of slave that a slave would own. She had a look on her face like the black people who use to sing and dance on the *Lawrence Welk Show*. They were stationed in the kitchen cleaning fish. My grandmother was on one side of the table, and she was on the other. They were supposed to scale then cut the fish. Suddenly she heard the worker yell for Missy. "Missy, Missy, come quick." As my grandmother looked, the worker pulled out what appeared to be a diamond ring from the fish's gut. Missy came in looked at the ring and placed it in her pocket and left, never uttering one word. My grandmother said she just looked at the worker who seemed proud of what she had done. My grandmother said that she had to do something else because she couldn't be around that woman with a knife in her hand. So she felt that in some way Missy owed us the use of the house while they were away.

I would still wander around. I would peep into their kids' rooms and look at all the toys, dolls, and things. I remember thinking, *Wow. I bet these kids never have to steal anything.* Now that was a revealing thought. The truth was they probably did or would at some point or another in their lives. Just then the overwhelming thought of the day hit me: Marsha was in the pool, in her bathing suit. I put on the raggedy trunks that I had and went out to the water. My family was already out there: my mother was sitting in a lounge chair making believe that she lived here, my grandmother was watching everyone enjoy themselves while picking up leaves, and my sister and her friend were already in the pool. It's amazing how a young boy never feels self-conscious about his body. I guess it's a learned condition response, because I looked like a popsicle stick with splinters. I got into the cool water and immediately went underwater. I nearly drowned myself staring at Marsha's thighs. I could even see a tiny section of hair sticking out of her bathing suit. I was in deep lust. I didn't know exactly why, but I sincerely wanted to touch her body.

This was the beginning of my wake-up call, placed by nature to my sex hormones. When I came to the surface, Marsha yelled, "Hey, swim underwater between my legs" as she opened them wide. It's amazing how a young male child could get so horny in cold water, the same element used to cool a man down from what I was feeling. What a world. I smiled and went right back under for a closer look. As I swam closer I could hear my heart pounding underwater as I approached her hourglass body, with the legs that could stop time. She gave new meaning to the word *breaststroke*. I began swimming with my arms wildly yet intentionally touching her legs with glancing blows, trying to touch every inch of her thighs. I was indeed having an aqua orgy with my emotions. When I came to the surface I didn't gasp for air. I exhaled as if I was smoking that after-sex cigarette. Yes, I could get use to this.

I looked over at my grandmother who was now sitting under a tree, looking up at the heavens. It wasn't exactly Barbados, but to her it sure was the same sun. Marsha got out of the pool and went straight into the house for something. Now I could act like the kid that I was and splash around in the pool and try to drown my sister. I did play with my sister for a short while, and I must have lost track of time. In fact we all did, cause when I looked up everyone was snoozing. My sister got out of the pool and lay down beside my mother. I wandered into the house looking for two things:

Marsha and the bathroom. I walked into the guest bedroom where we were allowed to change our clothes in. There was a tiny bathroom in the back of this room. As I pushed open the bathroom door, standing there next to the small window with the sun shining on her greatness was none other than Marsha, in the complete buff. She was stepping out of her bathing suit.

I froze still, but I never took my eyes off the prize. She was magnificent, like nothing I had ever seen before. I now understood the immense power of a woman's body; I would have eaten the entire apple tree had we been in the Garden of Eden and she offered it to me, seeds and all. Her shapely hourglass figure glistened as she radiated beauty. In her face was the look of both innocence and confidence. I was still frozen on this fixation. Who could have imagined that this was on the other side of the bathroom door? Can you imagine, here I was going through life minding my own business, when suddenly nature called, and I am beckoned to open this door? And just look what was on the other side? With experiences such as these, I will never fear death nor even mind what may be on the other side as long as I live. I will march double step through any door. This whole situation of me standing at the door seemed like an eternity, but it was only about ten seconds of me staring at her. Just then I heard a voice. It was is if an angel sang to me. Marsha said in a soft, baby-powered voice, "Come in and close the door."

Before I knew it the doorknob was being pushed back and forth from me by my sweating palm. She was now standing straight up in front of me. Her breasts nipples were firm they were dark chocolate, her body glowed like a bronzed polished statue, and her vagina was hairy and the hair formed a perfect V. Again she spoke. "Come here." I glided, floated, waltzed as if a magnet was pulling me closer and closer. I could now see three tiny bumps surrounding her nipples. I lost the natural sense of my own body. I was only a complete thought, a reaction to this moment, being divinely puppeteered closer toward this bliss, this spectacle of enchantment, this wonderment of creation.

This was my first completely naked female, with pubic hair; Lord knows how many times I lied to the guys about my experiences Oh yeah, my sexual genes were all up now, peering out through every part of my being. They were being uniquely calibrated, fine-tuned, pampered, and intrigued. My little Johnson pecker was as hard as her nipples. It was as if it was a little soldier and the national anthem was being played and the flag was waving high on its mast. I felt a sensation throughout my entire body, one that I have never felt before. The only way to describe it was that I wanted to fart, cough, belch, sneeze, and yawn all at the same time. I was now in physical and mental heaven.

Marsha gently grabbed my hand and placed it on her breast. I agreeably complied. It was the first full beautiful breast that I had ever felt. It was like reading skin Braille, and I was already mentally fluent in its meaning. We were now both mentally in sync. We both breathed in unison. We spoke with our eyes telepathically. I was basting while tanning in the aura of this moment. I may have been a young man but I understood completely. This was a moment that cannot be taught; it is purely instinctual. Tenderness is the highest form of nonverbal communication. All forms of life respond to it— adults, animals, fish, even flowers— yet it cannot be taught, it can only be inspired. It is instrumental, with nature as the conductor, and it always compels a different unrehearsed response. I always imagined that an encounter such as this would be good, but I had no idea that it would be this good. Her breasts were so soft I wanted to hold them forever. Had I had them in my hand on the roof with Dumpling, I would have spared the cop the bath; I would have reached for them and never let them go. The balloon in the box would have died a dried up orphan.

My hand was fusing with her breast. I glanced up at Marsha, who now had her eyes closed. She was winding her head slowly in a circle. Her hand was now pressed to mine, holding the back of my hand pressed up against her breast. I began to rub them oh so gently in a small circle. You may ask how did I know to do this, I answer you with this: how does a newborn turtle know where the ocean is and which way to go after it hatches from the egg as it emerges as a living thing? The baby turtle always heads toward the ocean exactly right. It is the intelligence of the universe. I was now in natures instinctual autopilot. There was no right way to hold them and no wrong way to hold them, there was only way. Marsha then diligently grabbed my entire hand and gently walked towards the bed which was in the corner of the room.

She slowly walked me over, and then she lay down still holding my hand very tight as if I would not have followed. Watching her lay down was poetic. I think that I may have experienced the first recorded case of visual eyegasm. I stood next to a small night table next to the bed. She gently ungrabbed my hand and placed her arm around my neck, gently pulling my head down. At first I suspected that I was going to get one big juicy kiss, but she made a sharp southern left turn at the lips, and I was then steered toward her vagina. Now I witnessed men and woman kissing in the movies before, so when I thought that I was heading for the lips I could adlib from love scenes that I once saw in the movies, but when my head arrived at the vagina, I saw no such flick up to this point in my life to advise me. I was totally in over my head. No pun intended. I was so close that the once perfect V now looked like a slice of pizza, with extra hair. The enchanted forest had just caught fire, the autopilot had been switched off, and I realized that I didn't know how to fly the damn plane. Reality sunk in fast.

Just then I heard a purring sound like a cat at first. I couldn't make out the words, then suddenly I understood. Marsha was saying "Kiss it, kiss it." I was now totally confused. Those words did not register. Kiss it, you mean where you pee from? Kiss your pee hole? Uggggghhhh. You mean like the kind of kiss I give my mother to say hello? While I was trying my best to understand her meaning, Marsha got more forceful with my head. It went from directing me in position to herding my stupid-ass head into place. The purring also stopped; it went from a purring suggestion to a roaring request then to a demand, and it was now approaching a direct order. As if things weren't bad enough, I was being totally confused and domineered by this crazed person. She tried to shove my entire head up her vagina. One of my senses was rudely awakened and was now in charge of my entire body.

My sense of smell had awakened and was placed in charge of all the other senses at that moment. As my cheeks were now being pushed into her hair, my face felt like those I'd seen on brothers as police would push their heads into the patrol car, I smelled a scent, one that I had never known before. Unlike the flower analogy that I gave, this was no rose. On top of everything else I was being asked to kiss something that I had no desire to kiss. I did not want to kiss it, but I did not want her to get up either. I just wanted to go back to the erotic palming of her nipples and looking at her splendor, kiss it, well I never. Maybe if I could kill the odor, then I could probably tolerate kissing it. Marsha was getting inpatient with me, grabbing my head tighter, pulling my hair.

Yes, I thought the only way to recapture the essence of the original moment was to kill the smell. Out of my peripheral vision I saw on the night table a blue small bottle with a rubber spray on top. It was a bottle with a skinny white tube connected to a plastic spray portion shaped like a pillow. One had to squeeze the pillow to spray the contents connected to a rubber spray hose. I was hoping that it was perfume or anything that smelled good, but I didn't actually care what it was. It had to smell better than this. I barely reached it with my arm as the other hand tried to push back. I finally placed it in my palm. *Got it,* I thought. I could see words on the bottle that read "essence of" something. With my free hand I stopped pushing and reached to spread Marsha's legs open so that I could get one good shot. She must have thought and figured that I was ready to submit because her moaning got louder and louder. I could already smell the scent of the contents of the bottle as I gently positioned the sprayer.

The essence of salvation, quickly will camouflage the original smell of this life machine. When I reached and moved Marsha's leg open, she voluntarily opened both legs as wide as she could. She thought I was coming to kiss this uncooked meal. Me in my own stupid way thought maybe she knew help was just a squirt away. She again said "kiss it" with a certain degree of expectation in her voice. I then pulled my free arm back to the squinter and sprayed two giant squirts into the hole where the scent ran rampant.

From my vantage point, looking up by way of her stomach, I immediately saw Marsha's eyes open as wide as they could open. Her hands immediately let go of my hair. I then got my head caught between two shut-slamming thighs. Now the problem was I couldn't breath. I could hardly hear anything, but that only lasted a second as I heard Marsha sing a thoroughly audible OWWWWWWWWWWW. She then kicked my head from between her legs and cast me aside. I felt used, not even a thank-you, my goodness, a little gratitude was the least ya could get. I was thrown away on the floor to get a full view of the reaction. The scene on the bed was remarkable. She screamed, she danced, she looked as if she was possessed by a choreographing devil. Had this been an ancient Indian rain dance she would have made it hail giant crap balls. Marsha then got up and ran to the window and screamed at the top of her lungs. My mother, grandmother, and sister must have broken a record getting to the room.

I nearly got hit by a flying door. As the door opened they all appeared totally confused. Marsha was now doing a dance on the floor, with one hand covering her eyes and one hand on her hole, with me on the floor laughing my ass off. I had no idea what exactly was happening but visually it was funny. I thought that she was over-joyed to get a fresh April smell. She tried to tell my family in garbled broken English that I had squirted something in her twat. As she tried to explain what had just happened, this didn't sound thankful to me; in fact it sounded damn accusatory, I remember thinking how fickle is woman. I get her smelling better and she turns on me. My mother immediately took Marsha into the bathroom and began flushing out her vagina. It really didn't matter what happened after that. My hormones had been stimulated: a woman's body equals much excitement. I was successfully initiated to sexual encounters with the opposite sex and exposed to tenderness by a young woman. The severe spanking that I got couldn't undo that which had been done. I wonder how Marsha was effected after that regarding sex. I bet she never closed her eyes or took them off any lover after that.

Now, why did I tell you that last story? Oh yeah, the manager at the luncheonette was after me, and that was the reason why I wasn't interested in him. My, how quickly a situation can get from bad to worst. The manager began singing "Hello Sunshine" every time he would see me; he also began to watch my every move. I mean everything that I would do, he would just stare at me, and now he even started looking at me below the waist and licking his lips, I had been protected by my youth in the beginning now he figured he had waited long enough. As I said I could have been happy just washing dishes the rest of my life had it not been for this kid-crazed manager who the workers began to refer to as the car with the engine in the rear. I tried. I sincerely tried to hang in there, hoping that someone else would extract the rendering of this unwanted attention. I was almost saved or so I thought. He hired another young, good-looking kid named Sammy to clean off the tables. I tried to make Sammy feel right at home so that he would stay on, but he soon fired him because he thought we were getting too close.

Marty R.

Sammy was the nearest to my age than anyone else in the place. We used to joke around a lot, mostly about the manager, so he fires my boy. The overtures became more and more aggressive and less and less discreet. I was still eating the meals he would have the cooks prepare. One sunny weekday, I guess he felt "OK, you're fat and old enough." I was at work eating the meal he brought especially for me. It's not that I wasn't warned by the other workers that he was also fattening a frog to feed a snake. I could see every time he looked at me eat he was probably imagining me on the table in the doggie position, with an apple in my mouth. Remember, this had been festering for years now and about to come to a head (no pun intended).

You see it was simply that the food was so excellent that I didn't give a damn what he wanted as payment. It's funny in a not so funny way that things can change so abruptly. One begins to wonder how you ever saw it any other way, and how did I get in this situation in the first place. I was miserable at work at this point; none of the other workers would even joke around with me anymore for fear of losing his or her job like Sammy did. I began really resenting Joe for putting me in this situation; I also hated the name Sunshine. It got so that the free meals weren't enough to fill me anymore. I should have seen it coming from the beginning as my grandmother used to tell me about human nature. "No one is that nice." I must have been a 10 on the fool's Richter scale. The problem was I had absolutely no money saved. Only old people saved money, I would think to myself, once they get to an age where they can't make anymore. One day Joe approached me and said that we had changed soda distributors, and that he would need me every afternoon to help him take the empty soda bottles back. The old distributor would pick up the empty bottles whenever he would bring in a new supply. How much sense did this make that we had to now bring the empty bottles back? And why would you ask the skinniest person in the place to help you do some heavy work like carrying full wooden crates, when he had big workers who would be happy to get out of the store for a break? This was it, I thought, he was finally going to demand to tan in this young man's sunshine.

This was one of the few times in my life where I began to question my brains. How could I let myself get into this mess? At what point did things turn around and get this bad? The lies one tells one-self as they are dancing to the music. The other workers would tell me as soon as he makes a move I was to make believe that I was going to kiss him and then bite his nose off and spit it into his mouth. Yeah, that makes sense. I was no fool and knew that I was still in America with a judicial system that didn't care what he did to me. I knew that if I would have done that, I would have gotten life in jail for nose snatching, and if I got the same judge I had before it would have been life plus reincarnation. That day I loaded the empty bottles into his car and we left. I sat as close to the passenger door as I could. He played the most awful songs on the radio. Someone with a voice like his, singing a song called "Tally Ho," it was as corny as you could get.

After we dropped the empty bottles in the crates off, he drove to his apartment under the excuse that he needed to get something. He turned to me and said, "You want to come in for a little while, Sunshine?"

I replied, "No, thank you, my stomach is hurting. Last night I had the worst case of diarrhea, and I think that it would be wise not to move too much. On top of everything else I drank some apple juice for breakfast."

He bought it hook, line, and stinker. The only thing about this excuse was that I could only use it once. After we returned back at the diner all eyes were on me. The men were searching with their eyes to see if I was the same person who'd left, and, I was proud to say, I was. But I'd had enough of this dance. If he tried to commandeer me to his apartment again, I might indeed bite the nose off. I was fed up. The workers were now taking bets on how long I could hold out. With people now losing their jobs because they got close to me, it was as if I had the leopard mumps.

When Joe offered me lunch the following day, I snapped back, "I am not hungry." You see, I do have some principles.

He replied, "Don't worry, there's no apple juice in it" and then winked at me. This was on a Thursday and payday was always on a Friday. Every day I kept telling myself to just last one more day and I would definitely quit. Enough was too much; there was now a large bet going on where some said I would give in for the sake of free food and possible advancement, but the overall consensus was from those who knew me best, and it was bet that I would probably bite his nose off.

That night was probably one of the worst. I thought about how I got so accustomed to having money. I mean, being on the up and up and taking care of myself was nice. I liked to dress nice, I liked not being hungry, and I also thought how this would affect any future court case, although years had passed since that time. My family finally had confidence in me that I was putting it all together. They still didn't know about me leaving school to work full-time; they thought I was on the straight. I was away from the neighborhood working sun up to sun down. They thought I was going to school then to work. The following morning, which was Friday, I got up and dressed and went to work. I was in no mood for any nonsense. I began doing the dishes from last night's meal. The cooks were already there and frying breakfast eggs. At 9:00 a.m., no Joe. I thought that this may just be lucky for me. If I got a pass today and got my hands on my pay, I would definitely tell the chump what I thought and leave. It was now reaching 10:00 am. This was highly unusual. He was always there on time, every day. I thought maybe he had a heart attack, or maybe he went swimming and his ass filled up with water and he drowned. Maybe, Maybe.

Then I heard in a musical voice "Good morning, Sunshine." Maybe I

Robby

was out of luck. Not only was he in, he was especially well groomed: haircut, aftershave, and a smile that would make a dentist cum. He stood behind me and said "Today I am making you an extra special lunch before we leave." He then stared at my ass. It's funny, once those words would have me licking my lips, now I dared not let my tongue out. Well, lunch was superb as promised, but this time I shared it with the other workers. I really had no appetite. I even asked for my pay right after lunch and the reply I got was "Don't worry I have your money, but you still have today to earn a week's pay. There may even be a little extra in it today if you're a good boy."

I began to get more and more scared and upset. He had another worker load the car with the empty bottles crates he then called me to ride shotgun. As I said goodbye to my coworkers, they joked and whispered, "Hope you like sausage for dessert. And after today you gonna have to sip soup on the toilet."

After he fired Sammy for getting too close with me, they some-what stayed their distance when he was around. Again we made the rounds to the distributor, but this time there was a lot of small talk. He would say things like "You know I couldn't handle all of my responsibilities without you. Don't you, sunshine?" and "I was thinking about promoting you to my assistant. What do you think about that, Sunshine?"

The more he spoke the madder I became. I thought he said "ass sissy tint." All I wanted was my pay, and if I had to tell him in no uncertain terms that I was not interested in anything else, then so be it. We were now traveling to a strange location; it wasn't the way back to the restaurant, and it wasn't to his house. I asked where we were going.

"It's a surprise, Sunshine. Don't worry, I won't bite you." We arrived at his desired destination under some bridge where he stopped the car and turned off the engine.

I looked around and saw no one in sight. I wasn't really afraid at this

Marty R.

point. I felt at this point I could knock him out if need be. He turned to me with a look on his face that said, "You could either fight, feel, or break out." I knew that this meant the end of my job, but I knew that I had to be tactful so not to blow my paycheck. He began taking off his shirt under the guise that it was hot. Man he was hairy, hair on his arms, on his back, on his neck, hair on his fingers and his palms. It was like a werewolf on a full moon. I nearly threw up. He then said, "I want you to like me so bad, Sunshine" as he propelled himself toward my side of the car, grabbing my left arm and throwing it around his waist. I was about to literally choke this bastard with my right, pay gone and all. When all of a sudden I felt something hard in my left hand, I mean really hard, a hard bulge in his pants. It was really strange to me, but once my hand felt it, it really, really turned me on. It was all that I could think about. Hitting him or running away was now totally out of the question. All I knew was that I had to have it. I began positioning my body so that I could get a real good feel, I never felt anything so big and so hard. I knew that I had to have it. Now I don't know what you may be thinking at this point. I was talking about his wallet in his back pocket full of pay. My Lord, it was huge. I already told you about my sex hormones: woman, Marsha, *remember?* Shame on you. I couldn't believe the size of this thing. One thing for sure, it was a lot larger than any wallet I've ever seen. As any thief's mind will always do, I already convinced myself that he owed me this. I tried pushing the damn thing up out of his pocket, but it was much too big. The more I tried to push it up, the more excited he became. He screamed, "Oh yes! Yes!"

Self-deception is indeed the greatest deception of them all. He began kissing my neck, breathing harder and harder, wrestling me around, squeezing me tight. He turned with his damn hairy back in my direct sight. I had both arms around him trying to get that damn wallet out, but I couldn't. The only way was to get him to take his pants down. It was too much of a tight squeeze any other way. I whispered in his ear, which incidentally also had hair in it, "pull your pants down."

He was still yelling "Yes! Yes!" and with one motion, one hand reached down and his belt was unbuckled, his button was undone, and the zipper was down. He was a regular Hairy Houdini. He squirmed out of those tight pants like a snake shedding its skin. I remember thinking, *Damn it takes me about ten minutes just to get mine down to use the bathroom.* Nothing inspires like the anticipation of sex. Lord, he was hairy; he even had hair on his knees. His eyes were now closed as he whispered, "Go, Sunshine. Do it, sunshine." I placed my hand on his back and motioned him to turn around and face the other way. He immediately readily complied. Now I had a free shot at this prize. It was still a bitch to get out of the pocket but I got it. Now I believe that our maker designed us in his image, and made us the best that we could be, but I sincerely think that he could have added something, which would have made life abundantly more tolerable. A puff button on everyone, so that when you're finished with someone in your life you only have to press it, and they go puff and disappear. I guess it wouldn't have done me much good in this situation; I would have had to look for it in this hairy ape's body. OK, I had the wallet. Now what? Now get the hell out of here, that's when I whispered, "Let me open the door to get my pants down. It's a tight squeeze in here, and I am not the Houdini you are."

He replied, "Yes, yes. Anything. Just hurry."

No truer words were ever spoken as I hopped out. I ran like a star quarterback slave being chased by a slave owner tackler who just released a Pit Bull with Aids, I held his wallet as my football placed securely under my arm. I must have run for two hours straight, I had no idea where I was, and I really didn't care. I got to a bus stop and slowed down enough to ask a woman if I was still in America. She answered yes. I decided to wait for the next bus with her. Many of these streets aren't safe; there's a lot of undesirables running around this city, ya know. The bus soon came, and I begged the driver to let me on because I was lost. The woman actually paid my fare. I didn't dare take the wallet out from under my arm. I kept the thing under my arm until the last person finally got off the bus. I then went to the seats in the last row and proceeded to count my spoils. When I opened it I couldn't believe my eyes. I nearly farted, coughed, belched, and sneezed again. I wanted to yell bingo, pokeno, black jack, yahoo. I've never seen so many one-hundred-dollar bills. The hairy ape was sure loaded. There was over 1,600 dollars and at that price I didn't care about revenge, reprisals, or retribution. I was rich, Jack! I guess you could say that I was a crude example of ghetto existentialism. Here and now, I was rich. Yet the voice of reason that we all have did try to guide me to do what was right. I heard a voice say, "Give the money back, it's not worth the trouble," but I ignored the mental fool.

I knew that this meant that I may have to leave home or possibly face another encounter with the judge; I had to think about this and think about it hard. I was somewhat secure, remembering that Joe never asked me for personal information, but did I ever mention it in passing with my coworkers. Could they find me? This money was also my co-workers pay, as well. I know if someone stole my pay and I knew something to help get it back, I would sound like a tobacco auction. Sometimes you have to decide if the price for the money is really worth it.

CHAPTER 4

AM-BITCH-ION

I got back to the neighborhood and couldn't wait to see and tell all my old buddies about my score. My life in the straight had come to a sad climatic end and all because of a hairy fool who liked me. Well, that's in the past. Sunshine had 1,600 dollars. You can now refer to me as "Sun Set for Life." I got back and it was still light outside, but the place was different. There were no kids playing in the playground, no old people on the benches; there was a deafening silence ... in fact, I couldn't find any of my friends. As I looked around I hardly recognized the place. Remember, I was waking up early to go to work and arriving home late at night. I hadn't had any conversations with any of my friends in quite q while. I just stood there looking around as if this was my first time here. It had a unique bad odor that I never realized before. It only took me a little while to find the answer as to why everything was so strange. After questioning some of the older residents as they came home from work and seeing some of my old friends, I had my answer. It was chilling to see, hear, and come to grips with the reality of its truth.

This was the summer of our most dreaded discontent. A demented destiny had descended upon the children of the ghetto without warning or reason. The plague that hit here did not attack the trees or the grass; they remained intact. Its victims could not get ready or prepared for their end by storing provisions; it descended on them in the form of the cruelest infestations known to man. Drugs.

It was not a drug season like kite or skate season, and no one saw it coming. Our locusts were carried into our dens in the pockets of scavengers, mental misfits, and social outcasts. It came unchallenged and assured victory by the inhuman conditions that prevailed. It came unmasked, uninvited, and was unrelenting in its ability to spread. It was more destructive that any army since the beginning of time, yet crueler because it took no prisoners. Its casualties were infinite and the shots fired were silent and self-inflicted. Its attack was swift, infernal, and complete; the opposing side stood no chance against it. You see with its promise of a better time, happier moments, and a feeling of self-assurance in their lives, they welcomed it, they laughed with it, they took it in their confidence, and when it turned on them, they were unaware, some were still laughing, but now at themselves. It became their master; it called and they came. When it demanded their allegiance, they knew no friends, no family, no religion, just heaven and hell. Heaven when they had it and hell when it was gone. They were willing to die for its pleasure, and both praised and cursed its power. They yielded to its control, they were hooked. Yes, drugs had literally wiped out my community; it was my meager job that saved my life. Most of my friends were dead, hooked, or curious; I went to see Tooths, and he wasn't smiling anymore. He told me the raw tale. You see I was lucky enough to look at a junkie, and know that I didn't want to be a junkie.

In any event, it was time for me to grow up. What to do with this money I just stole? When I got upstairs everyone was asleep. I packed a light bag and left five hundred dollars on the table. I wrote a note to say that I had become bored with the work I was doing and found a much better job that paid more and provided a room; it would also have a school nearby. I then snuck into my grandmother's room and gave her a peck on the forehead. I placed two hundred-dollar bills in her hand, and she woke up and asked, "Boy, what's the matter?"

I said, "Nothing, lady, go back to sleep."

She asked if I was in trouble again, and I said no. She got up and immediately grabbed her Bible and lovingly gave it to me. I told her that I now had a room close to my new job. She asked, "Does your mother know?"

I said, "I will be back tomorrow and tell her," my grandmother opened the bible closed it then handed it to me and then I left."

I was still somewhat worried about Joe finding out where I lived, but I remembered that in his eagerness to get me to work there, I never had to fill out any papers; no one knew where I lived because I never really socialized with anyone. I was the youngest person there, sort of like their mascot. Yet I wasn't entirely sure about this, so it was best to stay away for a while. I was off to stake my claim in the world with a pocket full of cash and a Bible. I was off on my life adventure.

I headed straight to the place where I heard that if you really wanted to see the world first class, you should make a reservation. I arrived at the Greyhound bus station later that evening. When I arrived at the ghetto airport the grayhound bus station. I still had about nine hundred and some change, so I grabbed the first bus going South. I wanted to see it all, experience it all, taste it all, and steal it all. The first stop of my venture was somewhere in Virginia. I sat next to this old man who smelled of chicken. He had on an old-style suit, which was about three sizes too big. He wore an old beat-up hat with an inch brim on it. He had age in his eyes and spoke in a soft voice with a heavy Southern accent. He immediately began schooling me about the perils of the South, his advice was "ta keep ya trap shut, and do whatever day tell ya." He just assumed that I knew who the hell he was talking about. He didn't have any teeth up front; I just figured that they jumped out to escape his breath, or he hocked them with the tooth fairy. He talked about the South like I was about to enter King Kong's ass and the ape was about to fart.

I had heard stories, but I never directly experienced the kind of fear inducing racism that this man was talking about. In fact it was hard to believe that such a thing existed. Deep inside, I realized that I didn't have much interaction with white society other than the storekeepers, schoolteachers, and bosses I'd had. I felt oh man that only happened to you because you're old and stupid. I was sure that once white America got to know me, they would learn to love me. I couldn't have been more wrong. I was naively projecting my limited view of the world. The old man had his warnings to me realistically illustrated once we arrived in Virginia; there we encountered a big, fat cop twice the size of Muldoon. His gun belt was nearly around his knees. His hat was on crooked and he didn't smile at all. We were all standing outside the bus as they cleaned the inside, while Officer Belly-go-Round approached the older brothers, one at a time. He started by saying with his drawl, "Bus driver tells me you been tearing up the bus, boy."

The old man quickly replied before the younger ones could answer "No, sir, twasn't us." I was praying that the cop didn't get a whiff of what he was spewing out his mouth, because he would have surely arrested him for assault with deadly spray pepper. The old man immediately dropped his head when the cop looked him in the eyes, I immediately followed suit. The cop didn't ask anything else of the brothers to whom he'd directed the question, the old man had deflected the question. Officer Butt-full then swaggered away to the next victim and repeated his verbal quatrain. "Bus driver said you been tearing up the bus, boy." This was another colored man about fifty years old, a colored man who replied, "No, sir, I would never do anything like that."

The crop of cop just walked away. He then approached a younger person around my age or a few years older who didn't have the wisdom or guidance of the old man who educated me. When confronted with the same accusatory statement, he replied, "I did what? That's a lie." Well, the handcuffs were on before he finished the word *lie.* The cop had him on the ground with one big-ass knee in his back. I felt sorry for the brother; had he only sat in my seat he would have been protected by this old man's wisdom. I began to look at my mentor in a whole other light. The handcuffed boy was taken away and for all we know executed. If it wasn't for the ultra bad breath, I could have kissed that old man. I learned an important lesson that trip. When in the South, *shut up.* Just think this was only the beginning of my cultural education. I decided while on the bus that my destination was Florida, sunny weather, girls in bathing suits just like the ones that I used to see in magazines, luxury motels all the thing I read about. I was a man now on my own, with plenty of cash and my own Bible. It was getting there that was the problem. I awakened to another fact very early in my pilgrimage- the bus ride was long, hot and boring. I enjoyed the scenery and after a while the old man even got interesting, I don't know if it was because of the ride or he truly had wisdom, but after a while I found myself listening and enjoying his stories. At one point. I even entertained the idea of slipping a twenty in his pocket. His stop was in South Carolina, which was about two hours away. His name was Yoseevas Williams, and he said that he had been married for thirty years to the same woman. He was a descendant of slaves and had lived in the same shack all of his entire life. He had two children whom he adored. He said he worked as a sharecropper. The more he spoke, the more I liked him. Now that I knew more about him, I couldn't smell any breath at all.

I actually grew to admire Yoseevas. He was calm and assured in the fact that no matter what life dished out he was divinely protected. He made this ride enlightening and gave me a million-dollar education. He spoke of the pain, the hardship, the hurt, the pleasures, and the abuse in his life. His face would illustrate every tale he told with animated emotions. I never met anyone like Yoseevas before in my life. An old man with a total American experience. I suddenly realized how relativity easy I had it, and how very much protected I had been. He was somewhat like my grandfather. My father was nothing like him. My dad would have probably gone to jail when the cop asked about tearing up the bus. My mother use to tell me a story about being on the bus with my dad, they were traveling through the south and they inadvertently sat up front. When the driver told my dad to get to the back of the bus he got up and walked outside to the rear and stood on the buses fender. The driver was pissed because they couldn't move with this fool on the fender. He told my father to get off and get to the rear, to which my father replied, this is the rear of the bus. The police were called and when they got there to arrest my father he spoke in his thickest Jamaican accent. They thought he had just arrived in this country so then escorted him to a seat in the rear and the bus left. When the old man got up to get his bag to get off, he peeped in my bag and saw my Bible. He smiled as he passed me and said what my grandmother said, "All the answers are to be found in the Good Book, boy, you gonna be all right."

He then waved goodbye as he gathered his belongings and went to stand up and wait for his stop. He taught me a valuable lesson that I will always remember in life, and that was to know when to shut up and keep your mouth shut.

Although I couldn't really imagine to what extent was his pain inside, I felt for this man. I couldn't even imagine a gang fight in my neighborhood where the gangs wanted to inflict cruel bodily harm because of the color of the other gang's skin, then insisting on them doing degrading acts. Or a gang who had physically conquered the other gangs then insisting on them doing degrading acts of inhumane antics just to satisfy a sick ego. I am sure I didn't understand the extent of the old man's words, but I thoroughly understood his eyes. He made my trip one of the most interesting ones that I had ever experienced. I sat and listened to all of his tales, thirsting for more. At one point I remember wishing that he could come and bring his family to live with us. Then it hit me. I was traveling away from my home and toward the place that the old man spoke of. I had a question that I couldn't make sense of that I just had to ask him. Before we reached his stop, he was now standing near the door. I went up to him and I said, "If the South is so bad and full of hate, then why didn't you move away and take your family?"

The old man just looked at me and smiled. He leaned forward and whispered, "Son, there was once a bird who thought that the winter couldn't be as bad as everyone had said. He decided that come winter he was going to be smarted than the other birds and put enough food away to survive. He was going to build a nest where no cold air could possibly penetrate. He worked on that nest all fall. When the tip of winter arrived he got in his nest and settled in, while the other birds had flown south. He was now secure that he had made the right decision. By the time January rolled in he started to get second thoughts, but still it was bearable. February soon appeared with the snow and the wind and the severe chill. He was nearly out of food and confronted with the fact that he would indeed die if he stayed in this frozen nest. He then realized that he should have done what the other birds had done and what was instinctually expected of him, and that was to fly South to a better climate. He knew that it was probably too late to try, but he had no choice. Death was certain in this situation. So he ventured out

Robby

and started to fly South. The wind was blowing hard, and the ice was forming on his wings. He knew that he had made the wrong decision. His wings became too heavy to fly, and he plummeted towards the ground. The ill-in-formed bird fell hard and smashed right through the roof of a barn. As he lay on the ground half-frozen and half-dead, gasping for air, waiting to draw his last breath of life, a cow who lived in this barn walked over and crapped on him. Now you may think that this was the worst thing that could have happened given the situation, but in fact it was the best. You see the crap was warm, and pretty soon our friend was alert and in control of his senses. He began looking around the barn and spotted a perch way up high, and he thought, *I could live here all year and never have to travel. This is a blessing.* He went to get up to fly to the perch when he realized that he was stuck. He fought and twisted but he was in deep. Finally he began to yell for help. He screamed, 'Help! Help me!' His cries were heard by another of the barn's residents. A cat heard his plea, dug him out from the crap, and ate him."

Yoseevas just looked at me for a moment with a half-baked smile on his face. I thought that this would have a happy ending. "Was that it?" I asked.

The old man said, "The moral of the story, son, is this: not everyone who craps on you is your enemy, and not everyone who pulls you out of crap is ya friend."

The bus driver then announced the old man's stop. In his slow, calm manner he grabbed the bag he'd been resting on. He looked me in the eye and stroked my hair. He bent over and again whispered in my ear, "And when ya living in crap but ya comfortable, *shut the hell up.*" I watched as he exited the bus and went back to my seat and thought of him the rest of my trip.

I arrived in Florida and immediately called home. Old girl answered and was obviously concerned. "Where are you, what kind of new job is this and where did you get this money from?"

I calmly said, "I saved it just for you. I got a better job and I'm helping get supplies. I am all right and all is good. I will keep in touch. Did anyone ask for me?"

"Like who?" she said.

"Like my friend's, my father, anyone." I answered.

She replied, "No."

Grandma asked, "did you read your bible?"

I answered, "yes."

"OK, we are all proud of you and thank you for the money. What about school?" she asked.

"I am taking night courses. Don't worry, all is good."

"Well, maybe it's best you are not here, things are bad."

"I know I saw it. All is good. Take care."

Well, I arrived in Florida and went crazy. What's the saying about a fool and his money? The hotels were like Joe at the restaurant; they didn't ask for anything up front, they just looked at my wad and said "Welcome"; not even my age was a factor. They couldn't care less where the money came from, they wanted it - case closed!" I bought clothes, food, sunglasses, and spent my time at the pool, relaxing and looking at the lady's bodies. My first days the only contact I had was an older German woman who didn't speak English well and once made me believe she was drowning. We were both on the shallow end of the pool, but she fell and made believe that she couldn't get back up. I reached down and grabbed her. She acted like she was grateful and asked me to walk her to her room because she was still wobbly. We got to her room and she opened the door and grabbed me. I was literally raped. She was no Marsha, but when she began to give me oral sex, I surrendered. I knew what it was from the guys in my neighborhood, but this was indeed a first. It was like she was trying to suck my soul out through my meat straw. I first pulled my hips back and then thought hey, that felt good. I then pushed them forward to where they had been and said, hey, that felt even better. I was nearly seventeen but looked a lot older. As long as I kept my eyes closed the entire time, it was good. It was when I opened them and saw she was now naked next to me that I realized how women's bodies differed. No hips, no shape to her legs, and no ass and somewhat deflated breasts. I felt as if I had to pee really bad, then all of a sudden the pee just escaped, and my body tensed. I soon realized that it wasn't pee; it was goey stuff. My first time cumming.

After that my penis died and there was no res-erection for this dead dude. I began to get embarrassed. I tried thinking about Marsha. I again tried making believe there was a flag in another room and my penis was now a general. *Nothing.* She kept sucking it, but he was gone. She asked what happened. I answered, "I don't know, let me take a walk."

"You coming back?" she asked.

I said, "If my mother lets me."

She immediately locked the door when I walked out. I left and went back to this unaccomplished lifestyle. The education I received on this trip was invaluable. The money I stole wasn't wasted, it paid for an education, a kind of twisted tuition. I learned from the old man to keep quiet when the time calls for it, and I learned from the old woman that I was capable of cumming and I liked it. I woke up about a half a month later at another hotel, nearly broke, hungry and with a head full of great memories. I had a real suitcase with nice clothes and an unopened Bible. I just had enough for a one-way bus ticket back to New York. I made my periodic calls home and painted a picture that I was doing great. Mom asked if I was taking care of myself and Grandma kept asking if I had read my Bible. I always said yes to both. Thankfully, no word of Joe or the police looking for me. That was good because his money was long gone. When I arrived at the bus stop in New York, I ran into an older woman from my neighborhood named Erma. She was going to visit her children, so we stopped and had coffee. Erma told me how good I looked and that everyone was so proud of me for doing so well. She also spoke about the drugs and the violence destroying the community and said that I had gotten out just in time. She told me she knew I had a good job but that she knew of a man in the Bronx who had a store and was always looking for good workers. She wished that I would meet him. I asked for his address and told her that if I ever got to the neighbor-hood he was in, I would look him up. Next stop, the neighborhood he was in.

CHAPTER 5

THE BROTHER SOLD

That same day my tanned, broke, but well-dressed self went to Erma's friend's store called Sold Brother. I thoroughly believed that the police were looking for, as they say in my neighborhood, "my loan from Joe." This was a corner store that sold damn near everything. As you walked in you were greeted by the noise of music being played, and a nose full of incense. They had records, books, combs, food, posters, candy, and drinks. They especially had very loud music blasting over a loudspeaker out front, which forced the residents to hear the songs that they played. It was a sight to see a woman walking down the street carrying two shopping bags swaying to the music. The store was next to a barbershop, and you could hear the culturally insignificant chatter permeate the walls. This corner was alive with culture. The people were a lot better dressed than the ones in my neighborhood. I walked in as if I was entering a Museum, I went to this man reading a paper and asked for the owner. This was a tall, well-built black man with short hair, and a well-groomed appearance. I introduced myself and smiled. The first thing he said, "I am the establishment's owner, Solid." Then he asked, "Why are you smiling? You really happy with you, huh, brother?" The trick was to make the other person smile. He asked me why I was here, and I told him that I came about a job that a mutual friend named Erma told me about.

He again asked why I was here, and I repeated that I came for a job. He then said, "And if I say no, there is no job, your entire reason for making this trip is shot. He then said, "Li'l brother?"

I didn't understand what he was getting at. He then said, "Boy, when you're asked 'why are you here,' that is your cue to impress the hell out of the person asking the question. You tell them exactly why they need you and what you will do to make their life better. Remember that."

He then told me that there were many kids in the neighbor-hood who would love the opportunity to work here. He then asked, "Why the bag?"

I told him that I had a job in Florida, which ended abruptly and I just got back to New York.

He then said ended abruptly, like fired? I replied, "No, sir.", "You in school?"

I said, "No, I finished."

He asked me to open my bag. He saw my clothes neatly folded and my Bible. He immediately reached for my Bible. He then asked me what I wanted to do with my life, and I said that I didn't know.

"I do know that for right now I just know that I want to work here."

He cast a half smile, still holding my Bible in his hand.

"You read this book, boy?"

"I am in the process of reading it now."

He placed it back in my bag and put his hand on my shoulder. I liked him right off.

He was very serious. He would look me dead in the eye when-ever he spoke, and there was no pretense in him. I got the job and was happy for it. This was a new beginning for me. He asked me to fill out an application and asked me every question he could think of.

"You ever been in trouble, son?"

"No, sir, I answered."

The Bible was my cushion. My grandmother was right, it could open doors for you. This neighborhood was like being in another country. I saw kids my age with baseball uniforms on, girls had on school uniforms, and everyone was polite and kind. People I didn't even know would say good morning. I didn't tell my folks that I was back. I couldn't go home broke after lying about working. I figured that once I was settled in, I would work in the day and I would sleep on the trains at night and get back to work in the morning, and hopefully find a place to stay in the interim. The drawback was the train ride; it was always loud and boring. After work I would just walk the streets and then catch a train. When I got bored I would usually pick up a discarded newspaper and read the comics. I would get a hot dog at the store when I got off, and that would hold me till morning. I would get to work early and wash up in the bathroom. My job at the store was to keep everything clean and sell as much as I could.

Soon after I started, everyone knew my name. The old people would come in for their newspaper and the young for their candy. I got to know the crowd of boys in the neighborhood. Now where I grew up in Harlem I was maybe a fair fighter when we would play fight. In this crowd here, I was exceptional. These kids would have been slaves back in Harlem, this was more of a middle-class neighborhood. I was amazed that there was no credit given, everyone immediately paid cash. In my neighborhood everyone used credit until payday or until their checks came in the mail. There was one girl who used to stop in on her way home from school. She was gorgeous and friendly and would always ask if I was all right and smile at me before she left, her name was Laura. Every day Solid would teach me something. His motto was to learn something completely new every day. Sometimes after work I would hang out with the other kids in the neighborhood, or after work we would just stand in front of the store and just talk, as young men sometimes do. One night we were just standing outside just shooting the stuff when a pimpmobile passed us by. It was fantastic and we all flipped over it and yelled at the driver to voice our approval as kids do.

Solid called me inside the store and said he wanted to speak to me in the back. This was the first of many backroom lessons, which started with a slap on the head. *POW!*

I said, "What did I do?"

He looked me dead in my eye and said, "Don't you ever settle for being an ohhh ahhh nigger. If you see a car and like it, then make up your mind to get inspired by it, and to learn all you can so you can go to college and get one. That was a poverty pimp who exploits his own people for his own selfish needs, don't cheer him on. Boo that asshole."

Made sense, but I couldn't understand why he didn't come out-side and tell everyone who was admiring the ride.

I worked and I rode the subway. I was scared of two things: 1. Someone who knew Solid or my family would see me sleeping on the train, and 2. Someone who knew Joe would see me sleeping on the train. Solid thought that I finished high school but in no uncertain terms did he accept the fact that I didn't strive for college. He stressed education, karate, and health food. I really tried my best to please him. I wanted to make him proud because I knew that he wanted me to always do my best.

Solid provided something that I never had before in my life, something totally new to me, and that was *expectations*. I knew that he believed in my promise. My mother expected me to always be good, but Solid expected me to always strive to be great. My conversation was getting better. I graduated from reading the comics from the discarded newspapers on the subway to reading the horoscopes, the sports pages, and some news articles.

I would work my butt off, and every day Solid would talk to me about current events. He would ask me questions and engage me in things he felt were important. It got so that when I got off I would jump on the train and look for the subject he was talking about in the newspaper so I could share something new when I got to work in the morning. Soon I started to emulate Solid and read the entire discarded papers before I got to work so when he would question me I would surprise him and sometimes have an answer. I didn't know then but my reading level went through the roof. I really wanted to impress this man. My proudest moments were when he would ask me a question about something in the news and I would answer with the correct answer and then give my opinion.

Solid would look at me with a satisfied look and say, "I'm impressed, li'l brother, I'm impressed.

I was what they called an everything man at the shop. I did it all: serve, clean, inventory, deliver." Solid used to call me his Wandering Generality who was striving to be a Meaningful Specific. Solid wasn't a college graduate; he was self-educated and said that he was born with a book in his hand. When he would sit down and read his face would become stone and his eyebrows were the only things that would move as he read. He was married with children, but for what-ever reason he didn't want his family at the store. I think because he singlehandedly got rid of the undesirables that used to hang out on the corner, bothering the patrons.

Yeah, this was the closest I got to college and much more interesting than the education I got from the streets. The young lady who came into the store to whom I was attracted to told me her name was Laura. Laura and I were getting more and more serious. We used to just say hi in the beginning, but I now found that I had something in my charm arsenal that I never had before, intelligent conversation.

I was becoming more multidimensional. Before, all I had was my street smarts and good looks, but now I had actual conversation. I worked there into my late teens and became very close to Solid. He was the responsible father I wish I had. One day I got paid and the plan was that I was to meet Laura at her house to take her to a neighborhood dance. I was looking at some new oils that just came in that we had never carried before, and I was telling Solid about my pending date. I then said, "Hey, what would you charge me for that coconut oil for my hair?"

Solid's face changed and he said those dreaded words, "Come into the back."

I walked into a slap right in the head. He said, "Where you going tonight?"

I said, "To a dance."

He said, "If Laura wants something to drink, will you pay?" And I said, "I guess so."

He then said, "Will you ask the waitress or bartender how much it costs, or will you just pay?"

I just smiled. He then said, "Li'l brother, when you want something for you, and you know it will help you make the impression you want to make, to hell with how much it costs, you just buy it." If I was wearing my street conscience, I would have thought that he was just conning me to sell me something that he wanted to sell, but this man was 100 percent in my book, and I knew that he was just looking out for me. Understand that with each slap I got either a book and/or an article to read to help me understand and learn what he thought was an important lesson. When I said that I regarded his word as total sincerity, that's a big jump as far as trust from me. My father would always say something to me, and I would then dissect and analyze it from a hundred different directions to see if there was truth in his statement.

It made me somewhat BS proof and gave me an insight that many children aren't afforded from their parents. Dad would have thought Solid was a sucker for working every day and being as honest and sincere as he was.

Well, I got the oil and smelled like a coconut tulip with special seasoning. I got dressed in my Sunday best, and I headed for Laura's house. I arrived at a beautiful two-story brick house in a lower middle class neighborhood. It was beautiful to me, and I just wondered what it must have been like to live there. Imagine getting to one's room without an elevator ride. I gently knocked on the door and it slowly opened. At first I thought Laura was wearing the best make up and girdle ever made, and then I realized that this was her mother.

She said, "Well hello, you must be George."

I said, "Yes, ma'am."

She went on to say that she heard very positive things about me. She also said that she would sometimes see me cleaning the outside window at the store when the weather was warmer, and I seemed to enjoy my work. Just then I heard clothes ruffling, and I looked to my left as he appeared from behind the opened door, one giant of a man who had to bow his head to clear the door's threshold as he entered the hallway. He was about six foot four, and he never smiled or anything. The mother introduced us, and he shook my hand like a damn snapping turtle bit it. I didn't want to flinch, but I remember thinking OK, Uncle, just let go. He asked me where were we going and what time we would be home.

I said to a local club and by midnight. He said how 'bout a local restaurant and home by ten. I answered, "Yes, sir, whatever you say, sir." *Just don't shake and hold my damn hand hostage with that grip of yours.*

Laura then appeared, and she looked beautiful. The first thing I thought was *Wow, was she a looker.*

The father said, "You look very nice, young lady, I can even smell your perfume over the coconut [a wisecrack about my hair]." The mother laughed. I stood back to let Laura pass, and she said, "You look nice." She then snickered and said, "And smell good too." The parents looked up in the air so not to laugh. We then left and were walking down the street. I wanted to grab her hand, but I knew that they were looking at us through the window. Laura asked where I was taking her, and I said to a restaurant. She said, "I thought you said that we were going to a club."

I said, "No, I said we could stop and get a club sandwich." She looked puzzled. There was a Caribbean restaurant about ten blocks away. I never ate there but loved Caribbean food. We got there, and it appeared to be a nice place. The music was nice and they treated us like royalty. At first I thought they was just treating me like a prince because of the coconut smell I emitted, but when I saw other people come in, I know that it was their custom.

We sat at a table in the back with a small flickering candle on it. They brought us two menus.

Laura was glowing in the candlelight. I was getting kind of nervous because I felt that she would realize that I did not live like this or dine out a lot; this was all a novelty to me. When I opened the menu and read the entrees I sighed with relief when I knew that I had enough money. When you live in the ghetto you usually read a menu from right to left and order what you can afford. I remember when the family went to White Castles and we would all have one hamburger each and swore we were splurging.

Laura asked, "What are you having?"

And I said, "I haven't decided yet. What are you having?"

She said, "Just some soup."

I immediately felt that she was concerned that I wouldn't be able to pay for a full meal, so I said, "Laura, please get whatever you want, I want you to enjoy yourself."

She replied in a soft voice, "I am enjoying myself. I just have to watch my weight." Luckily the filter in my brain that regulated what my mind thinks to what my mouth speaks stopped the thought that said, "I know, I just saw your mother."

You'd be surprised by how many relationships are ruined because one, if not both, of the couple's filters are broken and what they think comes roaring out their mouths. She ordered the soup and I ordered it as well. The waitress taking our order kept sniffling as if to say, "Who stole the coconuts?"

We sat and talked about everything. Laura mostly wanted to know about me: where I lived, who my parents were, how I got the job, did I finish school. I was honest in my replies. I told her that I had to leave school to help pay the bills. I just didn't tell her that they were all my bills. Laura was stunning; I was enchanted by her being. We slowly sipped the soup and laughed. Soon the conversation just flowed without thought or effort. I just reacted, and the company was enhanced by looks grins, smiles, eyebrows, arms, hands, and movement. I remember having a conscious thought that I really liked her, but equally important was the fact that for the first time I was not reciting things that I had heard.

I had developed true, honest intelligence from the newspapers and books I had read, and I owed it all to Solid. In the past when I was ever around a woman, I used a series of canned lines, which I thought were creative, and one size had to fit all. Now I was using my mind.

Laura was also just flowing in her many points, which she was making. She was also teaching me things I never knew before. She asked me what I wanted to do with my life. In the past my canned line would have been "I am going to get a thousand dollars and buy everything in the supermarket that was marked double your money back and then take it back and do that about a hundred times a year." This time I was blank; my mind hit a wall, but I immediately thought of this in terms of Solid's advice and knew that I had to show exactly why I was relevant to have around. I smiled with a tight lip and said, "I want to do something that will make me smile on my deathbed. When I reach my last thought and my last breath is about to set free my soul, I would be resigned and content with the thought that 'at least I did that.' I don't know what it will be as of yet, but that's what I want to do with my life."

Laura immediately asked, "How will you know that that was what you were supposed to do?"

I said, "Because it is what I was sent here to do how could that not be it."

There is a woman in the Bible, no one knew her name, but her claim to fame was the beautiful gesture she did when she wiped Christ's face when he was carrying the cross. Her name is and was irrelevant but her act lives on. I want my mission to be that kind of kindness. She looked at me, and I heard her just slowly breathing out as she looked at me and smiled. Now you're probably thinking, *Did he finally read his grandmother's Bible?* Right? *No.* My grandmother told me that story, and boy was it the right one to close with for this occasion.

As much as Solid tried to instill things in me, I still veered back and forth to my father's teachings when it served what I thought was my best interest, and impressing Laura was indeed in my best interest. Laura then looked in my eyes, I was feeling kind of bad that I used my street filling to impress her. I could see her begin to inch closer to me with every word. She then grabbed my hand and asked, "What's your favorite poem?"

P-O-E-M? This one stumped me for a moment. I thought hard then said, "When I peer into your eyes and gaze beyond your look, I can see the me I want to be. The person who makes you smile, and depend on, in your times of happiness as well as your lows. In you I see me. I will always strive to become better so that never a tear will wash away the me both you and I can see in your eyes."

She put her head down and said, "That's beautiful, who wrote that?"

I smiled and said I just did, inspired by your eyes. She pulled me closer and then kissed me. I suddenly looked at the clock and felt like Cinderella looking at the clock after a blackout. All I thought about was her big-ass father standing up and looking at his watch while holding a baseball bat. I asked for the check like I was upset and displeased with the service, and I wasn't. The waitress asked me if everything was all right, and I said yes, everything was just fine. I just didn't want to go to the hospital this night with Laura's father, so he could get his damn shoe back.

Laura asked me if I was all right, but the truth be told, I didn't want to let on that I didn't want to piss off her father. We had fun together. I looked up and saw that time had just flew by. I felt like Cinderella who knew her clothes would all disappear at midnight. I was concerned, but the most paramount thought in my mind was that we had a great time. It was the first time I really communicated with a lady, and I liked it. I was inspired to learn more, if just to keep her interested, if not to impress her. We got to her house and all of the lights were on. I walked her to her front door, and she began looking for her keys. She then suddenly stopped and looked at me; her face was glowing in the night's light, and her face was expression-less. Her eyes were softly open, and her lips were moist.

I said, "I really had a good time, and I hope that it was just the opening act of this play."

She was slowly moving toward me, as I to her. I could hear a heartbeat, but I couldn't tell whose heart it was. She moved closer, turning on each of my senses. As she was getting closer, I could now smell her perfume. As I extended my arm, we were now nose to nose, thought to thought, action to reaction, when suddenly the door swung open. Standing there in his interrupting glory was her father.

My senses immediately turned, off and they all went back into my body and hid. She was embarrassed and said, "It's me, Dad, I was just coming in."

He then asked her, "Are you all right? Did you have a good time?"

It wasn't an inquiring voice. It was more to me like he was asking, "Do you want me to kick his damn ass in and his teeth out?"

I didn't say a word. Why would I? There's a thin line between being a victim and a volunteer.

She replied, "We had a very nice time."

He then opened the door a little wider as if to say to her, "Come on in." Laura looked at me and sheepishly said good night. I said, "Night."

The father looked at me as if to say, "You leaving now? Or would you rather I chase you home?"

I turned and walked away. I walked away reliving the entire evening and deleting the moments with her father. As I got nearer to the store, I could vaguely hear the music still playing from Solid's store and I became thankful that he was in my life and exposed me to an entirely new way to live. I was proud of myself for the things I said and created, but knew I needed to learn more so I did not have to rely on my street smarts.

I wanted to learn honest, natural living, which to me was relying on educational smarts and wisdom and not entirely by my wits. I was happy and thankful at the same time. I went back to the store and told Solid to leave and go home, that I would close up because I knew that I couldn't sleep that night. Solid told me that Laura's father came in to buy something that he didn't need, to ask about me. He asked Solid what kind of a boy I was, and what kind of family did I come from. Solid told him, "He is a young man who is not just going through life, he is in the process of growing through life."

He asked was I in school, and Solid replied, "He is in the process of getting his education completed. As far as family goes, his mother is a good woman."

He then asked about my father. Solid then replied, "I under-stand that he's is an interesting man." Solid always said that the word *interesting* was truly an evasive word without one true meaning. He told me that I could use the cot in the back if I didn't want to travel home. That cot soon became my one true bed. There was a small apartment area in the back of the store that I thankfully moved into. Life was the best it had been for me. I was learning and living a whole new life. Each day, Solid would teach me something new. Laura would stop by from time to time, and we would sit and talk politics religion, culture, relationships, and us. It was all so very perfect. I literally never went back to the old neighborhood to visit my family. They didn't mind because they all noticed the transformation when they spoke to me on the phone or received the money I would send. Grandma would always ask me if I was reading the Bible, and I would always answer yes and thanked her for it. I was told that I was getting serious and turning into a young man. The best way that I could explain this transformation was by simply saying that for the first time in my life I had pride in myself and pride in the knowledge that I had. I threw away all of those one-size-fits-all clichés and replaced them with analytical knowledge. I was indeed happy, and life was good. I even stopped getting slapped in my head whenever there was something that Solid thought I needed to learn. I guess he now felt that he didn't have to activate my brain before sending in some knowledge. He even threw me a birthday party when I turned eighteen. It was a good time. I enjoyed working, I enjoyed learning, and I enjoyed being. I don't know what kind of family man Solid was other than the rare occasions when his wife and kids came to the store they would always look at him with love in their eyes, although his wife Marcie was a bottom line person and always wanted to know how much we made.

Robby

They all spoke of him, and to him, with respect in their hearts. His children would always call him "Sir" and answer him in proper phrases. I can attest to the fact that to me he was all he could be. Solid was the first and only completely positive man I ever met. I once saw a woman who purchased something and then lie and said that she gave him a bill higher than the one she actually gave him. While he was looking in the register at the bill she gave him, he gave her change for the amount she said she gave him because he knew that she really needed the money. She was a single mother who tried to make ends meet. He was the total opposite of my father. My father would have beat her out of her change then swore he gave her more than she was entitled to. It was somewhat puzzling to see a man without any need or desire to get something for nothing. I knew that the people in the neighborhood idolized him; they both loved and respected him and I mean a whole lot.

The old men in the neighborhood used to talk about their past lives and how much things have changed in the neighborhood since they first arrived. Solid could talk the talk of the street and then debate political issues with the best of them.

I used to sit in the barbershop whenever I could when Solid would get his hair cut just to hear the conversation. Easter was soon approaching, and I was saving money for a new set of clothes. Solid insisted that I go and spend the holiday with my family and bring them a good meal paid for with my *legal*, hard-earned money, which I agreed to do, but in truth I still wasn't ready to go back home. I liked working here; I didn't have to turn around to see if anyone was watching before I bent over and picked something up like I had to at Joes. I was keeping the shop immaculate, and business was doing great. We were selling a lot of things, and we actually tripled what we used to earn from when I first arrived to now. I think that the people knew that it was just a positive place to shop and the good music blasting was also a draw. They loved when we would play a soulful song on the speaker. Solid helped me go and pick out a dignified out-fit. It was really more business than street, and the colors all matched. I asked him who was going to work while I was gone, and he said "Who do you think worked the store before you came? I will and it will be as clean and as well run as before."

He then smiled and said, "Well, maybe not the floors, but the rest of the store will be."

Easter was now just a week away. Laura came by and asked me what my plans were. I told her that I was going away. She looked sad, but she also wanted me to go and spend some time with my family. I showed her the outfit that I had brought, and she asked me if I could wear it and come to her house before I left for the holiday. I told her that I would. The night I was to leave I gave the store one last kick-ass cleaning. I put all the new merchandise out, and I cleaned all of the store-front windows.

I worked my ass off. Solid just walked around the store and smiled and said, "Good job, young man, good job." I went in the back and washed up and then put on my outfit. When I came out the people in the store clapped. I felt good. I looked as sharp as a mosquito's penis. I even smelled like an angel's fart, not coconut, just pure nose candy. I was somewhat apprehensive about stopping at Laura's house; one need not be valedictorian at Sherlock Holmes's academy to know that her father hated my guts. She called and asked me to come now. I stood on her porch and hesitated but then said "What the hell," and I knocked. I could hear soft conversation coming from inside, asking who is it? The door slowly opened as if I were at some haunted house.

It was Laura, and she was wearing shorts and a T-shirt; she looked gorgeous. She told me to come in with a nervous voice. I entered and looked around for her family. I then asked in a hesitant voice, "Where are your parents?" Laura immediately grabbed me and laid the most passionate kiss on me that I ever had. It woke up my penis who asked, "What's going on up there?" She then led me to a back room where she began to undress, I heard a slow song being played. The best surprises are the ones that you're just not expecting. I was hesitant to take my clothes off. I imagined being here naked with her only to have her father appear suddenly behind me, putting his thumb in my butt hole and rolling me across the room like a damn bowling ball. I asked, "When will your parents be back?" And she said that they went to church. Her father was a deacon in the church. We slowly undressed one another, and both our hands were shaking. She gave me the most intense hug that I ever had. She placed both of her arms around me and just squeezed. I stroked her long flowing hair as I looked at her and then closed my eyes. She was all I could have imagined. She slowly fell backwards on the bed, and she coordinated the fall so that I landed on top of her.

She made some slight noises, and they echoed throughout my body. We were both completely naked, and there was no shame or feeling self-conscious. It was natural and beautiful. Our lips were touching as we telepathically communicated our desires. It was as close to heaven as one can get without dying. It was so good I nearly stopped thinking about her father. If there was even a sound coming from the door, I would have tried to tuck myself inside my butt and just hide. There was only the noise of movement. Now I had my experiences, which I told you about, but they were not like this. I never felt such emotion. It was once again as if I was blind and her body was brail and with every touch she was instructing me what to do next. We finished and just stayed there holding each other. Laura whispered, "You better go." I damn near had my pants on by the time she got to *better*. She asked me to come back that night so her parents could see that I came to say goodbye.

I left and then returned about three hours later. I knocked in a soft manner so that in case they didn't hear any knock I could still swear that I came and knocked. When lo and behold, standing there in his terrorizing glory was her father.

To put total confusion in my mind he looked as if he was even trying to smile. It was like he was using muscles in his face that went to bed with Rip Van Winkle. I didn't know what to think; he almost looked cheerful. I said good afternoon, sir? Is Laura home."

He said, "Yes, young man, come in." He said it as if he was reciting a confession to a crime written for him by the actual person who committed the damn crime. He wanted me to come in, and he was walking close behind me. I thought that he found out about what we did earlier, and I just knew that I would hear my head crack at any moment now. We got to the living room and he said "Sit down, I would like to have a word with you. May I offer you anything?"

"No, sir," I answered.

He then said, "You look very nice tonight. Where are you going?"

I told him that I was going home to visit my family. He asked me about them. He said, "What does your father do for a living?"

I was somewhat stumped. I said, "He's a salesman." "What does he sell?" he immediately asked.

I thought about the word "bullcrap," but I said "He supplies religion for the people in my neighborhood." He lifted his eyebrows and said, "Really?"

That wasn't an entire lie because every time my father would go into the bar, they would say, "Jesus you here again?" or say "Please, Lord, just keep that man away from me."

He then said, "I hear good things about you from the shop. You're slowly developing quite a reputation as a hard worker, I admire that. Were you always a hard worker?"

I said "Yes, sir, my last job really appreciated me. They gave me a big bonus for the job I did, and since then I equated giving and getting."

I heard Solid's voice telling me to sell myself. I went on to say that I liked working and doing the best job that I could do. Then his voice changed when he asked, "What about your schooling?"

I told him that I was a good student and enjoyed school, but I had to go to night school in order to help support my family. Just then I heard Laura yell, "May I come in now?" as if she was instructed to stay out. She walked in and smiled she looked at me and said, "Don't you look handsome."

Her father said "Thank you."

Wow. A half a smile and an attempt at humor, I must be dreaming. Hey, I still can't figure out why dogs don't need toilet paper. Laura sat down right beside me, and it made me a bit uncomfortable at first. I thought, *Poppa terror would get upset*, but he didn't. He continued to try to be friendly in his totally awkward way. Laura asked when I was leaving for home, and I told her that I was just going to help Solid close then get going. Laura's mother called her husband and he shook my hand goodbye and left us alone.

Laura said that she was going to miss me and enjoyed our new experience together, as well as our talks at the store and our night out together. She then said that she would like us to spend more time together, like go steady. I asked her what would her family say if I were to visit more often, and that was when she explained that her father and mother were OK with it. Then she asked, "Can't you tell?"

I said, "Your father did seem a little different tonight. It was like an Indian deciding whether to kill me with a blowgun instead of an arrow."

She said, "Point well taken," and we both laughed. I asked "So you mean we would be going together boyfriend and girlfriend?"

She said, "I would like that, if you would. Can't you tell that I already feel like your girlfriend?"

I answered yes, I would like that; inside I thought, 'my first girlfriend!'

Laura said, "You've worked hard in the time that I've known you. The people in the neighborhood have really grown to respect you, including my own father."

I was really proud to hear that. I told her that I had to get going so I could finish up and leave. We both stood up at the same time, and we looked into each other's eyes and were magnetically drawn closer to each other. My heart was beating fast. I could even hear it in my ears. My breathing was louder. When she grabbed my hand, I became a one-man band, with all the noises my senses were now orchestrating. She leaned closer and we kissed; her lips were again soft, wet, and inviting. She closed her eyes and I closed mine as well. We were now lip to lip, with her hand holding mine. I was in heaven until I heard her father cough, and then I was alerted to reality and mentally, quickly escorted back to the present. She walked me to the door and said, "Please be careful and come back soon." I didn't tell her that I wasn't going home. I was either going to again ride the subway and walk around New York or sneak back to the store when it closed.

I was in heaven, at least my mind was. I walked back to the store. I didn't dare turn around to spoil the moment by seeing her father looking at me. When I arrived back at the store, Solid was in the process of closing the store. It was empty, and as I walked in an older white man followed. Now you rarely see white people in this neighborhood unless they were the business owners. This one we never saw before. He looked at Solid and said, "Give me a cigar, boy." Just by his attitude, I knew that this was the kind of white man that would not have taken the three wishes if the genie was black; he just emitted evil. Solid just gave him a half smile and asked him which one would he prefer. He replied, "Just give me one, as long as it doesn't smell like this place and won't get me high."

Solid took out one of his best and handed it to him. He said, "That's a good boy. You got change of a twenty?" Solid took the money and gave him his change. He lit the cigar and asked Solid, "Why are you blasting that jungle music? Is that how you all get that rhythm? You just blast that crap till you just have to dance?"

Solid never answered. The man then asked if we had any ice cream.

I was standing there pissed by how he was treating Solid, and I was about to say, "Yes, we have some nutty vanilla in here," but Solid looked at me and shook his head as if to tell me not to say anything. Solid said, "No, we don't have any."

The man flicked his ashes on the floor and slowly strutted out like the head rooster in the henhouse.

Solid then looked at me and said, "Remember, son, you came a long way since you first showed up. You are not the same person. We all go through different people in the span of our lives. Jokes that were funny to you as a child won't make you laugh now. Always remember, it's not where you come from that makes you a good man, it's what you overcome. Have a good Easter."

I watched him leave and walk down the street. He was my hero. I loved this man. He taught me to think beyond the range that I thought was normal; he was like the old man on the bus only educated. He showed me that knowledge was the key to unlock all the doors ahead of you in life. I gave that store a second cleaning like never before. I made the soda machine and the coolers shine, and then I changed clothes and left and caught the train to go ... where? I did know that it was not wise to get dressed to ride the subway at night in New York. I was not the same person who left home to come and work here. This was Friday night and Easter was on Sunday. I left Solid's with a head full of good memories and hope. Life was only good when one has a new hope each day. Anticipation feeds happiness. I thought of going home, but I just wasn't ready to go back to that neighborhood. The drug wipeout was still affecting me. I did remember that Easter was usually a happy time in the ghetto: those who could get new clothes would get them, and those who couldn't afford new clothes would just put on their best, and those who didn't have best wore their suitable as if it were new. Poor people who didn't know about having money and things for the holiday had the best times during the holidays because their love of God was pure, and they could appreciate the grandeur and the spirit of the holidays. It was right before the holidays that the numbers runners made a killing. Most of the adults had a part-time job playing the numbers, and that was what provided much hope in the ghetto.

I sat on the subway reading a newspaper, and guess what, I even paid for it. It was my first unread newspaper. For some strange reason the news was even more interesting when it was unread.

On the subway you see a lot of people who don't really exist; they just go through the motions of life, repeating the motions of their lives just to get through the day, all needing a purpose for their soul. I felt fortunate to have a purpose. One thing I learned about life was that you never know how good you have it until you have some-thing to compare it to. I guess the drug invasion really got to me, but I know that I was also blessed with analytical reasoning. I didn't have to become a junkie to know I didn't want to be a junkie. I could look at a junkie and know I wanted no part of that. This Easter I was reborn; I had risen from the dead with a girl, a job, and happiness.

When the train reached uptown I saw an old friend who lived in the building next door to my family, and he gave me an update on what was happening, who died and who was still walking but just didn't know that they were dead yet. More than half of my friends submitted their will and therefore their being to drugs; it was bad.

They ravaged the neighborhood in order to support their habits. They begged, robbed, lied, and did whatever was needed to keep their Jones at bay. I heard that they even robbed the older people as they sat on the bench.

Robby

His name was Jocko; he gave me a real sincere greeting. He was saved by a vocational school he was enrolled in, and he had hope and expectations. A young person needs expectations in order to achieve something, someone to believe in you and give you a reason to believe in yourself. As he was about to get off at his stop, he just looked at me and shook his head and said, "It's bad at the home front, friend, you're lucky that you were able to get away from it."

I started calling all my friends by their names to get the specific lowdown on them, and everyone had a worse tale than the previous one. With each name I knew that it could have been me, although I was a bit luckier than the others. Whenever they would buy loose cigarettes, I wouldn't spend my money on them. I tried smoking with them, but I got dizzy and sick so I said hell no. They just kept on until their bodies surrendered to the price cigarettes collect before allowing you to enjoy them.

I guess I was fortunate that God made me the way he did, up to that point at least. When we finished talking, as he got off the train, I felt a pang of depression. Even Davey, my partner in crime from the roof caper, got caught in drugs and submitted to their demons. Tooths made it because of his father and the expectations he instilled into him. I asked about my dad and was told he was still killing people's trust with cons and capers. His running crowd was like crabs in a bucket; when one was just about to make it out, another would grab it, pulling it down, while trying to propel themselves forward. The bottom line was that no one in that crowd would make it out, and all were sentenced to the same time.

My dad would have laughed at the outfit I bought, and the newspaper I was reading. He would have asked me who I thought I was and said that I was trying to act and look white. He would have even laughed at Solid. That's another part of ghetto life that was hard to understand. If you tried to speak well, you were acting white. If you put on a shirt and tie, you were acting white.

If you were trying to be the best you could be, you were trying to act white. I never understood that, being the best you could be makes you white? I just sat and compared Dad's reaction to Solid's; I guess ghetto to Dad was a code for Get Toe Ver. I was told my mother and grandmother were constantly popping the buttons on their clothes, talking about me with pride, and the good job that I had. As Jocko got off we gave one another a genuine emotional goodbye.

Luckily all I had to do was divert my mind to thinking about Laura and Solid, and happiness would counterattack the depression. I fell asleep on the train and just kept riding all night. When we reached the outside on the elevated part, I could see the sun rise. I had some money and decided to go to lower Manhattan for some breakfast. This was now Saturday morning. I got off near Chinatown and had breakfast. I even washed up in the bathroom. I really liked just sitting and watching people just be themselves. The cooks at the place I ate at all had big smiles as they worked. I guess they were happy that Joe was not their boss.

I decided to walk around New York and just see the sights. I walked from the west side of Chinatown to the east side of the Bowery. There I saw a lot of street people who were in a state of despair. I could look at them and feel their pain. I didn't see a lot of black men there; I guess some of these men were lucky enough to have seen old age, while many a young black man died in the hall-ways of the ghetto overdosing on bad drugs that they couldn't even afford. I saw one white man sitting on a milk carton on the corner; his head was down as if in prayer. As he slowly looked up and caught my eyes, his eyes showed the pain of social rejection in them. He never said a word but the pain was apparent. I instinctively reached in my pocket and gave him all of my change. Not one word was ever spoken; his eyes said it all, in every language. All I thought was how heaven and hell on earth was simply a product of who was in your life. I walked uptown by 5th Avenue and saw the well-dressed part of New York. People who had all they needed and then some. I lived here in New York all of my life, but this was my first tour where I understood the faces that I was looking at. I felt fortunate to be in the situation that I was in. I passed by the waterfront on the west side and saw the mighty ships in the harbor. *The Independence, The Constitution, The United States.* I couldn't even imagine being lucky enough to be on one. I walked by 42nd Street and saw all its splendid glory. It was amazing how I lived in York but never got to know her by her first name. I walked and walked and finally got a great steak-and-potato dinner at one of the cheap restaurants in Times Square. I sat on a bench and just watched the people and listened to their chatter.

When I got back on a train and went to sleep, I was dead tired. I guess the police left me alone because I looked like I had a place to go. The next day was Easter morning. The train was at the exact station I had caught it at, as if it never moved. I again got off to get breakfast and walked around. I again washed up in the bathroom and ate. I then called home to wish everyone a happy Easter. Old girl was glad to hear my voice. She asked mother-inquiring questions. Are you happy? Are you safe? Did you eat? I answered yes to everything and kept repeating it. I was told that Grandpa was getting his house in the islands together, and they were all thinking about going down to the island for a while. Grandma had her fill of New York. I was told what I already knew about all of my friends. My mother was thankful I was able to get away. She was thankful for all the money I was sending to her. When Grandma got on the phone, you know what the first question was.

"Did you read the Bible?"

"Yes," I answered, "I read it daily."

"Did you get God's blessing?"

"Yes, many times. Thank you for the Bible, Grandma." I never even opened it.

"When are you coming home?" they asked.

I gave a big story about how important my job was and that it wasn't a good time to leave because the boss was totally dependent on me.

They all understood. We all said goodbye with a tear in our eyes. I continued my walk. I got back on 5th Avenue and saw the well-dressed families just showing off their clothes, walking, smiling, and taking pictures. I thought to myself how lucky these kids were not to have to deal with the ghetto. I also felt a bit sorry for them not to have ever heard the humor or lived the good times in the ghetto. I'm sure they had their own good times, but watching Tooths take Nunzio's cart was worth the price of life's admission. Saint Patrick's Church bells were loud and pretty. I remember thanking God for this moment. I thought it was time to return to my life at Solid's. I got back on the train and headed home.

CHAPTER 6

STREET SMARTS

Three years later I was now twenty-one years old. Solid turned much of the day-to-day operations of the store over to me. He even made a nice living area for me in the back. I guess the money he saved on a burglar alarm was worth the price of me spending my nights there. I was his trusted employee bestowed with vast responsibilities. I was also a part of this thriving community. My relationship with Laura was on solid ground; she was now in college, and I was a staple in the community. Even her father managed to post a half of a smile every now and then. I stopped thinking about stealing or getting over. I still used a lie here and there to fill in a blank when I was stuck for an answer to a question, but I regarded that as harmless. I had something I'd never had before, a reputation for responsibility, and I loved it. Every time Laura came to visit me at the store it looked as if I was just closing the Bible. I intentionally made it look like that, truth was, I never opened it, but it made her happy, so what of it? Never said I was perfect.

The neighborhood was changing as everything evolved. We now had our share of junkies here as well; they were just harder to spot. They were dressed better and spoke better English. Even the pushers were different. They all wore clean alpaca knit shirts and Gator skin shoes. The neighborhood kids still would sometime hang out in front of the store, but usually they would sing to the songs we were playing on the loudspeakers. They were a nuisance but they were harmless. I was now twenty-one and was book-taught and self-educated. I was directed to different books and articles that Solid felt I needed to read. I could hold my own in discussions about politics. Solid taught me that the most important thing that I had to learn and understand was knowing when to shut up and listen; somewhat like Yoseevas on the bus. I remember that one night as we were closing the store Solid was talking about a man in the neighborhood who was henpecked by his wife. I was laughing so hard at what he was saying, I hurt my belly. Solid looked at me and he pin pointed it and yelled *stop don't move*. I didn't understand what he meant by stop. He looked at me and smiled and said, "You're happy right now. Never take that for granted. Always take time to appreciate the happiness, because those moments are few and far between." He was right as usual; I was happy and he had indeed pin-pointed it.

The following week on one clear, warm night I was walking with Laura around the neighborhood when she asked me where I saw myself in three years. I said I didn't know and could immediately see that it was the wrong answer. Planning for the future was something we didn't do in my family. We lived each day as it came. My grand-parents would thank God for the day and then pray for a good one tomorrow. I then asked Laura where she saw herself in three years. I got a long, detailed answer with many specifics; nothing had my name or existence on it. Schooling was the main issue she spoke of. I thought about that answer long and hard. The next day I did some-thing I never did before. I asked Solid for Friday off, and he agreed. He said he had plans but since this was a first on my part, he agreed. He never asked me why I wanted to take off. My plan was to visit and surprise Laura at her college and see what was going on there. That Friday I woke up and showered, put on a smart outfit, and headed to Laura's campus. When I arrived I was amazed. I saw people my age who looked to me as if they came from another planet. They seemed assured and calm. They all acknowledge one another and smiled when they greeted one another. I was in awe.

I never saw so many educated people in one place. I walked around the entire campus and stopped and looked at everything. I stuck my head in the classrooms, the library, the cafeteria, every-where. I was there under the guise that I was going to surprise Laura, but I surprised me. The men my age looked as if they knew some-thing that I needed to know. They didn't look like any of the friends I had in the neighborhood; they looked like they were confident and curious. This was all new to me. I went looking for Laura, but when I didn't see her, I went into the bookstore and lost myself in books. It was like being in a spaceship. I wanted to see everything. I even heard a conversation between two students about a class they had and couldn't believe the way they described the course. This was nothing like any conversation I ever had. I started thinking about Laura listening to this daily then coming back to me as I cleaned the store. I felt as if I was depriving her of being the best that she could be. I guess one would say I began to understand her father's point of view concerning me.

There were young ladies looking at me and saying hi. I believe that this was one of Yoseevas' and Solid's moments when they said to know when to shut up. I sat outside reading a newspaper I'd bought and just listened to everything being discussed. There were those who had valid opinions about things and some who I would dispute things they said. I wanted to be a part of this. I stayed there all day and late into the night. There was a Health Food place down the street where the students would stop and have a drink. I went in and got into a conversation with a group of students on the subject of about having knowledge. Some thought that people who were smarter were happier. My opinion was if you were stupid and didn't know you were stupid, how were you any sadder? I think that I held my own, and all the young men and woman seemed to actually like me. I also learned something else that day. I thought that the young men here at college would be more appealing to Laura because of their scholastic intellect. I learned that what I lacked in scholastic ability, I was made up for by my amazing memory's ability to inject long ago learned precise facts or keen wit into current conversations.

I also noticed that some of the women were more attracted to me than others when I filled in the blanks with wit. I was tall, slender, with curly hair and light eyes. I wasn't loud or pretentious. I really had a good time and enjoyed the challenge of engaging. I wanted to be here and never even once thought of Laura once I sat with these students and conversed. I didn't forget about her; I was just thrilled with the moment. I totally lost track of time when I finally looked at the clock and it was nearly --nine 9 o'clock. I immediately thought that I should get back and help Solid close and tell him about my day. As I walked closer to the store, I realized that something was wrong. I couldn't place my finger on it, but something was definitely wrong.

I soon realized that there was no music playing. Even though it was night, I still expected music. The barber shop was even quiet with all the lights out, it was closed, but they usually left one light on. Solid's store appeared locked and the gate was up, so I kept walking to Solid's house. This was not supposed to be; Solid usually stayed open till 11:00 p.m. I thought that he must have decided to close early and go home. I arrived and knocked on the door. When it opened a tall, light-skinned man who I've never seen before was standing there; he was dressed casually and asked who I was and what I wanted.

I saw Solid's wife, Marcie, who was coming down the hallway. I said. "Hi, Marcie, is Solid here?"

Marcie looked at me and said, "Haven't you heard? Where have you been? Solid is dead."

My heart dropped as if she just stabbed me with a sword. I waited for her to say, "April fools, got you, joke." But it never came. Dead? Why? When? How?

"He was at the store and was shot and robbed at about 4:00 p.m. today. They robbed him and shot him."

"Who?"

"We don't know yet. The police are investigating it. They want to see you tonight. You better go to the station."

The light-skinned man then grabbed her and sat her down and kissed her on her lips.

Marcie didn't look as if she was in mourning. Actually she looked somewhat indifferent. I walked over to her and said, "I am so sorry."

Marcie said, "He just wanted to be in that stupid store. We were supposed to have gone out tonight, and he cancelled with me to be in that store. I knew that I was the reason he cancelled."

Marcie looked at me and asked, "Where were you tonight? I didn't know you to ever take a day off."

The light skinned man looked at me and also said in an accusatory voice, "So where were you? It's amazing that you weren't there tonight."

I was too numb to react, I couldn't even speak. The light-skinned man said, "While you're here, let's call the police now."

What could I say? He called and I waited. The police soon arrived, and the light-skinned man answered the door. He whispered something to them, and then opened the door and said, "There he is."

There were two white cops who looked me in the eye and introduced themselves. They began to question me one right after the other. No one saw the pain that I was in. They took out a pad and wrote down my answers. Name, address, father, mother, school. I answered everything honestly unlike what I did with Flub-a-Dub on the roof without even thinking. When they asked for my previous employment, I immediately said Joe's Diner in New York City. I then heard Joe laughing at me. "Got you, stupid. 'Hang him, burn him,' give him some gas. Let some 'lectricity flow through his ass." Then it hit me. When they check with Joe and see what I did to him and his money I knew I would spend the rest of my life in prison.

"Is today your regular day off?"

"No, sir, I asked for today off."

"Where were you? Any witnesses?"

"I went to my girlfriend's college."

"Did she meet you there?"

"No I never saw her."

Everyone just looked at one another.

The two officers kept drilling me, looking me straight, deep in my eyes. I was afraid to even cry for Solid. I was scared even though I knew I had nothing to do with this. I did know that there are lots of innocent people in jail. I was told to go back to the store with them.

The light-skinned man said as we were leaving, "Well, this may be an open and shut case." He then yelled to the police that he was taking over the store's operation. I then looked back at the door, and he was embracing Marcia in a way that was beyond comforting her. I was now totally confused. I was still half dead with pain. I didn't want to see the store, but I knew that any wrong emotion might be misunderstood. We arrived and I hesitated in entering. When we got inside I saw blood on the floor. I couldn't help it, I began to cry. The two officers just stood over me watching. They took me to the back and searched my room. I sat on the bed silently crying. They never said a word. One cop went over to my dresser and picked up my Bible and asked, "Whose is this?"

"It's mine," I answered. They looked at each other. They asked, point blank, "Did you do this, son?"

"No, sir, Solid was like a father to me. I wish it was me who was working tonight." I then added "There was a group of people I met at a café on campus who will tell you that I was there."

These were the students I wanted to be a part of. Can you imagine what they would think of me if the police contacted them to investigate a murder?

The two cops went outside the room to talk. When they came back the short cop said, "Don't clean up the store, we will be back tomorrow. Do not leave the area."

His tone was similar to the bus driver who said, "You were tearing up the bus, boy."

I answered, "Yes, sir."

I heard the old man say, "Just be quiet" as he placed his hand on my shoulder. When they left I cried my eyes out. A part of me died inside, a great part of me. How could this happen to a man so good? Solid would have gladly given the robber the money if he really needed it. There was still so much to learn and share with him. Death is so final and unwelcome. It barges uninvited into your life at the worst possible moments, then demands your full attention for months. Death makes you think about words and encounters usually forgotten and taken for granted as long as more memories can be made. It's kind of like sitting near a waterfall taking the sound of the water hitting the water for granted, until the last drop hits the water below the falls before it stops forever.

Robby

Then you remember the beauty of the sound that you took for granted each and every time you heard it, and all of those rainy days that contributed to that sound. Solid pinpointed the exact moment that I was happy, and now I can't even imagine how to recreate that feeling. Solid is dead, and my life is now held hostage and dictated by the past actions that brought me to him in the first place. Who writes these scripts called life?

Was my father right? Was Solid a chump for working? Did he die in my place because I needed to see what college was like? What was now paramount in my mind was what will happen when they talk to Joe about me. I can hear it now, "He already robbed one employer, it's not a stretch to think he killed another one for the money."

I could see Laura's father saying to the police, "I knew it all along. He was a wolf in cheap clothing, who stunk of Coconut."

I knew one thing for sure: I had to get out of here and quick. No one would take my word over Joe's about what really happened. I felt my father's logic, street smarts and Social Darwinism over take my mind. I had to get out of here. I packed my bag and put my Bible on top. I cried my eyes dry and took my last look at the store.

I placed memories on every inch of store that I looked at. From here on I was to be known by one name, Robby. I couldn't contact my Laura, or anyone. I needed to get lost in the crowd. So ended my dreams of college and Laura's questions about three years from now. There was only this moment, now and me. They say that when one door closes, another one usually opens. I felt no door, window, or hole open up.

As I walked around the store and soon realized everything that was happening, I began to think about all the times Marcie came to the store. Solid would always stop whatever he was doing and give her his full attention. She would always ask, "How much did you make today?" I never gave it much thought as it happened, but seeing that light-skinned man holding her hand and kissing her made me think about things I wouldn't dare think about before. I called her at home to talk with her.

Marcie's answered and her voice had a nonchalant demeanor to it. She asked me where was I and I said the police told me to stay put. She told me about Solid in a by-the-way, unattached manner, like she was conducting a sightseeing tour. I cringed inside because Solid didn't deserve any of this, none of it. It was told to me like she was staring at me and said, "Well, the good news is that you don't have to work in that store anymore."

I asked Marcie where the kids were, and that I wanted to see their son Sean. She said that the kids were with her mother.

I felt anger surge into my thoughts I began to get really upset, but I kept my emotions in check because I knew that Solid would have wanted me to comfort her no matter what the situation was. I was kind and considerate not because of her but in spite of her. I asked her when the funeral was and was told that she was having him cremated in a small private ceremony

I told her that the neighborhood would all want to pay their respects; they would want to hear loud music playing, and she replied they can gather outside the store. "If they plan on doing that, you can work that day and sell the food if you are still around, she still talked about Solid in a by-the-way type manner."

I felt sick to my stomach. Anger was like a drug that took control of my thoughts. I said good bye and hung up. I walked outside and just walked. I didn't have any destination in mind; I just walked with the tears running down my face and the anger now in my heart. I remember thinking that Solid didn't deserve this, he didn't deserve this. I also kept asking myself who the hell was that light-skinned man?

I then heard my father's voice calling Solid a fool for living a lie and believing in things that never really existed. Here was a man who believed in education, hard work, and honesty, and look what happened to him. All the street-smart slicksters who haunted the street lived longer, safer lives. I walked totally disenchanted at the life that I had been exposed to. I really thought that all was well and everyone was happy, but I realized that it was just the illusion of happiness; the picture was beautiful, but the X-ray was terminal. I don't think I slept at all that night. I knew that the next morning a vigil would be held in front of the store. I tried to believe that Solid was in a much better place. To be completely honest, death confused me. I use to hear them speak of it in the barbershop and it never made sense. The people who didn't believe said everything had its opposite, and the opposite of life was death. Life was consciousness, and death was the opposite. I would just sit and listen as all the men argued, but I would think that it was not a precise analogy. Isn't the opposite of a life that ends with death a death that never ends with everlasting life? I would also get confused on the story that the people would tell about how beautiful heaven was, but they would then tell stories about voices from the afterlife warning them and keeping them safe from danger.

Let me get this right: life is beautiful, but the souls there warn you of what dangers exist, to keep you from coming to the other side? It just didn't make any sense.

I knew that Solid would have wanted me to stay and take what-ever awaited me. Solid would have wanted me to face the police go back to school and find another job. I was numb inside with anger and rage in my heart. I felt that all that crap about being righteous and living the straight life was as my father said was for suckers. Why would a man that good, that honest, and that caring have something like that happen to him? That death made me believe that no one ever escapes the street no matter where you are. I thought about seeing Laura, but that was a passing thought. I just wanted to be alone. I had my packed bag and Bible, and I just kept walking. The only thing that I wanted, believe it or not, was something I never even thought about before. I wanted a drink. I got back on the train and went downtown because I needed to see lights. I didn't want to be alone in the dark anymore on any night. So I went downtown in New York. I had a little money left, and I was able to secure a bottle of wine, so I sat on the curb with my bag in tow, and I said a prayer for Solid and said grace for the wine, and I began to try to drown my soul.

One bottle would serve as the master of ceremonies who introduced me to another and another, and when I ran out of money, I didn't look for a job. I only looked-for ways to get another bottle. I sat and drank more and more. I woke up on a milk crate in the city. I had a puddle of drool on my lap, and I slowly lifted my head up. I didn't know what time it was or even what day it was. I slowly looked up and saw a man standing next to me. He was wearing a suit and he looked into my eyes. He then reached into his pocket and handed me some change. I knew that just like the man I encountered my eyes were now fluent in the universal language of despair.

I took his gestures to mean that this was now my new job. I looked for people to ask for money day-in and day-out; I panhandled. I either slept in the street, or if I had a good haul I would buy a bed in a flophouse with my bag in tow. This became my routine, and the anger and rage never left me, but I substituted the facts of reality to make it seem as if Solid somehow was a fool for loving that woman and a fool for letting me take off that day then winding up working my shift. He died instead of me.

Sometimes I ate, and sometimes I was so hungry I would settle for digesting the plaque on my teeth, but I was never thirsty; I was drowning my sorrows in cheap wine. The kind of wine that I drank wasn't made in a family-owned winery with the grapes being treated like children who will one day make their parents proud. The wine I drank came with a cork taped to the side. The cork was to be used for when you get the extreme diarrhea from drinking this rotgut. This wine's grapes weren't pressed by experts;

they would place the grapes in a whoopee cushion and then they would run over the grapes with a donkey cart. I would sometimes get the urge to call home, but those thoughts were few and far between; though one time while high I did call, still pretending that I was on that vertical path, making believe that I was running the store. My grandmother would always get on the phone and ask me if I have read my Bible, and I would always say "Yes, Momma, I get my inspiration from it and it fills my soul with peace."

My heart would beat a double rhythm as I waited for them to tell me that the police were looking for me. Then I would get off the phone and get another drink. I was dirty and smelly and didn't even know me anymore. What most people don't understand about life, was a lesson I learned on the streets of NYC. The me from the store was dead, and this me was a strange, smelly, unfeeling, uncaring thing who tried to break relations with all the positive things that Solid tried to implant into my head.

I could have gone another way and chose to make him proud, but the things he taught me and the things my father taught me waged war with one another inside of my body, and all I could do was stay drunk and wait to congratulate the winner. I couldn't give a bedbug's bugger about the outcome. I only knew that when I was drunk, I didn't think about anything, and when I didn't think, I wasn't angry, and when I wasn't angry I wasn't sad, and so on, and so on, I guess.

There are times in one's life that sense makes no sense. I guess I could have chosen to go in the positive realm of what Solid tried to teach me, but don't make the mistake of trying to intellectualize emotion; it just can't be done. I saw what drugs did to my neighbor-hood, and now I saw what alcohol was doing to me and the world. Some men in the flop house could recite Shakespeare; some were mental giants, but they all wanted to do what I wanted to do— anesthesize their truths with liquor

Already at this young age of my life, I saw what drugs and alcohol did, and they both offered something unique, but each one demanded everything. I saw people who just couldn't deal with what life had to offer on its own terms.

Sadly I was now one of them. I missed Solid, and I tried to hide those feelings with resentment toward life. I didn't want anything to remind me of him, and I didn't want to be in the dark alone. I would sometimes go down to the pier when the ships were in, to just sit and look at the bright lights on the ships.

I even tried to dirty his memory to try to validate his demise. The truth was I was hurt to the core, and the alcohol was the only way I could anesthesize and stop the pain. I went out and asked everyone who looked like they needed air to live for money. Some days were good and some were not so good. There were many in the flophouses who just wanted to steal your day's pay because they believed that their pain was greater, and they just didn't give a damn about anyone else. I wasn't in the habit of fattening frogs to feed snakes. I was approached for my money, though it proved to be first and last. A man with a Santa Claus beard approached me and said, "Give me some money." I acted as if I was going to go into my pocket to get it, when I turned completely around and sucker punched him. His beard was not a cushion; it was like hitting steel wool. He went down with a thud, and word spread fast. It was amazing how many men would steal the nothings that other men had. I lost dirty under-wear that was in my bag. I was dumbfounded how a man could steal dirty underwear, but no one ever tried to steal my Bible.

This was a very confusing time in my life. I didn't care about anything and only thought that if Solid hadn't agreed to work for me, I would have worked that night, and it would have been me killed. I spent a lot of time thinking about who the murderer was. Was it a junkie? Was it an angry white shopkeeper who hated the blasting music? Was it someone the wife put on him? It hurt and that was all that I knew.

I searched for donors all day then drank all night. When I didn't go to the flophouses, I stayed in the warm subways and slept on the trains. It was not the life I planned, but who exactly lives the life that they plan. When your homeless your somewhat invisible to every-one. I kept thinking about the me I was before I became this me of now. It's totally amazing how many times in life one starts the day seriously believing one knows it all only to wake up the following morning and realize that you don't know anything and never did. I was now in my stupid stage; the fight between good and evil was waging war in my mind, and rage and anger were staging their last stand in my heart while confusion and ignorance decided to stage a coup in my soul. Hence, I was thoroughly messed up.

I drank, and I wandered around, and I observed. I began to get in a routine of just sitting and watching people on the train, on the street. Wherever I was I would just stare at people. My mind would be blank, and I wasn't taking anything in, but I noticed that other than the crazy ones, all people did and reacted the same way. I was just a staring freak. In my mind I would go back and forth between my father's way to live and Solid's, and whenever Solid's name or philosophy entered my mind and was about to beat my father's way with common sense and win the comparison, I just took another drink and washed it out. I never had any peace while on the street. I thought that every cop I saw was going to stop and question me about Solid, or Joe, but to them I was invisible. I didn't even want to hear any music playing. This was an awful existence.

CHAPTER 7

CLIMBING DOWN

I jumped into the ocean. My body got wet. Did you reach the bottom? No not yet, I have to touch it, not just to stop. Cause with its foundation, I can push off for the top. Can't hold my breath nor swim any longer; I see the surface light getting stronger. I'm nearly there, and I won't stop. I'll either die or reach the top.

One day I was sitting on the side of a building I went to often. The fishing was great, and I usually reeled in some loose change. There was a bed of flowers behind me that smelled really good. I would ask everyone passing by for a handout with a seriously dejected look on my face.

This was a classy business district in lower Manhattan. Even the blacks looked like foreigners; they were well dressed, and they all complied with my begging and handed me a sweet deposit for my next go-round of stale, fermented grape juice. I liked this neighbor-hood, and it was all new territory. The people were extremely generous. I believe I had a monopoly here; I didn't see any other homeless, senseless beggars such as myself. On days or nights when I made enough I'd sometimes call home from a pay phone. Even though I was usually very tired and very hungry, I wanted to just check in so they knew that I was still alive. Old girl would always answer and was glad as always to hear my voice. I lied with authenticity. I told her that I was taking care of the store and working hard. She asked if I was eating well. I think my stomach heard her and tried to commandeer the call and yell, "Hell no, help me, he's starving my dumb ass," but my voice calmly said yes. I then swallowed and sent a wad of saliva down to quell this uprising. My grandmother then came to the phone and again asked, "Are you reading your Bible?"

I said, "Yes, ma'am, it fills my heart and soul every time I pick it up, thank you for it."

She would again say, "You're very welcome" and end with "bless you, we're all proud of you." Nothing said about police. I needed something to eat and drink. Anything. I had a pocketful of begged change, but I didn't know exactly how much I had.

I wanted to go someplace and count it. I saw a guy selling hot dogs and smiled thinking about Tooths; I went up to him and said, "How much for a hot dog?" and he just pointed to the price on the cart. I said "I can't see it well, I haven't eaten for days." He wasn't fazed; he pointed to the sign again. I asked, "How much for some mustard and hot-dog bread?" He said fifteen cents

I asked for one; that way I would have more money for wine. I said, "Is there a liquor store around here?" and he said that he didn't know. I gave him the fifteen cents and went back to the place where I was sitting to try to get my fifteen cents back from the generous crowd. I literally squatted at this location for weeks at a time. I still couldn't believe the money I was making.

I even enjoyed watching the people dressed in their very nice clothes.

Marty R.

One day a man came out of the building and stood next to me. I remember that it was a Friday. He was white, tall, and slender, with a Clark Gable--type mustache. He smelled like a rose garden and had a suit that looked as if it cost the price of a house. He asked me what I was doing and why was I just sitting here daily, begging. I was still a little high, and the last thing I needed was a Solid lesson in wasting your life. I told him that it was a long story. He told me that I did have a choice, and he gave me a dollar. He saw a cheap wine bottle in my pocket and said, "If you're going to kill yourself, at least go inside and get yourself some good liquor."

I replied, "Good liquor is expensive, and that doesn't look like a liquor store."

He said, "Boy, you really don't know where you're at, do you?" I replied, "Yeah, at this point in time I am in the small intestines about to pass through the bowels of this dimension of reality into the Abyss of the earth's toilet."

He said, "Well put, young man. You some kind of down-and-out poet? Young man, right through those doors is everything you need for a whole new life."

He asked me if I had any clean clothes, and I said, yes. I had my outfit and my Bible in my bag, which I had to hide in a locker at the train station.

He said to meet him here tomorrow with some nice clothes on. I really didn't know exactly what he meant by this place "had every-thing I needed" for my whole life, but the good liquor intrigued me. I mean, what did I have to lose? And although my clothes were out of season and probably very wrinkled, what did I really have to lose? Everyone who I saw going in and coming out those doors looked happy and well maintained to me. I wasn't looking for a change, or maybe I was. I had literally drunk the sorrow out of my dumb ass, and I still hadn't made up my mind about my internal fight with good and evil. I was kind of tired of being hungry. I did notice that every time I passed a television set in a bar or store window, it had on a

Robby

commercial about really good-looking food on it, and all the billboards had a family sitting down to a feast.

He lit a cigarette and was about to walk away when I asked him his name and he said, "You can call me Blue. Or at least I thought I was till I met you."

I said, "What time tomorrow, Blue?"

He said, "Be here at noon, and be neat, take a damn bath. What may I call you, boy?"

I replied, "Robby." I said, "I will be here, and I will be neat, and I will pray for rain tonight so I can get that bath delivered."

He laughed and kept walking.

I was starving and wanted my nightcap, but the bottle in my pocket was nearly empty. I still had change, but I had to go to the locker and get my bag. I went to the locker and as always my bag was still there even though the locker was unlocked. I don't know if I was just lucky or thieves didn't have a thing about stealing wrinkled clothes and a Bible. I grabbed my bag and looked inside; everything was still there. I grabbed my Bible and just stared at it. I remember hearing that Jesus fed a crowd with just two loaves of bread and some fish; I would settle for another hot dog-roll with mustard. There was no Jesus around to feed me a meal, and I didn't believe that miraculously my stomach would somehow get full, so I just put my Bible back in my bag and pulled out the outfit I had brought for Easter.

It was in bad shape, really wrinkled. I decided to go to a flop-house that night and forgo my nightcap because I could either borrow an iron to press it or put my outfit under my mattress and self-press it, ghetto cleaners' style. I found a place with a bed by the window. I just sat in bed most of the night and stared outside at the stars. It was dark except for the streetlights. Usually right about now I would head for the lightest area I could find to avoid the darkness. This time I just sat and thought about everything that had happened in my life up to now.

I thought that I was finally ready for a new experience. I have to let go of all the pain and hurt and move on. I was about to open my Bible and finally read the first verse on the page. I always believed that I would randomly open it to something that the Lord wanted me to know, but I felt sleep catching up on me, so I gave in and dozed off. It was amazing that I could sleep at all; the people here would either snore, fart, or talk in their sleep, and some would even curse at their damn rock-hard pillows. I was part asleep and part awake.

I thought about everything as I mentally skimmed through all of my experiences which had led me here to this point and time in my life, and I asked myself the questions that only sane people ask themselves. Was I happy? I then asked myself when was I ever happy, so that I had a point of reference to compare now to. I then remembered that when I was really, really young there was a time when my father and mother were alone in the room, and they just hugged, and I would run between them as they both looked down at me and smiled. I remember being happy when I would laugh in the kitchen at Joe's before I became prey. I remember the time I spent with Laura, but most of all, which was paramount, was the time I spent with Solid when he pinpointed the exact moment of my happiness. How was I going to get through life without a slap in my damn head followed by much-needed insight and intelligence?

I know that this may not make sense, but I wondered how I could ever recapture that happy moment again in life; I didn't have an answer to that question. I drifted off to sleep and wrapped the rock-hard, smelly pillow around my head so I would not hear the sounds of the people asleep. The following morning I woke up sober and excited with no telltale signs of a hangover.

I immediately looked under the mattress at the outfit I was pressing. It looked OK, but the odor was a little off. I went into the bathroom and washed really good. I even thought about eating a breakfast. It's funny but it just felt a little different this morning. I don't know why, but it did. Eating a breakfast was a novelty. I washed my face, my hair, even under my arms. I didn't have any deodorant and didn't want to waste my time by asking anyone for any; the one thing you never see is a homeless person carrying deodorant. Any person who had deodorant here must have gotten thrown out last night by their wife and had nowhere else to go. I got dressed and looked in the mirror. I nearly didn't recognize this person. It was like seeing a long-lost twin. Most of the residents were still asleep and still snoring. I still had some of the change I collected in my sock, so I limped again when I walked. It was like being back in the old neighborhood. You see, in the ghetto, you had to keep any money you wanted in your shoe.

I went downstairs and got a sincere good morning from Granny, the lady at the front desk. She said, "You look good today. Do you have an interview?"

I stopped and thought about her question. I didn't know what I had today, or why I was excited, but I was. I guess the prospect of just breaking my negative, go-nowhere routine excited me. She then said something I'd never even thought of. She asked, "Who interviews on a Saturday?"

I told her that I had an appointment with a friend but said to myself, she's right. I had my bag with my other dirty clothes and my Bible.

I sat on the front step of the flop hotel and counted out fifty cents, just the price of two eggs. I may even have enough for coffee and a muffin. It had been so long that I ate a real breakfast, that I didn't know what real food cost. I even thought of asking for money from passersby on my way to the place, but dismissed that thought. No, not today. I picked up my Bible from my bag, and for absolutely no reason I kissed it. I sat and ate and felt good. Everyone was eating in the diner and reading a paper.

Marty R.

I was even going to open my Bible and read it just to fit in till I saw a discarded newspaper on a table. The smell of all the good food was all I needed. It was like an old Thanksgiving dinner at my grandparents' house, I even left a ten-cent tip for the waitress and I felt good doing that.

I finished and just walked around wasting time, enjoying the novelty, for the first time in a long while, of having a specific place to go. I was paying attention to the time. I went through a big department store and walked real slow, hoping that a perfume person would splash me with a free sample of their product. It would have been like putting a rose petal on a dog's ass with diarrhea. I never let them spray me when I would walk through here in the past; being sprayed with cologne and going to a flophouse was like putting a welcome mat in front of your bed, but I figured what the hell, even I could still smell the flophouse on me. I passed by a counter that had woman's perfume on it and immediately sprayed myself. I arrived early at the building and sat where I usually sat, near the flowers. This was a lesson in human nature for me; people who previously passed by me before now saw me dressed nicely and said hi or nodded their heads. When I was there before in my bum's garb, no one would even look at me, and when I would ask some of them for change, they would quickly look down and hurry to take the change out of their pockets, then pelt it in my direction, and be done with me. Some would say "Aren't you kind of young to be out on the street?" but would not wait around for an answer as to how I arrived at this destiny, or how they could refer me off it.

I sat and waited and to tell the truth I, myself, never even thought about the homeless when I was eating regularly. I would see them, but I wasn't a bit curious about them or their plight. I felt that they were people who just couldn't cope with life, and they were probably weaker then us plain folks. It wasn't till I got here and looked out of their eyes did I understand that they all just wanted what all people wanted, a valid reason to get up, a sincere kiss good night. A look of approval, a smile of pride, a sense of belonging, and the ability to cry at the end of a good movie, to feel a tight throat when you try to swallow while looking at a beautiful Christmas tree, dignity, and to be able to feel love.

I had heard some stories as I got to the down-and-out point that would make an onion cry. Sometimes I felt that I really didn't have a right to be here as far as hard times go. Yes, I'd lost my mentor and friend, but many of the people who resided here lost a piece of their reason for wanting to inhale after they exhale. I sat here and waited, and I couldn't believe what was going through my mind. I guess it was the clothes. I sat and wondered if it was the suit that made Superman. I sure felt as if I could fly right about now. I sat and waited. I saw a bunch of well-dressed men arrive and go inside the building. Many were carrying packages. They had big ones, small ones, and even ones that looked as if there was a human body wrapped in tarp, but they all were smiling and seemed happy, and they all said hi to me as they passed by. I saw a homeless man across the street, one whom I'd never seen before, and I didn't even feel that he was infringing on my spot. He came over and asked me for some money; boy, was that strange. I reached into my pocket and gave him about two nickels. I started to hand him my Bible for luck, but it was the only thing that I had of my grandmother's.

He smiled and took the money. He looked as if he had also hocked all of his teeth or drove a hard bargain with the good fairy. I knew that the nickels that I gave him were going straight for wine. I was more curious with my surroundings to have anything but a passing thought concerning my street-walking protégé. Just then Blue showed up, and I heard him say "Well, well, well, so you can appear human." He got closer and sniffed me and said, "Even smell human." I turned and smiled and extended my hand. He said, "Boy, you're sharp as Dracula's Fangs." He said, "Now tell me about you. Are you doing what you want to do in this life? Is this the reality you used to dream about?"

We sat there for a while with my head down and then I began to talk. He just listened. I thought I was in a free psychiatrist session, and I went through everything in my life. Even I couldn't believe how much was coming out of my mouth. I talked about damn near everything. All he did was listen; he never even interrupted me. I spoke about the good in my life as well as the bad. I left out the possibility of the police looking for me. He again asked if this was the life I wanted to live. He asked if I found a magic lamp and could ask the genie for anything in the world, would I ask the genie for complete happiness, or would I waste a wish asking the genie to please make me panhandle a lot of money, or ask for a bus stop closer to the corner I was sitting on so I could more easily bum the passengers getting off.

When I finally finished answering and telling my tale, all I knew was that he was sitting there just staring at me, never uttering one word. He asked about my family, and I told him that I was alone in the world. This time his stare lasted a little uncomfortably too long; he just stared. When he finally broke the silence, he said, "Follow me" as we walked toward the front door to the building. I started feeling kind of stupid for talking so much, but to tell you the truth it was good to get it all out. Actually, it was somewhat therapeutic to get it all out. He walked in first and told the guard at the door that I was his guest. We walked through an office area to a large auditorium. There I was amazed by what I was seeing. It was like we just walked into another place in another country, another time There was a large crowd in the middle of the room and in each space next to the walls were men selling things. I don't mean things like you see for sale in the hood; these men were selling things you just don't see for sale in everyday life. I asked, "What is this? What is going on?"

He then told me where I was and what was happening.

This building was the home of the United States Seamen's Union, and these were seamen who had traveled on ships to all parts of the world. They worked on the ships doing all kinds of different jobs, and the things that they were selling were brought back from the different countries they'd visited.

You had one guy selling the finest perfume from France, one guy selling bottles of rum from the Caribbean, gold coins from South Africa, silk from China; they even had French and Italian wines. It was like being in ten different countries at once. Every man's item had its own unique flavor and culture, and these were not men who were trying to make a living, as most men were, out on the street. These were really well-dressed men who were not going to haggle over price. They all had their price, and the people who patronized them were just as cool. The buyers asked questions as if they were already thoroughly educated with the products.

It was amazing to watch. Blue just watched me watch them. I never smelled any perfume or cologne like the ones they had; it was like a summer's vacation for my nose.

I wanted to buy some cologne and just throw some through a window at the flophouse. The liquor and wine they had compared to what I was drinking like rotten grapes to Golden Garden of Eden grapes. After I had my eyes and brain filled with amazement I asked Blue what was the deal. I asked how did they all come to be here. Some were from the United States and many from different other countries.

He just stood there and smiled. When his smile slowly left his face, he said to me, "Seriously, son, where did Jesus go when he needed men to build his church?"

I said I don't know. He said, "My young friend, he went to the sea and gathered his flock. You see friend, seamen are called to the sea and Jesus called the seamen to be fishermen of men. This is the offspring of the flock, these are seamen. This building that you are standing in is the United States

Marty R.

Seaman's Union. Just as Jesus was building his church, we are building a union here."

I still didn't totally understand but acted as if I did. He continued, "These are the men who work on the ships, the ones you see in the harbor when you travel in Brooklyn or down the west-side highway.

We are the union that represents them. "The things that they are here selling," I then interjected with understanding and total comprehension in my voice, "are things that they brought back from other countries?"

"Precisely, my man, we have our own world here. Here we look out for one another, we take care of one another, and we are a union in unison with one another. Which is a word derived from the words *unity* and *unite one. Union.*"

I was completely, thoroughly, totally impressed. I used to see some of them coming and going from the building when I was out front, and when I would see them I had to notice that they even walked differently.

They carried themselves as if they belonged to something much bigger than themselves; they just looked like they knew something. Just then it got quiet, and all eyes followed a group of men who just entered the building. They were all walking slow in a circle that formed around a man in the middle of them. The man in the middle wasn't particularly impressive looking, but he had a confidence about him. Everyone he passed bowed their head and said hello or just nodded their head to acknowledge his presence and pay homage. He was walking towards us when we made eye contact. I nodded and smiled. He said to Blue, "You smuggling children from overseas and selling them here?"

Blue laughed and said, "No, sir, he was looking for a change and wanted to see what we did here, and now he wants to join us. He may be a good recruit for what we were looking for."

All of the men in the circle began looking at me. One picked up my bag and asked, "Is this yours?"

I was kind of embarrassed because of the condition it was in. I answered yes. He then looked and reached inside and pulled out my grandmother's Bible. He asked, "Is this also yours?

I replied yes. He asked if I was in search of religion and I said, "No, sir. I just came where Jesus came for the people he needed to build his church."

Blue just smiled and said, "Good for you, son."

The man in the middle said, "Blue, on Monday take him to Lavajeskie and let him talk with this young man. We need good men here."

He handed me my Bible and they all walked toward the elevator. Blue then asked me if I knew who that was. I just stood there thinking, *I don't really know who the hell you are, Blue.*

He said, "Well, son, you started in here at the top. That was the president of the union, JC."

I said, "Jesus Christ?" and Blue smiled and replied Jon Cappa. I again asked him what the story was here, and to please speak plain, simple, straight truth. We walked into an area of the building with offices and desks, and we sat down. He then again slowly explained that this was the seamen's union, the United States Seaman's Union, where men who so desired came to expand their horizons and feed their eyes and memories with the sights of the world. They come here to be an active part of progress and to live full lives.

I just sat and listened and dreamed the words spoken in my mind's eye. I visualized me traveling, seeing the world, living the better life, and not having to worry about any police looking for me. Living better than I ever lived before; it all sounded good. I really wanted to join. I wanted to be a part of this, I was sold. I wanted a better way of life. Blue explained everything to me. I sat there and listened like a child being read a fairy tale. Like a kid on a roller coaster being instructed what not to do before the ride starts, yet in the rear corner of my brain was my father's negative explore the negative first mind. Was this just some man-made crap created to lure suckers like me here to pay dues?

I was harshly taught by my experiences with my father to always reserve the right to doubt and think that this just can't be true, and if I just looked really good at it, I would see that it was probably a con. It was like when my father would promise me something, and I would look forward to getting it, and when it came to the time he was to deliver on his word he would walk in with a crap-eating smile on his face while wearing that imaginary T-shirt that read, "IF I WAS YOUR LAST HOPE, YOU NEVER HAD ANY HOPE." I cautiously asked what did I need to do to be a part of this.

I was told that I had to get a letter to take down to the US Coast Guard in order get my seaman papers. Then he asked me, "Do you have any money at all?"

I said, "Blue, I don't have enough silver to fill a tooth, unless you know anyone who wants to buy a Bible."

I then heard my grandma's voice say, "Are you reading your Bible, son? All you will need is in your Bible."

He just looked at me and said, "Let me speak with the man who just spoke with you. Sometimes they make exceptions and sponsor special people who can work off their debt in favors when needed." I asked what kind of favors, and he said not to worry. "If your family asked a favor, wouldn't you do it?"

I reluctantly replied, "I suppose so."

"Well, we will now be family."

I so badly wanted to believe that all he said was true; I wanted so bad to get back to living and resume my path on a somewhat normal life.

I was tired of the funny looks from people, the smell of the flops, the long nights, the uncertainty of tomorrow, the miseries of the moments of putting my stomach through the pangs of being on an endless and never-ending fast. Going to bed then waking up always hungry was a habit that I never really got used to.

It was just time to leave the street, and I just knew it. Blue said, "I will fix it, just be here on Monday and keep your Bible handy. You're gonna need something to read on the ship. I left there with my newfound inspiration whose name was hope. I felt as I felt when I visited Laura's college before Solid's demise, the possibility of new possibilities, made me internally happy. I left the building and just stood outside. I started to notice things, which were probably in front of me the entire time. I saw people with smiling faces, I heard music coming from some of the stores. I saw the beauty of the afternoon. I really didn't care if this was a con or not; I took it as it was, even if it was just a believable lie that I wanted to accept. Now I had to get past the rest of today and Sunday. I wasn't even concerned that I couldn't afford the good liquor or wine being sold in there. I didn't feel like any shelters. I walked down 5th Avenue to St. Patrick's Cathedral and just went inside and sat. I watched all of the people who came in and felt the power of hope firsthand.

I watched the people sit and pray. As I watched I realized that everyone had their uncertainties to bear, their challenges in life, their reality and routine interruptions that were all called a part of life. I did something that I hadn't done before: I sat, closed my eyes, and prayed. I gave thanks for everyone who came into my life and tried to help me, and even the ones who simply helped me think, but had no intentions of actually helping me.

Was I a changing person? Was I trying to purge all of the evil out of me before the next experience? If you're thinking the answer is yes, and if I saw a well-dressed man come into this church to pray and as he was getting up from praying with a tear in his eye his wallet fell out of his pocket, would I go over to him and say, "Sir, you dropped your wallet"? *Naaaah,* I would have probably thought the Lord wanted me to have it, that's why he dropped it, but the way I now felt I might have taken a dollar out of the wallet and left it in the collection plate, depending on how much he had in it, of course. Redemption comes in stages; this was just a stage I was going through, not an abrupt change.

I was just happy for another shot at a somewhat normal existence. I was warm, calm, and happy. I sat in the church just thinking how mere people can make one's life heaven or hell. Although man cannot be perfect, he can create perfect things. One can make other people happy, and one can also create hell in one's life. It's amazing how many different experiences can come from one person. I was still searching for what kind of person I would be. I still had my father's teachings about life's experiences which somewhat trumped the teachings of Solid. I thought that good people got taken and evil people got over; I knew nothing of karma, because what did Solid do to get the end he got?

I just sat with my eyes open, at peace with the world. I knew that life was again changing for me, I was beginning a new page in this book called my life. I was even hungry for food again, I mean really hungry. I guess everyone near me thought my belly was praying by the noise it was making. As the old man on the bus so eloquently put it in his analogy, I was living in crap, but I wasn't comfortable. I sat and held my bag with my Bible and just stared at the altar. I didn't want to get up until Monday when I was due back at the union. Negativity never crossed my mind as my father used to say. The early worm gets killed by the bird. For the rest of the day, I ate, I prayed, and I wondered.

Monday morning, I woke up on a subway train, happy, excited, and nervous. I couldn't wait to get to the union hall. They let me stay in the church most of the time and didn't even bother me when I would close my eyes to nap. Even though every time I heard a noise I would pretend to move my lips like I was saying a prayer. They would close the church at about ten, and then I took the subway to the hotel. I went to a public bathroom and gave myself another deep sink bath. I scrubbed myself like a freshly plucked Turkey on a Thanksgiving morning. I put soap pieces under my arm as deodorant. I brushed my teeth with a ragged fingernail and brushed and combed my hair with a handful of toothpicks. I decided to just wear another T-shirt and pants and hope no one noticed the stains. In the back of my mind was that catchphrase which Blue had said about owing a favor, but truthfully speaking I would have screwed a herd of flies with a pack of toothpicks in a 42nd Street peep show if I had to, just to belong to that group of seamen. I got neat and clean and walked down to the hall. I arrived and just stood there looking at the building. It was a six-story older building with a spirit and flavor of its own.

The guard recognized me as I entered, and I bowed my head and went inside. I think that it transformed me just by walking through the doors. These men who belonged here have seen the world, and that was an accomplishment that we never even dreamed about in my building in Harlem. Unless you were a gun for hire for the Selective Service and had a government rifle and a bull's-eye on your back, that is - in the military. I thought that just by seeing other parts of the world gave one an immediate understanding of world events. I even thought that once you were merely standing in another country you could immediately speak the language. I was in awe of this opportunity, still at war with my ethics and beliefs, but I knew that this was a chance not bestowed on the people where I came from and never thought for a second, why me?

Instead, I thought, why not me? When people had the first vote recorded between Jesus and Barabbas, they didn't choose the good one, they chose Barabbas; he never thought he'd get chosen either and he probably also thought, why not me. I arrived at Blue's office and was given a sincere welcome.

I was immediately taken to the top floor where all of the executive offices were. I couldn't even imagine working in such a place; it was beautiful with really beautiful secretaries and beautiful potted plants. I went into an office of a very short white man with curly dark hair; he had a Napoleonic look on his face. I was then introduced to Mr. Percy.

He was the right-hand man of the president, JC. I was again told the reason I was here was because every once in a while they allowed a new person to join without having to front the fee for the papers, but again in no uncertain terms it was stated that I would owe them for it. I asked what exactly would I owe, expecting a monetary reply. Without batting an eye he answered, "allegiance." I guess for whatever they had in mind for me, I was approved. I got the signed papers I needed for sponsoring me, and they invited me to the conference room for breakfast.

I remembered Solid's advice about making a good impression and looking everyone straight in the eye. I tried my best to sell myself without saying too much and looking like a fool. Percy asked me if I had common sense. I thought, *How do you answer that question?* I said, "I think so," but I found out firsthand during my stay in the streets of New York that *sense* wasn't at all common. He smiled then said, "Let's test your common sense. If a light sleeper sleeps with the light on, what does a hard sleeper sleep with?"

I just smiled and said, "A hard-on."

Percy said, "If you would have said 'with the light off,' I would have made you leave here."

Blue then asked me what was the difference between a peeping tom and a pickpocket. I thought about that one then said that I didn't know. He laughed and said that a pickpocket snatches watches, and they both laughed.

I shyly smiled. Blue asked me what skills I had for ship work, and I told

Robby

him of my time in Solid's store. Percy said, "That's great, you can work in the galley helping the cook."

I was now in a state of suspended nonsense; everyone just laughed and joked. I only wanted to get my hands on the actual seaman papers. After the meeting, the understanding was that I was now in debt for the papers, and I owed either my rights to heaven or hell, plus my soul and allegiance. I was then given a letter signed by the union royalty with instructions to take it downtown to the United States Coast Guard building on the west side and get my papers.

This process was still all very confusing. I didn't even know what these papers should look like. I arrived at the coast Guard office, in a building, on the first floor and handed a man in uniform my letter. The next thing I knew, I was being photographed and fingerprinted. The letter from the union was so powerful that they didn't even ask me for any identification. I intentionally dropped the George and told them that my legal name on my birth certificate was Robby. I was then told to wait in another room. I sat there just looking out the window at the Hudson River, trying to imagine that this was what an ocean probably looked like. Soon another man came into the room and handed me a small piece of laminated paper. I thanked him them looked down at it. It was beautiful; it said "Mr. Robby Robinson, United States Merchant Marine." I belonged. I just looked and threw my head back in laughter. Now I had identification that no one would question; George Robinson was dead so no police would ever find him.

I had no idea what being in this organization even entailed; all I knew was that I belonged, and I once again had a family. I left the Coast Guard building, never even aware of where I was going. My eyes never left my papers. I did notice that it wasn't any kind of seaman's paper at all, it was a card with a picture of me on it. I went right back to the hall, as proud as anyone else in the hall was, maybe even more. This was like graduating school with an unknown skill.

I went straight to Blue and showed him my prize and got my first congratulations. I then looked down at it all over again and relived getting it. Blue asked me if I had any plans. He joked about the name Robby Robinson and asked if my parents were high at the time they named me. He said it was like naming your child Marty Martin or Bill William. I had no idea what was next. He asked me when I wanted to ship out, and I said how about today. The thought of being safe off the street with my new identification insuring against the possibility of the police finding and booking me was a thrill pill in itself. Blue just smiled and walked me into the large room. There was an older white man on the podium who had a vulture's neck that looked like it came out of his chest and hung a little too far out, and much too low. He had an Adam's grapefruit attached to it, not an apple. He was the one who gave out the jobs.

He didn't smile at all; behind him was a blackboard with some writing on it. He would look at the blackboard and then say some words, and the many people in front of the podium would slap down these small cards on the podium's counter. It was like they just got the right card for the winning hand and was putting their cards down. Blue went up to him and whispered something in his ear, and the next thing he did was cross out something on the board and pointed to me. I had no idea what was going on. Blue then walked over to me and told me I was shipping out that day at 5:00 p.m., and that I should bring Lavajeskie back a bottle of Scotch. I thought he was joking. I had a million questions, and he said, "Just make sure you make the ship. Once you get on, there will be many people on board to help you understand everything that you need to know. I will tell the Deep Sea to look out for you."

I was thankful, but I still had no understanding what exactly was happening. I was also told that I really lucked out because I was to work in

Robby

the galley under the best trainer I could get. I didn't know what the hell a galley was, but I acted as if I was fluent in ship lingo. I wanted to ask where would I eat and sleep, what would I need, then it hit me: all the time I was living on the street I didn't know or care about that; why was it important now? I never even asked where the ship was going. I couldn't care less if it was just the Staten Island Ferry as long as I was a part of this family. All my vibes said that this was the right move.

My nothing-filled days and worthless nights of exploring the nuances of cultural insignificance in the Pollock-ridden bowels of society has finally ended. *I didn't even remember traveling there, but the next thing I knew I was at the dock.* There was nothing to pack.

I do remember standing at the dock looking at that giant ship which was just an old freighter, but to me it was *The Queen Mary*. I remember thinking that maybe prayer in a church does work. It was pure beauty; I was engulfed in her beauty. I stood at the gate and watched the other seamen show their papers, walk past the guards, and slowly walk up the plank. They even looked like seamen; they wore brimless hats and carried duffel bags. I looked like a confused, out-of-place, panhandling landlubber.

I was in awe of everything; the smell of the water in the bay was like smelling new seasonings and spices of life. I was excited and thankful to be there at all. I walked slowly, taking in everything, and missing nothing. All of my senses were in overdrive. I showed my card to the guard and waited to walk up to board the ship. I was cleared to enter and slowly walked up the gangplank, which separated this reality of land with the experience of the sea.

I again noticed the men who were aboard; their demeanor was different. It was as if they knew a secret about life that no one else was let in on.

Once I entered the door, I was met on the top by a man in a white uniform who asked for my papers. Here was when I really thought that this was just one big joke, which was about to reveal itself. I gave him the papers that I was given at the union, and he looked at it as if he was a doctor. He then folded the papers and handed them back to me and said, "Welcome aboard. You are to report to the galley." Holy crap, I was really a player in this game. Shyly, I asked him, "Where do I go now?"

He mildly laughed and said, "You are assigned to the galley, the mess hall, so go see your master."

I got very lost looking for the mess hall and didn't want people to know that this was my first time, but the only one I was fooling was myself. After my last wrong turn, I was told by a man who I asked where the galley was. He said that the mess hall would be in the last place you looked right before you found it. He laughed and said, "Just follow the sound of the loudest mouth on the ship, followed by the smell of coffee." Shortly thereafter I found it.

As I entered the door, standing before me was my boss. He said, "Hello, young blood, you Robby? I am the ship's motivational speaker, spiritual adviser, and professor of the Ocean, Mr. Deep Sea." Now I finally understood what Blue meant when he said that Deep Sea was to look out for me, I had thought he meant the ocean. He was a tall, stout, very dark-skinned man with severely bloodshot eyes that seemed to pierce through you. I said, "Good day, sir, I am reporting for duty," and I handed him my papers. He slowly reached for them as he gave me the visual, up-and-down look over.

His eyes then shifted to my papers, and as he read them, his lips moved slightly. He looked at me and said, "You are a sea virgin."

I said, "Sorry, sir."

He repeated with clearer detail, "Is this your maiden voyage, boy? Your first time on the sea?"

I smiled and said, "Yes, sir."

He said, "Put your gear down and have a seat, boy, I have to give you years of education in about five minutes." I sat down and he stood straight in front of me. "Boy, I am your boss. You are in my gal-ley. I am the leader, dictator, and king of this space. You will beckon to my command and make sure that I am happy. You will be the best you that you can be on this voyage. You will strive to please me. You will sleep in my cabin since your new meat here. I will formally introduce you to my lover, my mistress, my religion, and the glory of, and to, God's creativity. Understand, she is temperamental and *dominating*. Her skin is that of soft beauty, and her inside is timeless, she is the ocean, Mrs. Deep Sea. Is that all the gear you have, son?"

"Yes, sir, I replied."

"You look a bit worn, as if you have been fighting instead of flowing with life. How old are you?"

I answered. I was going to tell him more, but he interrupted me and said "That's OK, time answers all questions, son. Did you bring anything to read?"

I reached in my bag and took out Grandma's Bible, which I still hadn't read. He reached for it and opened it and said, "You just impressed me, boy." He then said in a stern voice what Blue had already told me, "Do you know why Jesus went to the sea to get the people to help build his church, son?"

I replied no so not to spoil his moment, and he laughed and said, "You will. I would have never guessed that you would have this. Have you read any of it?"

I replied, "Yes, sir."

He then skimmed the pages of my Bible and opened it to the middle, and his eyes lit up. He looked over the book and said, "I was wrong in my opinion, boy, your stock just shot up. You may indeed have some sense, and maybe even won a round or two in your fight with life. I see you save your money."

He then reached and pulled out two one-hundred dollar bills, the same bills I gave to my grandma. I could have died when I saw those bills. I must have lived on digesting my plaque most of my days on land, and now I am going to go out to sea and I find that this was there all the time.

I can't remember how many times my grandma asked me, "Did you read your Bible?" God does indeed have a sense of humor, but the joke is always on the slicksters.

He handed me my Bible and the money. He then told me to go to deck 2 and look for cabin 12. As I was leaving, he then called after me, smiling, and said, "I sure hope you rested because you will work on this voyage."

"Yes, sir," I said.

I somehow found my way to the cabin. His things were neatly put up like I've never seen before. The room had purpose and order, something that I was just not used to. I tried to emulate his way of neatness, but it was a lame try. I sat on the bed and wondered how I got here and just reflected on all the time from Solid to this, still surprised by my grandmother's gift. I couldn't tell you how long I was on the street. I drifted off and was awakened by a loud noise. It was the ship's horn. Soon the rocking of the ship put me in a deep hypnotic state. I was calm and very much at peace.

All I know is I then had the most beautiful, deepest sleep I'd had in years. It was interrupted by Deep Sea's voice, saying in a soft calm manner, "Wake up, son, time for work."

I asked what time it was, and he said work time.

The cabin had no windows, so I was totally confused as to what time it was. However the dark didn't seem to bother me. All I knew was that I felt totally rejuvenated; my nose was clear, and my senses were on full alert. I got up and started getting dressed. Deep sea was putting his socks on when he said, "Follow me." We went out the door and through a maze of corridors. We stopped at the showers and washed up, then went up the stairs to the galley. The lights were turned on and I could now see that it was around 4:00 a.m.

There was a porthole in the kitchen, but outside it was totally dark. I actually thought at first that it was a picture of a hole hanging on the wall. Deep Sea shouted out commands, and I immediately followed. I tried my best to impress him as I once did for Solid. Deep Sea spoke with his eyes as he telegraphically implanted his order in your mind concerning what he expected. He started preparing the meals, and before I knew it my stomach was being seduced by the scent of food. It was a good experience.

I worked until I saw the hole-in-the-wall picture slowly changing colors and become somewhat visible. I could now distinguish clouds in the sky.

People started arriving for their meal at 6 a.m. I was now serving, and Deep Sea introduced me as Youngblood Robby. After the last person ate, we had to clean up everything as if what just happened never happened. Deep Sea then said, "Not a bad start, kid, we will do this three times a day. Now go take a break and get ready to do it all again."

After we finished and I had nothing to concentrate on, my stomach began to feel queasy, and I didn't know why. I left the galley and started walking around. I didn't know where I was going, but I knew I had to find a place to sit down. I got to this metal door and had to strain to push to open it. As I placed my left foot out, I was looking down at my stomach feeling queasy. When I was outside, I slowly looked up and saw it for the first time. Deep Sea's mistress, the ocean.

It immediately engulfed my vision and filled every area of my mind. She was beautiful. I was overwhelmed with visual splendor. The living manifestation of God's perfection. She was abundantly more than everything I had heard about her, she was all that she was, and all of everything there was. Suddenly while looking out the strangest feeling came over me; for the first time in my life my only thought was to just think of immortality and how small one's life was just a quick snapshot in the grand picture.

I only wanted to stand there and indelibly stamp my memory with a picture of this beauty so no matter what ever happened in my life it couldn't be said I didn't appreciate all I now saw. She was just as Deep Sea had said. I just stood there and watched. She moved like an angelic ballerina; her body was soft, her blue color was consistent, and the perfume she wore was one that infiltrated beyond one's nose, straight to your spirit. Her soft mist sprayed kisses that hit my face. It was like being romanced with a perfume of fresh tears. I don't know how long I stayed there staring, but I knew it was a while. The next conscious thought that went through my mind was that my stomach was still feeling a lot funny. Yes, those who are to adore her must be initiated into her splendor; all new life begins with great pain. To try to understand this feeling I got from looking at her, one would have to first live in the ghetto, walk the streets of New York, stay in some flophouses, go to sleep and awaken here where I was.

Because for all intended purposes, I was asleep as I lived. Funny how we all think that we are awake through the entire times in our lives, but we do things that only a sleeping mind would do. A mind that did not appreciate the gift of life itself or appreciate what was created for us.

Looking at the ocean, I couldn't understand how much time I wasted trying to understand good and evil. Although my moral pendulum was moving back and forward, I wasn't sure exactly which side my true nature belonged to, but at this moment I began thinking about how many people would never get to see what I was witnessing. My thoughts were pure and positive, and I was thankful to see her.

It was now time to get back to work and do my best to impress Deep Sea. He was a perfectionist; whereas Solid wanted to teach, Deep Sea expected you to already know. When he wanted something he wouldn't tell you where it was, he just would expect you to get it.

He worked my tail off, yet the captain and crew all spoke glory to Deep Sea's name. He had the reputation of having the best-run kitchen on the ocean. I did my absolute best to please him. After a while we clicked and made a pretty good team.

I was never afraid to work hard. My days were filled with work, and my nights were spent doing what most of the other seamen did on a ship, *read.* I didn't even know or cared where we were going; the sight of the ocean was worth the price of admission and it was all I looked forward to seeing each and every day.

Work was a sincere effort. It was only by Solid's teachings that I was able to perform with consistency and professionalism. I had to wake up before the sun did daily and get to the kitchen. This was not always easy to do with Deep Sea's snoring; although it wasn't anywhere near the snoring in the flop houses. The difference was that here the ocean gently rocked me back to sleep.

I had some of the deepest, soundest sleep of my life, and after work getting into bed was like a religious ritual you looked forward to as some people looked forward to church. Deep Sea and I would talk all day, but all the conversation stopped as we walked back to the cabin, and then we would each go shower in the bathroom, and we would come, back to the cabin and grab our books and read until we went to sleep. Deep Sea was a perfectionist as well as a workaholic and took immense pride in having the cleanest, best-run galley on the seven seas. He would talk with his eyes and expressions that I understood fluently. He would sometimes talk about his family, but his main love was his mistress the sea, which he worshipped daily. He would constantly ask me if I ever saw anything more beautiful in my life. We traveled to different countries in the world, and once on shore I would leave with the other seaman. Deep Sea would always stay behind and sit in his folding chair and drop his fishing line over the bow into the water and sit there with a peculiar look on his face. I never actually saw him catch anything, but he was totally content and at peace sitting there, drowning worms. While I was with the seamen, we would hit every brothel in every country. I was probably the youngest and maybe the best looking, so the boys seemed to like to hang out with me. I would often pay my money to the ladies and sometimes fall madly in love with my chosen mate for the time we spent together, and then I'd leave. The first time was in a port on the island of Martinique. I was taken to a brothel by the ship's electrician named Gary. He was well known, and he spoke about the place we were going to as if we were going to a museum. When we arrived and went inside I saw some of the most beautiful women I'd ever seen. Many times I couldn't make up my mind who to choose. My first time, a young woman who looked about my age walked out of the back room, looked at me, and slowly walked over and grabbed my hand and took me to the room. It was really my first experience with a professional woman. I rubbed her full breast like I was Aladdin expecting a genie to appear and grant my wishes. She moved in bed like she could disconnect her upper body from the lower part and then move the lower part as if it had its own spinal engine.

She would then moan like she was both humming and singing a song, oh so softly. Just looking at her was once again like my penis was in the army and she was our country's flag. It would stand at attention and pledge physical allegiance to her. I was in complete love until I had to pay and then reality brought me back to normal, and my penis was honorably discharged. Whenever I would get back to the ship, Deep Sea was still on board in the exact same place and position, casting his fishing line in the water. He would ask me where I went, and I would say we just looked around and explored. This existence went on for about two years, and I loved this life, I loved this routine. When we would get back to home port, we would all get paid and get a talk from the union official and then go to the hall to pay our union dues. I would sometime see Blue, who would say to me, "Don't forget your obligation."

I would call home but I would never go. I just wanted to get on another ship and go out again the same day, if possible. Deep Sea was always in demand and ships' captains requested him constantly, so we stayed at sea, and we stayed busy. He cooked and ran the galley like a mother, and he was not above telling anyone to go wash their hands before they ate. I traveled, ate, and worked, it appeared that now both Deep Sea and Robby were always in demand; I was now his assistant. We always surpassed regulation guidelines and expectations by keeping an extra clean workstation and preparing the best meals around.

We always kept the captain and crew happy and well fed. Deep Sea knew every port and had probably been there a dozen times before. He once told me that he had circled the globe about fifty times. We talked a lot in the kitchen and he told me of the large family he was supporting, so he stayed with his mistress, the sea, constantly. As always when we would finish work and reach the cabin we would both get our books and read until we fell asleep. Then as scheduled the sea would gently rock us to sleep. The only time Deep Sea would leave the ship was when we were in a country known for its spices he would shop for cooking goods. He was unique, to say the least; he wasn't a Solid-type spirit. He wasn't trying to change the world or even inspire anyone to try to change it; he just wanted to be the best at what he did and be appreciated for his way, and indeed he was. When the ship would reach home port, we would wait until the patrolmen from the hall came to pay us. A patrolman was the person sent by the union with a suitcase full of money to pay us and tell us what we needed to know as far as changes or union expectations. Life was once again sweet. I became an avid reader, and I really enjoyed and needed books. I even scanned the Bible until I knew what I was talking about. Deep Sea could quote any passage in the Bible and believed that the sea wanted him to understand her heavenly father, and he did. The sea taught us patience and humility. When there was a bad storm at sea, I would be surprised how humble that could make a man.

Life indeed had a strange way of teaching a lesson, even to a person convinced that they knew it all already, i.e., *me*. The men who were on the ship were a very mixed array of all classes and nationalities; they looked at being a seaman as one of the best-kept secret profession in America. Where else could you get paid for seeing the world and come home to a large paycheck waiting? Seamen were like racehorses who while at sea just patiently waited for the gate to open at a new port, and then they would run wild. At sea they would read, tell jokes, play cards, share family stories and talk of life's experiences. Once we arrived and the gate opened, they would raise hell at whatever port we were in. There was a man named Buster from a Caribbean island that had the record for the most women. He, like the electrician Gary, knew where every whorehouse was located and who was the best star to reach for. It was funny in a strange way that Buster was married and as soon as we arrived in home port, as soon as he could get off the ship, he would call his wife and tell her that he was back and would be home soon. Deep Sea used to say that he was the most dangerous kind of a married man. He knew exactly what he would do if he ever caught her cheating, so he made sure she had time to clear house; that was if she had any of his nature in her, pardon the pun. He once brought her back a box of scented toilet paper, now that's love.

Every man on board had another sea-earned name; these were really fun-loving, worldly, educated guys. One was a guy named Manny; he was from Puerto Rico. He was obsessed with women's feet. He would go to the houses and pick a woman totally by the way her feet looked. We called him the toeceanographer. Another was a man named Cordell who suffered from bad gas after each meal, he was called the fartographer. The men on the ship consisted of every race and ethnicity, and they were all characters. We joked, played cards, argued about politics and life, but we all worked hard, and we all took pride in the jobs we did. It was a totally new experience for me, and I guess me wasting time in the flophouses and streets in New York made me appreciate it more than I would have before. It's amazing how one can go through life just bouncing off experiences and living between good and evil. This life was more related to my time with Solid. I loved the sea and my time on the water. I only wished that I could be with some of my friends whose life was short lived and unacquainted with God's beauty. I spent the next two years working, reading, and buying and selling all of my ill-gotten imports at the hall. I didn't realize it, but because of my avid reading, I was actually becoming interesting to talk to. I used to hear some of my shipmates' tales of their first loves, and some stories were quite endearing. I guess one of the most important things that I learned was that true love just finds you where it may.

I was most happy with our ongoing constant haunting of the leisure houses on whatever continent we happened to dock on. The crew changed, which assured a completely new entertainment experience on every trip, and sometimes the ships changed, but I stayed with Deep Sea who was always glad to have me. Back in the city I would pay my dues and support the union by buying freedom stamps. It was a stamp to show union support. It didn't matter what it cost because one would always sell whatever perfume, items, or gold coins one could sell. I was sending some money home, not a great percentage of what I was making, but just enough to say that I sent some money home, and to reimburse grandma for giving me back the money I gave her. I didn't stay in contact with anyone in my family because I was having too much of a good time, and I just wasn't ready to see anyone. I guess when I looked in the mirror, I still saw me as I looked while on the streets. One time I was in the hall on a Saturday between ships. I was laughing and joking with the men when Blue came up to me and asked, "are you ready to pay your debt?" He said it in a way I would imagine Satan would have said it at the end of your life, if you had sold your soul to him. "Your contract is now up, wanna bring your soul over here?"

His tone completely shocked me, but I was obligated to do whatever he asked because he was responsible for this new and exciting life that I had. I swallowed and answered meekly, "Yes." He said, "We have a special job for you to do, and it's something I know you could and would do well. Come to my office on Monday, 10:00 a.m."

I then asked, "Is it safe?" and he burst out laughing. He laughed so hard you could still hear him when you could no longer see him. Now I was really concerned. I was in a box and knew that to maintain this lifestyle I now had to pay the piper, but my mind was too destructive to imagine anything good. I thought that I would have to maybe deal with a union enemy or something that was going to be really secretive. It was the way he laughed that made me skeptical. I wanted to just get on another ship and leave, but I knew that was just not an option. I wanted to talk about it with Deep Sea, but this was one of the few and far between times that he was with his family. He would usually call me when we were to leave again. I didn't have anyone to ask or talk to, and my agreement was between me, Blue and the union, and only between us. Thinking about what payback could be made time stand still.

I don't even remember Sunday happening. I was in the hall early Monday morning at 9:00 a.m. As I arrived at the waiting area near Blue's office, the president, JC was just walking in. He came over and said hi to me and shook my hand. I waited on a chair outside in the reception area. Blue then came out with a look on his face as if he was Snidely Whiplash and I was Sweet Nell about to have my family's farm foreclosed on. Blue then said, come in, son."

I remember that I was walking as if I had to literally kick one leg in front of the other to get traction. He smiled and said, "How are you? We have been keeping track of your performance and heard a lot of good things about you. Actually I just got off the telephone with Deep Sea this morning."

I didn't know which part of his statement to respond to, so I just cracked a crap-eating smile and listened. He then asked, "Are you a part of this union?" and I said in a resounding voice, "Yes, sir."

"Did I tell you that we are a special organization who looks out in every aspect for the hardworking seaman? Do you know the story about Frankenstein?"

I said, "Yes, sir."

Blue then told the story that Frankenstein was a doctor who created a monster totally put together by his creator, the doctor. The doctor had to find all the special body parts to make up his creation in order to make sure it operated at its maximum best. "We the people in charge are all like that doctor. The monster is this union, which we created to operate at its best, and in order to continue to be the monster that it is, we have to make sure that all of the parts continue to work together and at its absolute best."

At this point I wasn't sure if I should smile, cry, or run. I just nodded my head yes. "Are you ready to repay your debt to the union?" I nodded again. "What I am about to tell you will never leave your ears or this room, and once I tell you, it will never past your lips. The union election is a month away. You do know that, right?"

I felt like Davey on the roof just agreeing with everything Flub-a-Dub had to say. "We have been entrusted to make sure we remain the monster that we are. Understand?" Nod. "We need your help in making sure this happens." I was going to ask how, but I knew he would just tell me. I was more concerned with not appearing to look scared or uncool. I just knew that he wasn't going to just ask for my vote. He said, "We have a special job that requires the right person who can stay calm and cool and ensure success."

I asked him, "What is it you want me to do?"
I was going to ask if it was safe, but as I was always taught, time answers all questions. He then reached inside a desk drawer and pulled out a slender long piece of paper and held it up. "Do you know what this is?" he asked. I was totally confused; my head nodded and I said no, completely out of sequence. "This is a voting form, we have elections here every four years for the president as well as the administrative staff. We need you to guarantee that Frankenstein remains the monster that it is."

My curiosity was peaking at this point. I knew that I wasn't being asked to be anyone's campaign manager. He then came around his desk and sat in the chair next to me. He was a lot more animated and secretive. "This is a ballot form. As you can see, all one has to do is put a check next to the person's name they are voting for and then deposit it in a box. These elections are monitored by the hierarchy from Washington, DC because there was once an allegation of corruption. Are you with me so far?" Back to the nodding. "We need you to count each form and make sure that the present body parts of the monster stay in place."

At that point I thought I was just being asked to help the people from Washington count the vote. I replied, "I would be proud to help and do whatever I can do." Blue said, "Remember when you asked me if it was safe?"

A nod yes. "Well, after the election is over, these ballots are taken to a bank and secured by these Washington people, until the other people who count the actual votes arrive the following day. You still with me?" I still thought I was going to help count the vote the following day. "Your task is to remain with the ballots and keep a count of each one and make sure the monster remains intact. Understand?"

How could I make sure that the people he wanted to make sure would win, would win, with a room full of vote counters as well as the observers from Washington?

He now leaned closer to me as if I was going to get the kiss of death. "You will arrive at the bank with the ballots in hand, but instead of handing them off to the Washington observers, you will accompany the ballots inside of the safe where they and you will remain for the night."

"You mean they will leave the door open, and I stay with the ballots all night, right?"

"No, they will lock the safe's door, with you and the ballots inside. You will then begin counting the ballots. We will give you a list with the names of the monster pieces which need to remain part of the monster in order for him to continue efficiently."

I now pictured myself suffocating in a bank vault half-crazy with fear. I didn't want to ask a question revealing my fear, so I asked how could I change the outcome of the election if the people already voted. "Good question. If there are too many votes for the wrong person, you would simply place another check next to the other candidates name, therefore nullifying the card. If a card had two checks on it, it will be discarded. You will have to keep count of every vote and then place the checks where you need to."

"Won't the observers be suspicious of me being left in the safe that night once the door is opened?"

"That will be taken care of, and once the safe is locked they would just stand watch until the following morning. We will take care of any concern they may have. Your job is to take care of the ballots."

I then asked, "Suppose I suffocate while inside the vault, then what?"

"As long as you don't light any matches or panic, you will have enough air until the next morning."

I wanted to say, "I'm about to panic now just listening to this." "Son, I saw something in you when I first laid eyes on you to make me believe that you were a trusted soul. You help keep our monster intact, and the union will always protect you when you need protecting. We are all counting on you. We will supply you with some flashlights, water, and food. You just stay awake and do your job.

Understand?"

"Yes, sir."

"We're all depending on you."

I was in a state of shock. Never had anyone ever asked me any-thing like this. I now felt sorry for the people who got stuck inside the elevator after we kicked the door. Locked in a vault for a night was way beyond that!

"We will meet again and go over everything the week of the election. You are to discuss this with no one, not even Deep Sea."

"Yes, sir." I stood up just praying that my eyes didn't squeal on my thoughts. He extended his hand, and I shook it. He smiled and said, "You know what we are asking, right?" A nod yes. "You know what the two things not to do are, right?"

I said yes, one was to keep my mouth shut and two, don't panic. He laughed and said, "Good, but make that three things. Don't eat a lot of beans the night before." He laughed.

I smiled as if I also thought that was funny. I turned and began to walk out of his office. It really didn't totally hit me until I got outside the building and looked at the sky what he had just laid on me. What the hell kind of luck do I have? How ironic is life? To save Frankenstein, I have to be Dracula and spend the night in a damn coffin. They first get me used to the open air and sea, and the payment is being in a locked box. I was wondering with all the splendor and beauty that I have seen and experienced, would I have signed on if he had revealed his plan to me at the onset of my joining the union? I got a resounding yes, although I really didn't know how I would react once the damn door to the safe was closed. I took the path of least resistance; you know, Einstein's theory that water traveling downhill hits a rock and just goes around it. I kept telling myself that on the night when I arrived I would ask, and they would agree not to lock the damn door; this was my mental path of least resistance, knowing in the rear chamber of my mind that it made about as much sense as the good fairy buying false teeth. I had one more cruise to do before the election. I didn't know where the ship was going before I would be called upon to do this task.

I could hear my grandmother in my mind giving me the worst analogies when warning me not to do something.

Like "Boy, don't run, you may fall and split your kneecap open and get gangrene, and once it gets infected you die." Or "Get down off that chair before you fall and hit you head and could only speak & write Jibberish." This time she was saying "Boy, they gonna lock you in a safe and suffocate you and then collect the life insurance and say you snuck in to kill yourself." It's amazing how life plays pingpong with a person, hitting them between good and evil. I couldn't wait until the ship pulled out from land so I could just think clearly.

Once at sea, Deep Sea kept asking me if I was all right. He didn't want to pry, but he knew that something was up when he got the reference request from Blue. He looked at the people in the union as if they were politicians. All the talk about their faith in God, then they accomplish the task of getting elected and immediately begin committing false witness against their neighbors.

I thought that he may have known the plan and was in on it with them, and they just wanted to see if I would talk, and if I did they would change the election day to a Friday so by Monday I would have been deceased, judged, and long gone. I hit this mentally from all angles and settled with Deep Sea knowing nothing about this.

Out at sea again was like being reborn. When looking at the ocean, now I always thought she was beautiful, but this time she was spectacular. The open sky, the waves, the enchanting splendor. I must have really been scared. In the back of my mind, if I would have described anything in the ghetto with the words *enchanting splendor*, the guys would have said, "Limp your wrist when you talk like that." I must have been evolving into a person who could now express their thoughts because of my intense reading. Sentences like *that's messed up* or *screw you* now became animated. The more I learned, the less I cursed, knowledge can do that to you. The problem was that in the ghetto, you didn't know someone who knew someone who would have agreed to this Frankenstein crap, and if they did it was to get to the cash inside the safe. They would enter the safe skinny and leave very fat. This trip was like being told I had a month to live and was packing a lifetime into one trip. Again, the time flew by. It's amazing how time creeps by when you're a kid in school; it's all slow motion, and when you become an adult it's like a moving in a Chaplin movie. When we docked back in New York City, Deep Sea said something to me on the gangplank that was profound. He smiled and said, "Good luck, boy, whatever you do don't sell your soul."

Wow, that had two meanings for me: one symbolic and one at face value. Before I knew it, I was back in the union office. It was a Monday, and the election was that Wednesday. I had a lot of dumb questions, which I was too afraid to ask, like "Suppose it's obvious who the winners are, will you call this off?"

I was immediately called upstairs to Blue's office again. They asked me what I wanted to eat once we all sat down. I immediately asked, "Suppose I have to go to the bathroom once inside the safe?" and they all laughed and said to cancel the food, bad idea. I was then introduced to a man named

Jackson. They called him Bummy. I asked Blue why the name Bummy, that wasn't a seaman's name. They then explained the obvious, I was told that he got his name because no matter what he wore he looked Bummy. Bummy could have a tuxedo on and still look bummy. He was somewhat an expert in changing these ballots. He told me they would make sure I had sufficient light, different-colored pens, some pencils, and some champagne. I asked why the champagne, and he laughed and said, "Boy, you will be in there all night. If you really have to go to the bathroom bad, pour the champagne out and stick the cork in your ass."

I was the only one who failed to see the humor in this. He knew everything about changing the ballots, but when I asked about the air supply inside the safe and if I would be all right, he would shrug his shoulders and say yes. The more Bummy spoke, I figured that if there was indeed a Frankenstein monster made up of different parts, then Bummy was part of the asshole. He had on a suit about three sizes too big and had a severe bump on the bridge of his nose and short nappy hair. I immediately assumed that he was the resident ballot counter before they recruited me. He was now promoted to training fools.

I was wined and dined by Bummy that night and told how important my assignment was and how they were all depending on me. The day before the election I was taken to a big beautiful hotel, where I was told to just relax and rest. I was provided with the best of food and drinks, and just like the manager of a prizefighter, Bummy said no sex; it would zap my strength and make me tired, and the last thing they wanted was a person who would go to sleep in the safe. Little did they know that I wouldn't be able to sleep in the safe even if I attended a marathon orgy for a week straight. Hearing this man even mention sex was odd to me; I couldn't even imagine Bummy knowing that such a thing as sex existed, but as my mother said, for everyone there is an anyone. He looked especially bummy and out of place in this beautiful, plush hotel and I mean this was a real high-class hotel. I never ever dreamed I might even deliver something here, let alone be a guest. The people who I was allowed to speak with from the union came by, and they all told me that I had to stay calm and get to work immediately. I had many, many ballots to count. After they left, I sat with Bummy and we talked. I asked him honestly, "Could I suffocate inside of that safe?"

He said "No, that's not your biggest problem. Your biggest problem will be dealing with your negative thoughts, and if you let them get the best of you, you're screwed. By the time the door opens the next morning, if you let fear and panic get the best of you, you will be able to speak and understand a bowl of Rice Krispies fluently. Just stay calm and stay focused and you will be fine."

He looked nationalistic and said this was a great honor to have been chosen to do this. "These guys can make a jackass into a real fine racehorse. Do them well, and they will do you proud."

That was a good thought for him to leave me with, one I never thought of. I guess I was the jackass. I had thought that I was merely paying back a debt, not creating one payable to me.

Once he left and I was in bed staring at the ceiling, I knew and accepted that this was really going to happen, and I had to accept the fact that I must do my best. I kept thinking about Solid saying, "If you're going to do something, then do the hell out of it." The following day was Election Day. I woke up and was going to order a feast, but Bummy came in and limited me to one hard-boiled egg and a thimble full of juice. He asked if I was mentally ready, and I took a deep breath and sighed and said, "Oh yeah." I asked, "Will the people from the government be all right with this?" And he said all the pieces have been placed on the board, everyone knew their moves.

"Do not engage in any conversation with anyone. They will probably not even look at you in case they have to take a lie-detector test. You go in carrying the ballots, take them to the safe, and then hide inside until the door shuts. Once you hear the locks engage, go to work. Here are your supplies, and remember what I said, the only enemy you will have inside there will be your imagination."

I asked him directly if he ever did anything like this. He smiled and said, "I will do whatever is asked to keep this monster alive. I wasn't even allowed to vote that day." I asked if I could go to the hall and vote, and Bummy just burst out laughing. "For what, young blood? Suppose you do and later have to nullify that vote?"

I felt kind of stupid by the question. He then told me to try and take an afternoon nap at noon. At four thirty, we got ready to leave. Bummy was on the telephone with someone and said that I was ready, that I would do fine. He then came over to me and said, "Here is a pill to keep you up should you need it, but this is a double-edged sword. It will keep you up but ignite your imagination, so just take it as close as you can to 9:00 a.m. when the door automatically opens. Once the door opens, you will have on this suit. You will then just slowly walk out of the safe and into a waiting car out front. You understand?"

"Yes sir."

"Young blood, your mind has to be strong and you have to control it and not allow it to control you. Understand?"

"Yes."

We got into the waiting car and drove straight to the union. I waited in the car while three security goons brought the ballot bags out to me; they looked heavy and full. Bummy was slipping cash into the goon's hands. One government official got in the front seat; he never said a word or turned around to acknowledge us. We then drove downtown to the bank. It looked like an average bank, about to close. We stayed in the car until all the people

Marty R.

left at four fifty-five. We calmly grabbed the bags and walked in. There were two men in suits in the back by the desks looking out the window. My heart was pounding as if I was robbing this damn bank, not making a deposit. The man who was in the front seat then came inside and spoke with the men by the desk.

When we got by the safe, Bummy began handing me all the bags and said, "I will pick you up in the morning. There's plenty of air, just control your mind and do your job. Hear me?"
As I got closer and looked inside, I heard my mind yell, "I'm not going in there for any damn monster!" I told it to shut up and continued to walk inside. Once I saw how small and enclosed it was, my mind began to campaign for panic. It told my body, "You have to first piss, crap, sneeze, cough, fart, yawn, swallow, cry, anything to stop this madness." I thought to my mind, just shut up, it was trying to cause mayhem with my body parts and create a panic rebellion. I took a deep breath and just stood still. Bummy was now outside the door. I could see the arm of a man next to him but not his face. He gave me the thumbs up. I smiled. Bummy said in a stern voice, "Young blood, give me the thumbs up."

My mind yelled at my hand to stick the middle finger up and run the hell out of here. I looked down then looked up and flashed the sign. The door slowly closed, and I then heard locks moving. I immediately lit the flashlight that I had and took out a small lamp-light. My mind yelled, "You damn fool, you're about to lose me." It took me a minute to compose myself, it was somewhat hard, but I did. I looked at my watch and knew I had sixteen hours here.

I was at the execute hour, the point of no return, the commit stage of this plan, and the only thing I was sure of was that I had to emerge from this with my mind totally intact. My first thoughts were brutal. When I would feel panic coming on, I would have to take a deep breath and be thankful that I was chosen for this great responsibility. It was dead silent inside there, and all I could hear was my heart beating, my blood circulating, and my mind calling me an asshole. I figured that I should begin counting to try and take my mind off the moment. I took all the ballots out of the bag and made separate piles. I tried to make them the same level as the others. I then spread the lights I had around the area and even began humming a tune. When I completed that task, I was going to begin counting each ballot. I figured I must have wasted about two hours already putting everything in order, then I looked at my watch, and saw that it only took me ten minutes, time was now standing still. Now I know that the mind is a powerful entity, but I was now learning exactly how powerful it could be. My mind had a mind that seemed to be on its own, and every so often it would try to appeal to my weaknesses to join it in a revolutionary takeover.

At one point my mind tried to recruit my nose. It gently said, "Mr. Nose, you're having trouble breathing. I believe that we are running out of oxygen. What kind of man would subject someone he loved to this?"

My nose quickly checked with my diaphragm and asked in a panicked sneeze, "Is that true, are you having trouble breathing?"

The logical side of my brain would immediately intervene and assure everyone that things were all right, and that it was impossible to run out of air in the short while we were in here. I began my count. I had a pencil and a piece of paper and tried shallowed breathing just in case. Man, it was quiet in here, you could hear a flea fart without even trying. I kept busy and occupied, and every time my mind would attempt to recruit a co-conspirator, I would do my best to calm them down and appeal to logic that this was all in my mind's mind. It looked as if the president of the union, JC, was a sure winner, unchallenged. It was the lesser positions, the monster lower body parts, which were in trouble of being toppled. The monster appeared intact; it was just some legs and toes in trouble. I was now through with half of the ballots; I had absolutely no appetite and was getting tired of being in here. Not tired as in sleep, tired of this damn confinement.

I tried to close my mind and picture the vast ocean, Deep Sea's mistress, but my mind would say, "Oh yeah, you're out at sea now, right? Then how come we're not rocking? You smell any salt, asshole?" I was afraid to look at my watch again. I kept chugging along and was now nullifying quite a few ballots to coincide with the names on the list that I was given. I just kept going and going. When I was about finished, my mind had successfully recruited my eyes; it did it in a very clever manner. I was near the end of my count when my mind said, "Hey, fellas, Mr. Eyes, I know that you're both busy and that this is very important, and far be it from me to interrupt, but aren't these damn walls closing in on you?"

I slowly looked up and damn if it didn't appear to be true. I immediately beckoned my logic, "Where the hell are you?" I quickly closed my eyes in an attempt to spare them and wiped them both thoroughly, and when I slowly opened them again and looked to assure them that everything was fine, my mind said to them, "Ignoring the situation won't stop this." I was about to experience the mother of all panic attacks. My nose then abandoned its post and joined the other side. The smaller it gets, the harder it is to breath. I looked at my watch, and to my surprise it was working. It was now 6:45 a.m., two hours and fifteen minutes to go, but man this was brutal.

Every part of my body was advocating joining the other side in opposition against me and my will. I think that I even once muttered the word "help" and shut my eyes. My mind was trying to enlist every part of me, yelling, "Shut this asshole down! It was he who brought you all here, it is he who should pay!" Just then, as I was about to lose it and give in to the masses of the asses, I closed my eyes and took three or four deep breaths and heard my logic say in Solid's voice, "Only two hours to go, and you're going to throw it all away, for what? You're nearly there! You want them to open that door and find you balled up in a corner farting in the thermos and smelling it, or standing sure and tall with confidence and self-assuredness, with the job completed and done well, wouldn't Solid want you to do the job well and make the best impression you could?"

Well, not all but most of my body parts listened to my logic and allowed me to finish my task at hand. I didn't peer at any walls or take my eyes off the ballots; I didn't even look at my watch again. When I was finished I just sat there with my eyes shut, still unable to sleep, not hungry or thirsty, just waiting for this to end. Soon I heard a slight noise; it was faint at first as if something turned, then it grew louder. I looked at my watch and it was 9:00 a.m. I stuffed all the ballots back in the bag and pushed the bags behind me. The door then slowly opened, and I could smell fresh air, cold air.

It was like I was waiting for the doctor to just slap me on my ass. I saw Bummy's face; he was standing there, smiling. I placed my hand against the wall and posed as if to say, "Finished already?"

He said, "You all right?"

I answered, "Did you ever doubt it?"

I was led out of the safe and thoroughly searched in case I had any latent ambitions. As they searched me, I thought, "Damn, I never even thought about the money inside of there." My mind said in a stern voice, "That's because you're an asshole." We walked past the men inside and into a waiting vehicle. We drove back to the hotel, and all Bummy said the entire trip was "You done yourself proud, son, you done yourself proud."

I lastly remember getting in that bed at the hotel and closing my eyes. It took a while to get that safe out of my mind's eye and re-recruit all of my facilities back to my command, but slowly they all came around. Even my mind said, "Boy, I was just testing you, and you passed with flying colors. You know that you're my main crap stain."

I smiled and went off to sleep. I remember that my last thought was *If*

Marty R.

by serving this monster I could maintain this life-style, I would enjoy upon waking up hearing the ringing of the dinner bell, ZZZZZZZZZZZZZZZZZ, anytime, anyplace. ZZZZZZZZZZZZZZZZZZZZZZZZZ ...

CHAPTER 8

GROWING NOT GOING THROUGH LIFE

Life was meant to live and laugh not sit and hesitate. God provides the fish my friend, but you must cut the bait.

I woke up the next day feeling like a new person. Even my mind was trying to get back in good with me. It whispered with glee in my head, "We did it, we did it."

I asked it, "Are you speaking French? What's with the *we*?" The phone soon rang and it was Bummy. He said he would arrive in ten minutes and he asked me to get dressed and be ready to leave. He also said to order a good meal or six and say goodbye to this lifestyle. It wasn't until I was in the shower when I really thought about what I had just accomplished and survived. I was a little concerned that my mind may have sabotaged the count. I thought, *Suppose I was off and the people didn't get in, and Frankenstein was now mixed with someone else, maybe a black Frankenstien, or he had long hair or a mustache?* I enjoyed a hearty meal and dressed. Bummy then came and sat down in front of me. He asked if I knew what time it was, and I said yeah it's morning time. He said it was 4:00 p.m. on Friday. I slept nearly two days. "The count is finished, the election is officially over?" I nervously said.

"Anddddd," he replied "urine."

I thought he was calling me *piss,* but he meant "you're in." Everyone was grateful.

He explained that no one would ever speak of this to me, but I should rest assured that I made some friends and that Frankenstein was intact alive and doing well. I may not have been a body part of the monster, but I felt some pride. I could at least say that I was once a Frankenstein builder. I asked, "What now?"

I was hoping he would say, "It's finished, your debt is paid in full," but he answered, "Take some time and go back to work, but don't get too comfortable, they may need you again."

I just wanted to get back to the open sea and the salty smell. If I loved it before, I would worship it now. He dropped me off at the hall, and everything was as it was the days before this adventure. Deep Sea was out at sea on another run, so I asked the dispatcher what was available to sail as soon as possible. He said "Hold, on let me look on my desk in the back."

He came back out and said, "We have a trip going from the downtown dock to Bermuda."

My job would be to just to make up and clear off the tables and serve water at dinnertime. I was to be paid three times what I usually got for washing the dishes and cleaning with Deep Sea. He went on to say that this was on a passenger ship and not a freighter, and when I was not working I could enjoy the amenities on board. Holy bird crap, was this some sort of reward for that safe job? It really didn't matter. I said I would take it and then went shopping for casual clothes.

Marty R.

The ship was leaving that evening at 8:00 p.m. I couldn't understand why no one else grabbed that job. But when Lavajeskie even broke tradition and cracked a smile; something he never did. I thought to myself, three times as much, I'm rich. I got my gear and went shopping, I was in one of the big department stores downtown and just took my time: the me who got on that ship was not the me who got off the last one. I had a newfound confidence. I felt that if I could survive the ordeal of the safe, I could survive anything, even jail, which wasn't a good analogy to make or way to think, but I did.

I lost all restraint and was a different person. It was like that safe was an oven and the person who was put in to bake came out a finished 'bird', well-done indeed. I had no fear of jail, as in the past, or anything else for that matter. Once you sincerely believe that you can totally control your thoughts and actions, you are somewhat liberated from the shackles of life. I got to the dock on time and checked in on board; these seamen who were on this vessel were very different. They were more refined and appeared well kept and better educated. The ones who didn't look educated were smart enough to just smile at you and say nothing. This was a new experience for me, my first trip without Deep Sea. I was even given a cabin to myself, which was unheard of on the freighter ships I previously served on. We set sail and I reported to the galley. The man in charge was an Indian man named Fiad. He shocked me when we met by calling me sir. I was told that all I was here to do was to pour water in the glasses for the passengers at the table. This was unheard of with Deep Sea. I cleaned, washed, scrapped, swept and mopped. I later found out that this was a battle won by the union. If your job was to clear the table or serve the food, you were not allowed to serve the water. Frankenstein was indeed exerting his authority.

I spent my time pouring water and relaxing in my single cabin with a porthole in it. Frankenstein must have said something to Fiad because I was treated like a king. The sea looked as magnificent as always, but the added pleasure was again seeing the really beautiful emerald water of the Caribbean. I said to myself, I could do this for the rest of my life, but sometimes life's destiny and reality have other plans for you. I was now reading books designed to make myself interesting. I memorized jokes and quotes. The trip was a good one. After dinner was finished and I had off time, I would put on a nice shirt and sit at the bar. There were a lot of older single women on the boat, and being a young single stud was a real attraction. I began to realize that my tall, slender frame with my curly hair and light eyes were an attraction, but the truth be told, many of these woman didn't care how I looked. Many wouldn't even look at me when I served them water. I was just a Pour Boy to them, but sitting at the bar drinking water was like advertising a new product in a store with no other stock. I became a novelty aboard this ship, a man who was available. It was the epitome of the law of supply and da man.

Now I had already lost my innocence, so it wasn't like I was inexperienced. What was new was being exposed to women who were very much older. Some were funny and sweet, and some acted like they were giving me a special treat and that I should be eternally grateful. There was one in particular who was somewhere in her fifties, but this was champagne in a beer bottle. She smelled like the ocean with perfume, and she would make the sexiest cooing noises when we made love. She told me that she was on this trip because she just got divorced after twenty-five years of marriage. She asked me in the most sexy way a woman could ask, "I know that you don't mean it, but while we are making love could you keep repeating in my ear, 'I love you?'" The power of suggestion was powerful indeed. I kept saying it and depending on the position we were in, I would even believe it myself until we both exploded with the passion time bomb. Then we would wake up and look for each other's puff button to press to make one another disappear. It was a good experience. Here they didn't have a Deep Sea; they had white and Indian cooks who didn't say a word.

Being in a quiet mess hall was totally new to me. I missed my friend Deep Sea, but the meals served here were like the difference between Joe's Diner food and the food at the hotel I had stayed at. I would sometimes go to bed at night thinking about my time in that safe. When I was a little boy and used to hear about people being locked up, I would always project myself into their feelings and feel that it must have been terrible being locked in that tiny cell daily. For the most part my perceptions of what it may have been like some-times controlled my actions, preventing me from taking unnecessary chances; sometime, not always, but sometimes. Once that fear was gone, I could feel myself back on the good and evil scale, and I was tipping back toward evil. Sometimes fear is a good thing. We got into home port on time, and the union representative met us in the dining hall to pay us. He would always carry suitcases full of cash to give each man their pay. I would just sit and watch as he reached his hand into a bag and pulled out a stash of cash, as if there was no bottom on that bag. He would always have two protectors or union goons on each side of him. At this point I would still send money home, but would never call. One thing I knew was that I never wanted to see the ghetto again. Once we docked, none of the female passengers would even ask me for any contact information, which was fine with me.

I rented a room at a nearby hotel. It wasn't like the one Bummy put me up in, but it wasn't a flophouse either. I now would never pass a man in the street who lacked material possessions, who most people would call a bum, and not give them whatever I could. I would look at them and always know exactly how they felt and how lucky I was.

The next morning I headed straight for the hall to see what I could get into and check on old friends. I heard that Deep Sea was still out with his mistress, and doing well. I was in the great auditorium at the hall, looking at silk that someone was selling, when an official from upstairs named TJ Smith said to me that if he had some of that silk he would wear the best suits in New York. It then hit me like seeing the stabbed dishwasher and thinking that there was a job opening. I should buy enough material for six suits, then take the material it to the garment district. Two hours later I was in a small tailor's shop named Ben Dover. He was a small Jewish man with a thick mustache and glasses. I thought his name was odd for as Jewish man. I thought maybe it was code for a man who swung both ways. I introduced myself and explained the truth. I was a merchant seaman with access to this cloth, and that it was all legal.

I was looking for a partner who would make me suits and keep the rest of the material for payment by selling the other suits to their customers. The training at Solid was in full swing. Having a slender frame was an incentive; because I didn't use much material. Ben put on thicker glasses and immediately grabbed his measuring tape and began measuring me for a suit. He measured everything but my private parts and told me to come back in two weeks. I took another short junket on another cruise ship and returned. I got my pay and headed straight to Ben's shop. He brought out the most spectacular suit I'd ever seen. I took it from his hand and was putting it on in the same room he measured me in. It was like placing a crown on my head. Once it was on, I didn't even recognize me. I went from a jackass to a racehorse. I nearly gave myself an eyegasm. I felt like I was finally looking like I was always meant to look. I wish that all my Ghetto friends could have seen me. Ben looked at me and smiled and said, "Anytime, just come back with different colors and materials, and I will take care of you."

So went my routine short trips, buy silk cloth at the hall, see Ben. When I would now sit at a bar on a cruise, I would be the star of the room, and I knew it. It's amazing how people seem to endow you with attributes that don't exist just because of the cut of your garments.

I didn't even have to buy drinks anymore. They were placed in front of me, ordered by female passengers, and the bartender would just point to the buyer. I would raise my glass and smile. I also incorporated something that Solid used to teach me. It was that the most important thing that a man can learn in life was when to shut up and just look. Sitting at the bar with a silk suit on was like flashing a sign that read "Very Open for Monkey Business." Another reason I was comfortable at sea, there was no chance that anyone would question me about Solid, even at port I started to relax and let that concern go. I was now a man in a silk suit with identification that read Robby; no one would mistake this me for a store clerk. It got so that once again I was drinking my ass off, but the difference now was that the drinks were actually good, and most importantly I cared about how I now presented myself. I guess all alcoholics are separated by a thin line; if you don't care about yourself, you'll wake up anywhere. If you would suddenly realize that no matter how much you have to drink, but looked forward to tomorrow, you will make sure your clothes are folded when you sleep wherever that may be. I guess the term to always remember to pattern your invention to make sure it goes from generation to generation, was a good one.

I often thought that the guy who invented the wheel once said to himself, "Why am I pushing this damn cart over the ground, when I could have circles on the side and a horse pulling it?" I soon got the idea that the same way I was able to capitalize on the silk to help me, all the things at the hall that the men were selling and all the things I purchased overseas could be sold or traded here in the bars, liquor stores, and perfume stores to fund a greater lifestyle for myself. I began taking my pay and purchasing damn near everything they were selling at the hall, then taking the items to the bars, outlet stores, and to the liquor stores. These items didn't have a government stamp on them, but really when was the last time your purchased a bottle of booze and checked to see if it had a valid government stamp on it? I was the best-dressed hustling, enterprising entrepreneur on the streets, and my source was limitless. Frankenstein was growing by leaps and bounds. Each day there was at least ten new faces, all here to trade their lives on land for the life at sea. Each trip I would now take would result in my bringing back goods. The other men who had other goods were glad to do business with me. I would buy all they had when they had it. As soon as they came off the ship and already had a pocket full of money, I knew that this was the best time to buy what they had to sell. I mean, who haggles when your pockets are already full? I looked like a movie star in my clothes, and that gave me a dapper sense of being. I was now able to stuff the pockets of my suits with cash.

The only thing I truly missed was the ocean, Deep Sea's mistress hooked my heart, she really did. I would run into Deep Sea from time to time, and he would always give me a sincere friendship greeting. "I hear good things about you, boy. You must be doing well, huh? I hope you're showing everyone what hard work and cleanliness can do."

Then he would always ask, "Do you still have a soul?" He was like Solid, except he was only truly at home on the water. I was catching the eyes of Frankenstein's doctors, who were also giving me hearty handshakes and sincere hellos when we met. When someone would mention the elections to me and say something that could begin a conversation about the safe, I would place a puzzled look on my face and just shake my head and walk away. I never said yes, no, or anything about my safe experience. My tailor Ben was now giving me orders for different colors of silk and was even supplying me with shirts and ties as well. My mother would have been proud, my father envious. My friends would call me the white wannabe dressing like this.

Marty R.

I called myself "Cooooool." It was just about now that I learned another one of life's lessons, one that school never teaches you. One that only successful people learn and that is greed has no end and never says enough. Greed wants more and more and more. Why? you may ask, because it just does. In the hustler's mind one is never saving or preparing for tomorrow. I was enjoying today to the fullest, eating, drinking, and loving, just to get to tomorrow when I can do it all over again with different food, alcohol, and women. I was selfish, self-centered, and arrogant, but I did give to the homeless whenever I saw one. One day, while I was at the hall in the auditorium just talking to someone, lo and behold, the man who should have been inspired to have thought of the suit exchange long before me walked by and gave me a Bummy half-smile of approval. Bummy worked upstairs with the hierarchy, but no one really knew exactly what his job was. All I knew for sure was that it was not near election time, so I figured it was safe to acknowledge him, so I waved and smiled, no pun intended

I guess that whoever coined the phrase "the clothes make the man" really knew what they were talking about. It's kind of like the reason clowns have to wear funny clothes. A clown in a business suit would be deemed unfunny. The better I dressed, and the more money people thought I was making; I was really impressing every-one. I guess if you were to put a pile of crap in a decorated plastic bag, you could convince people it was magic mud. Dressing well really shaped my image. All I did was take the same goods that were being sold at the union's auditorium and market it outside, creating demand. Again the liquor and cigarettes weren't legally government stamped, but if you owned a bar and could sell the same alcohol that you would usually pay twenty dollars a bottle for but had just paid only eight dollars a bottle for, wouldn't you pour this alcohol into your old finished government stamped bottles? Cuban cigars and liquor were a big seller as was the French perfume. I was still ship-ping out on passenger ships, but now every time I was out at sea, all I could think of was how much money I was not making. I remember that we were at a port in Grenada, and me and some of the crew went to a bar for some drinks.

The women were fabulous. One lady had an ass that was so beautiful, I could not even imagine her taking a crap with it. I told my buddies this ass didn't take a crap. It was much too beautiful, it gave birth to crap. I was at the bar just staring at her and just smiled. A man who we called Pimping Sam from Alabam was standing next to me. He looked at me and then at her and echoed something Solid once said to me, in different words of course: he said only fools and idiots smile for no reason. He then asked, "Did she once look at you and smile?"

"No," I answered.

"Then why are you so damn happy? Young blood, a man's technique is what makes him unique. Make her want to be the reason you smile. Unless of course you're already so happy that she can't do anything for you." Sam also said, "I noticed when I walked in you stood up to shake my hand, a man never stands to shake another man's hand unless he wants to pay homage to him, were you paying Homage to me?

It's amazing how when there is something that you need to know or reinforce something in life, it will come to you with a remark a whisper or on the radio. I stopped smiling right there and then. Both Sam and Solid were right about looking serious and establishing a serious first impression; it made me a completely different person. After that was reinforced again, I was now presenting myself as a man, and realized that half the effort in selling something is pack-aging. No, I didn't get the girl that night; everyone was buying her drinks, and I wasn't but the lesson was learned.

When I got back in port I immediately went back to my business. I picked up and delivered the goods and put on my flashy clothes. I was renting a room from another seaman who had a large house a family and a spare room, it was actually where I dropped my bags. I would literally live at the hall when in port. I looked like I was the only part of Frankenstein that people could relate too. I often used many of the quotes I learned while at sea and used then in analytically precise instances. I was well liked and even admired by many. One day while I was collecting goods for my customers, once again lo and behold Bummy walked up to me and said, "They want to see you upstairs."

At first I thought I did something wrong. Bummy must have studied at the Pimping Sam University of Social Development. He rarely would smile or even crack a grin. I asked what the problem was. He replied, "You want to stay here and question me and find out nothing, or go upstairs and find out?"

The main executive offices were upstairs, but this was an office only a few steps above Blue's office with a very private entrance. I had heard stories about the executive offices upstairs. I heard everything from "heaven on earth" to "it's where they keep the Frankenstein monster." I slowly walked up the stairs instead of taking the elevator, thinking what could this possibly be about. I thought my debt was paid in full. When I got upstairs, I was directed to those steps located in the rear of the other offices. I opened the door and thought I walked into heaven. There was an atrium with flowers, trees, and a waterfall. The sights and smells were like being in a rainforest. I walked over to the secretary's desk near the window and introduced myself. I was immediately announced by the secretary. She was a beautiful Italian woman named Adonis. She said, "So you're Robby. Your reputation precedes you."

Now I was really scared. Reputation? I replied, "As does yours. I was told that the flowers up here were beautiful, but I thought that they were the kind that grew from the earth, not bloomed from a mother, and worked in this place."

Robby

She smiled and said, "Wait here."

Adonis was as pretty as she could be: long auburn hair with a face that showed intelligence and sex appeal wrapped in a slight smile, with full lips, blue eyes, and the sexiest legs wearing stockings and heels. She was about ten years older than I was but wore it better than most women my age. She was much better looking than the women I comingled with while at sea. I sat and tried to show the cool side in case someone was watching me.

I saw the elevator open and watched as Bummy walked off and went straight in the back, and yes he was still Bummy, even while wearing a really expensive suit. I still did not understand what his job was, other than to make sure no-one never ever spoke with any of the hierarchy about company business. I sat there a good half hour, convinced that someone was watching me, so I tried to remain as still as I could. Every so often Adonis would look up from her desk and shoot me a smile. Her phone rang and she said, "Yes, sir." She then looked at me and said, "You can go in now."

As I walked in the back, I saw her eyes follow me. I couldn't even imaging having a job where you had to report here every day. I never dreamed of anything like this. There was one thing I knew for sure, and that was that I looked good. Outside this office I saw those who were sitting t their desks all looked up at me through the glass partition when I stood up. These were people I've never seen downstairs before. This was like the top of the clouds, and downstairs was just earth. I got to the back office just when the door opened. Bummy said, "In here."

I walked in and another man who I've never seen before and who looked like a prizefighter gave me the once-over twice. He looked me up and down and then grunted and walked out. I watched as he walked down the walkway and didn't see anyone look at him leave. I entered the office and saw Blue who was with another gentle-man who I didn't know. Blue saw me in my suit and said, "Look at you. I hear you singlehandedly organized the merchant seaman into viable merchants. I remember when I first saw you outside, sitting at the tree well. Now that person has died, and this one was reborn. I'm proud that I played a role in assassinating that lost looking other person. Here you are working, traveling, and more importantly organizing and recruiting. That's what we are all about, providing a better life for those who depend on us."

He then asked me, "That other person at the tree well, do you miss him?"

I said, "Some parts of him have stayed, some have evolved, but I have to say no. He accepted and made the best of whatever life gave him, and this man here, the one I am now, he plans his life."

They both laughed. Blue then said in an evasive way, "I remember you played a good role in the preservation of the status quo."

I didn't reply because I was told to never discuss it. I just nodded my head. He said, "The monster needs you again."

I was relieved because I thought that this had everything to do with my exploits downstairs. I asked, "How may I help?"

"Do you know what the job of a patrolman is, and what is expected of him?"

I answered, "Yes, sir, the patrolman is the one who pays the sea-man when they return from sea. He's the man with the suitcase full of money. He handles their grievances and tries to offer solutions even if he only makes them think that something has been done."

He laughed and said, "Well put, my friend. We need a man to replace one of the patrolmen who is about to have a health crisis." He said, "Do you know Frenchy?"

I replied, "I know of him."

"Well, he's going to leave here soon."

Robby

"I thought to myself that he looked in good health the last time I saw him."

"We need a replacement until the next election, and we thought of you for two reasons: 1. You look and dress like a man who should be representing us, and 2. We wanted to say thank you for what you did."

My first thought was, no more time at sea? That was hard to think about, I really liked the sweet job I had on the cruise ship, but it would also mean working my business full-time. A patrolman could get anyone on any ship he wanted, so I could triple my supply of goods immediately. I said, "Whatever you wish."

They said they would announce it next week and asked me to go downstairs and see patrolman Mr. Silver, and that he would begin my education.

Blue closed with "I expect you to do us proud, and remember, as long as the monster is respected and feared, no one will even think of messing with us. As usual, you are to repeat this meeting to no one. Understand?"

"Yes, sir," I answered.

I got up shook hands and left. This was the longest I ever saw Bummy with his mouth shut. I remember leaving thinking about Frenchy. I just saw him and he looked fine to me, but what did I know?

As I passed Adonis, she waved me over and whispered, "Even office flowers needs attention, and nurturing now and then." She placed a small piece of paper in my palm. I nodded my head and held back the smile. I took the elevator down and read the note. It was her telephone number. All I thought about was watering her two lips.

CHAPTER 9

MR. PATROLMAN-ME-VERSUS-ME

The patrolmen were the guys with the bags of money who sat at a desk all day long looking good. They handled all of the seamen's grievances and problems. They were the liaison between the hall and the shipping lines. I went straight to Mr. Silver. His name was because of his silver hair. He was an Italian man who looked like the father figure you would have painted if asked to create a picture of a dad. Nice smile and a low whisper in his voice. His fingernails looked professionally manicured, and his suit was impressive. I walked to his desk and introduced myself. He damn near cut off my circulation with his glare. He said, "A seaman can recognize another seaman a mile away. I've seen you in here, and you appear more like a ship's captain than a seaman."

I said, "No, sir, I am a seaman who loves going wherever the ship is headed. Couldn't imagine having the responsibility of a captain and taking it there. I just got the call from upstairs."

"Well, you really hit pay dirt, didn't you? You have one hell of an opportunity before you, are you ready for it?

I replied, "I once read that when opportunity meets ambition, if they play the cards right, they can be the parents of success."

He smiled and said, "I like you, young man. A patrolman is an elected position. We are the problem solvers, the paymasters, and the backbone of the beast. Your education begins tomorrow, be here at 9:00 a.m."

I left and looked at Adonis's number all the way to my room. I called her that evening as soon as I got home. "Hello?" she answered, "who is this?" I said the person interviewing for the gardener's position.

"Where are you? I am home now, can you pick me up at my house?"

I told her that I didn't drive and didn't own a car. She asked, "How do you get around?"

I told her I had a chauffeur who drove an iron horse from station to station.

"I will get my car and meet you downtown at Ovations at eight tonight. We can celebrate your new position." I immediately took a shower and put on a tan suit and a tie. I arrived at the meeting place about ten minutes late on purpose. Ovations was a quiet, high-class establishment in the Italian section of New York. Adonis was already there, and she looked and smelled like a dozen roses. Her lipstick was as red as blood, her eyes sparkled, and as soon as she saw me she flashed a full-teethed smile; it was sincere. She said, "Well, what do you feel like doing tonight?"

I answered, "May I see your menu before I order?" I looked in her eyes and said, "What's your definition of *celebrate*?"

She said, "Let's first get to know each other. You seem really young to have all this responsibility and opportunity trusted upon you. Do you have any idea what you're in for?"

I said, "I hope you're talking about tonight."

"No, I'm talking about your new position. You are as close to the executives as one can be. You are relied upon to keep the peace. Didn't

Mr. Silver explain everything to you?"

I replied, "No, my formal education begins tomorrow."

She then said, "Let's order a drink to celebrate. You do drink, don't you. You are of age, right?"

I just looked at her and winked. We were at a private table. She motioned to the waiter and ordered a bottle of champagne. We sat looking into one another's eyes.

She then leaned forward and said, "There's something mysterious about you. You appear innocent, but you don't speak like you're innocent, unless you're just one of those young men with an old soul, yet there is experience in your eyes. Are you one of those seamen who gets into port and rushes off to the leisure houses, never leaving a stone unturned?"

"Adonis, I don't upturn stones. That not how I get my rocks. I have to be attracted to the entire mountain to want to climb it, not just up turn and collect stones."

Adonis laughed and replied, "Uh-huh, you knew I would like that answer, didn't you?"

Adonis then went into what she knew about me. "I heard that you are reliable. I never saw anyone capture so much trust here so quickly."

I wondered if she knew about the safe but I wasn't going to mention it. Suppose she was a plant to see if I was going to talk? Tell me about you lady. The next twenty minutes were about her telling me her story. It was about how she was in a crowd and lonely. She knew everything about the monster and impressed me with her insight. She even referred to the monster as Frankenstein and said that she worked with the monster's brain. We sat, and she talked, and I listened until most of the champagne was gone. She said, "I hope you can drive a stick shift because this champagne has my head spinning."

I said, "I told you I don't drive."

She smiled and said, "I can teach you. You see, a car with a stick shift is somewhat like a woman. You must know when it's time to move, when to go faster, when to downshift, and to know what gear is expected at that precise time. You must have a gentle hand and total command to do what is needed and what is wished. I could teach you how to drive a stick if you would like."

At this point there was an energy in the air that revealed excitement on both our parts. I said, "Let's order something to eat and take it back to your house. I will get another bottle of champagne."

She quickly bit her lower lip and said, "Let's go."

We left with supplies in hand, and she drove slowly home. We got to her apartment in the city; it was complete with a doorman, and it was fabulous. Now when working at Solid I met many women who said that they were secretaries, but no one could afford a place with a doorman. I thought she was either the best secretary who ever lived or was well taken care of because of the secrets she kept. As we entered her apartment we put the packages down, and she walked over to me, looking into my eyes and facially beckoning a reaction.

"You ready to test for your first driver's permit? I replied, I have been watching you as you drove home. I think I can take it from here, but I may need help with the signals."

Adonis opened my pants and grabbed my stick, and said, "Let's make believe that this is the stick-shift and my lips were the clutch." As she freed it from my pants she laughed and said, "Wow, you are indeed a longshore man." She manipulated it in a sexy manner. Her eyes were slightly red from the drinks, but she held it firm but not tight. It was like heaven in here; she smelled good and tasted better. I picked her up in my arms and she still held on to it. I slowly walked into the bedroom and whispered to her.

"I can take it from here."

She said, "You sure you know what to do? This is your driving test for your permit."

I laid her gently on the bed and said, "I got it from here. Let me first adjust the mirror, as I saw you did in your car."

I then walked over and manipulated the mirror on her dresser until we could see ourselves. I then placed pillows under her body and said, "One must be comfortable inside the body of the vehicle." I kissed her all over and then whispered, "Are you ready to begin the ride?"

She squeezed the clutch and moaned. I whispered, "I am about to begin." I gently opened her hand and took control of the stick. "I believe that in order to begin our journey and move you, I have to slowly put it in first." She laughed and sighed at the same time. The next thing I knew we were listening to our bodies giving us a standing ovation as our skin clapped together, a continuous sound made by doing what I was doing all over again. This was nothing like making love with the women in the houses at the ports we visited. I couldn't decide whether to keep my eyes on her breasts, her face, or her thighs. When I looked at all three at the same time, I would try to use all my efforts to control myself so not to speed this ride up. I took small doses of each not to flood the engine. Making love to Adonis was like tuning a Stradivarius violin. When she would moan or liter-ally sing an emotion or feeling, I would try to again make her recreate that sound. Adonis inspired my best, and I was more than happy to try my best to please her because in pleasing her I was giving myself total joy. This was the ultimate conjoining of a man and a woman. It was the first time I made complete, unselfish, spontaneous, uninhibited love. This is not an indictment or comparison of any other woman. This is a tribute to the natural, self-assured experience of an older woman.

When we finished I knew that her flower was well watered by this seaman. She was much older than I, but she was one of the sexiest women

I had ever seen in my life. To experience her in passion, to hear he moan as she composed her sex song, was indeed glory to behold. I didn't stay the night; I had to be ready at nine the next morning. Adonis was asleep when I left, and the doorman asked if I wanted a cab. I said no, thank you, and gave him a five-dollar tip for asking. He gave me a thumbs-up sign as I left.

I got home but couldn't sleep the entire night. The next morning I was up with the last of the moon glow. I showered and put on a blue suit and light blue shirt with a maroon tie. I arrived at the hall and had some coffee in the small café area. At 9:00 a.m. everyone was there. I calmly walked into the office area and spotted Mr. Silver. He was at his desk, and sitting on his left was a patrolman named Archie Bella. He was sitting at his desk sipping coffee and reading the paper. We would acknowledge one another in the past, but we never had any conversation. Now Archie looked like what you would draw if someone asked you to draw a gangster. He had a large head with curly dark hair. Clean-shaven face with skinny very chapped lips.

I said good morning, and he looked at me but he never responded. Mr. Silver said, "Good morning, son, this is Archie Bella, he was assigned to help with your training."

Archie Bella still didn't acknowledge me. After he finished reading his article he slowly looked up at me and reached for his coffee. He said fifteen people died in an apartment fire last night in the Bronx.

I said that's terrible. He replied, "Why? If they were still here they would be breathing my share of the damn air."

I didn't know whether to laugh or how to react. He never cracked a smile.

He said, "You getting married today?"

I just looked at him with a perplexed look on my face. He said, "You dressed like that to impress the patrolmen? There's only one thing that impresses us, son. You know what that is? Bread, bulging pockets,

Christmas cash. So they want me to help train you. You ready to be trained? You ever had real responsibility? Were you ever depended upon to achieve? This isn't a job, son, it's a profession, you will represent us. Your job is to make members understand and believe that we are their family, and they must stay loyal to the family. They must feed the family, they must protect the family, and the family will always have their backs. You understand me, boy?"

"Yes, sir, you're saying I have to get behind the members." "You're looking at me, boy, but you aren't hearing me. You don't get behind anyone, you get in front of them."

I just stood there looking at him and Mr. Silver. I wondered what Archie Bella saw when he looked at the ocean. I bet he thought it was whale piss with salt. This was a cold-hearted, no-nonsense, "hurray for me, screw you" type of person. I sat and listened to his every word.

As they both spoke and exchanged their renditions of what this job entailed, I understood that this new position would make me banker, lawyer, police, mediator, judge, jury, family counselor, husband, and pimp. I wasn't sure if these man were really dedicated to helping the members, or just making sure that Frankenstein stayed full. Was I really to do an important service for the members, or were we just fattening frogs to feed snakes? For every line about helping the members, he contradicted it with "make them need us, make them want to take care of us, make them know to call us before calling their wives their fathers and mothers."

The next session was about the aura of a union official. We walked like our balls had diamond scrotums; we listened to every word a union member told us even if they spoke another language, and we really didn't understand them. We looked as if we were on a first-name basis with the creator, and we dressed like a neighbor. "You can wear the suit, but don't look like you know you got it on. Understand? Here is your first test. If you ever get into a situation and you don't know what to do, what would you do?" After he asked he just stared at me.

I said call you or Mr. Silver. He just stared at me in total disgust and then slowly replied at the top of his voice, "Hell no, ain't you been listening to anything I said? Are you half stupid? You would never get into a situation where you don't know what to do. Stay the hell out of those damn situations. You are to go into the main hall and mingle, get the hell out there and make them look at paying their union dues and supporting our programs as they look at put-ting money in a collection plate at church. You are now an apostle of the eminent Reverend Frankenstein. Go forth and multiply our dollars."

Once again, I didn't know if I should laugh, cry, fart, sneeze, or belch. I wanted to do them all at the same time. I just watched the two of them. Archie Bella slowly picked up his newspaper and placed it in front of his large head. I walked over to Silver's desk. He pointed to the desk that belonged to the man I was replacing, Frenchy. He said, "That's your desk. Sit down and observe everything that goes on in here."

I had no idea what to do next. I didn't even have a newspaper to hide behind. I looked into the top drawer and found an old union paper called the *navigator* and stuck my head in it. I sat at that desk for two weeks listening and watching everything that went on in this office, pretending to be reading the newspaper. I watched the others do what the union patrolmen did. These patrolmen were nothing like the ones on the police force, the only thing they shared was the title. These men's responsibility was to *collect* and *serve*.

There were six patrolmen at their desks, and everyone much different from the next. White, black, Hispanic They all were known by their sea names. There was Harry Snow, Soup Jenkins, North Star Williams, Chili Perez, Norris Smith, and Frenchy Struts. They all had their own clientele who asked specifically for them. The one thing they all shared was the air of confidence that dripped from their brows.

I watched the men collect dues, listen to grievances, get ships for men in distress. I saw grown men turn in to Santa Clauses, genies, and leprechauns. Every so often Archie Bella would glance my way and shake his big head. The same way he would shake that big head yes as he listened to the member' concerns.

This was a large room with many desks; there were no pictures on the wall. These guys who occupied the desks here were smooth. It was apparent that these were Frankenstein's fingers. Their purpose was to get the money. At one point or another every member would have to come in here to either pay dues, discuss a grievance, or just buy a freedom stamp. A freedom stamp was a small postage-like stamp that members would buy to show their support for the union. Each patrolman was a character in his own right. Some were elegant speakers, some were just personalities. The patrolmen were also the ones who would pay the union members when they docked after a trip. The patrolmen would handle whatever problem the members would have with the shipping company. The ace in the hole that they had in their arsenal that would usually resolve anything when all else failed was the word *strike*. I had to recruit someone to handle my business affairs. I was making a great deal of money buying and selling the wares the seamen brought back from their voyages. I knew this young man who liked the way I carried myself. He was a man about four years younger than me. He use to always compliment the way I dressed and follow me around. He was a good-looking boy whose ambition exceeded his intelligence, but whose doesn't?

I thought that I could trust him, as far as I could trust anyone, and when I got him his first suit I could tell from the look on his face that he was hooked. He gave me a sincere thanks. His name was Dell; he was a full-

Robby

fledged mulatto. He had this unique hairline as if his hair was professionally landscaped. All he really had to do was pick up the supplies and deliver. I had all my connections in order, and at this point it was easy. I made a hundred dollars for every twenty I spent. Not bad, huh? I learned about marketing and markup from Solid.

 I became totally fascinated and enthralled watching these master patrolmen deal with issues, sell useless stamps, and curry favor from the members. I also had Adonis upstairs telling me when I was on overdue and needed to get off of my ass and look like I was dealing with my responsibilities. Adonis gave me the lowdown on what was being said about me upstairs. They didn't expect much at first; they wanted me to cook slow and simmer until I was completely done. Learning from the patrolmen was higher education, and most days I didn't want to leave the office. It was like watching ten godfathers at their daughter's weddings daily. They would make the seamen feel as if their problems were already solved by just talking to them. I remembered what the neighborhood told us to write on my father's tombstone when he dies: *if I was your last hope, you never had any.* They were the opposite.

 One day as I was paying total attention to the goings on in the office, I heard a familiar voice say, "You abandoned the company of my mistress to be here with these men." It was Deep Sea. I was really glad to see him. I thought he was going to make me clean my desk. He smiled and asked, "You still have a soul, boy?"

 I said, "Yes, sir, it's just that now I spell it S-O-L-D." He didn't think that was funny. He was somewhat like brother Solid; he wouldn't have thought that was funny either. My coworkers liked it. He asked me if I missed the sea, and I whispered yes, but man does not live by fish alone, and at some point one must surf the wave goodbye. Again I thought I was being witty, but Deep Sea didn't.

"Boy, the sea is the bath of knowledge, the well of one's soul that refreshes the spirit. It's what makes God great without ever having to brag. I hope you don't forget that, son. I hope you don't forget it. Don't lose your soul, boy."

He then left and the other men just laughed, and said the sea's a nice place to visit, but who wants to live there? I really felt a twinge in my stomach when Deep Sea left. I did really miss the serenity of the sea.

That started an argument about biting the hand that feeds you. All the patrolmen started as seamen, but they were bona fide land-lubbers now. About a month from when my training began, I was asked to cover a ship that just returned from a short trip. I was asked to do the payroll. The patrolman named Soup Jenkins went with me. I went to the cash dispatch office and was told that I needed to take sixty-two thousand dollars with me. You get the cash and pay the men upon their return. Any man owed overtime because of emergency service was paid that when they brought the forms signed by the ship's captain to the hall. I was given a suitcase full of cash and vouchers stating what every man was due.

I was advised by my coworker Soup that because I was liable for any miscount to sit and watch them count it three times, then I was to count it three times. I was then told to go downstairs to choose a security detail to go with us. These were the men known as goons. The goons were the bodyguards who would accompany you to both protect you from danger and, in some cases, protect you from you. That was a lot of money for anyone young and ambitious to have.

Soup told me to talk with the goons and find someone I liked because most men always took the same goons with them. The Goons were Frankenstein's fist; they did an array of assignments from keeping the peace, protecting the hall, and intimidating opposition. I went downstairs next to the coffee station and saw a room full of muscle. Some of these guys looked like they lived in a gym. They looked like they could squeeze the earwax out your head with one headlock. I was told that your goons were your salvation, so choose wisely.

When I walked in, all eyes shot my way. I was told to pick no less than two. The men just locked eyes on me; they never smiled or spoke. Some just moved their heads to acknowledge me as they locked eyes. In the back of the room, I saw these two guys talking and not paying attention to me. One guy who was big, but he really didn't have a threatening look on his face. It was kind of friendly but in an optical-illusion kind of way. If you looked at him long enough, the friendly face would appear serious. It all depended on how long you stared at it. At first glance he looked approachable, compassion-ate, but stare too long, and it said, "Keep out of my way, what the hell you staring at?" I asked him his name, and he said Foushay, Ronnie Foushay. I asked him if him where he was from, and he said the South. As I spoke to him, the one next to him walked around me and stood behind me. I turned to see why he stood behind me, and Ronnie said, "That's my kid brother, Marcus. He's just making sure you're covered."

Marcus was the youngest; there was no misdiagnosing his look. It said, "You have ten seconds to kill yourself before I begin to kill you."

They were full brothers, but Ronnie and I had the same complexion, and Marcus was three shades darker. I said, "You're both hired."

I walked out of the room without having to lock eyes with anyone else. Ronnie was in front, and Marcus was behind me. I'm sure feelings were hurt because of how fast this happened. When the patrolmen saw who I had chosen, I got high marks. The Foushay brothers were known and respected as no-nonsense guys. We picked up the money, and Ronnie drove us to the dock. It's amazing that whenever we got paid in the past after returning from a trip, I really didn't pay any attention to the goons around the patrolmen. I guess their job was just to get you there and back safely.

Marty R.

Soup Jenkins accompanied us on the first run, and it was smooth as gravy tea. We got to know one another like family. When I traveled with my goons, I felt like money in a safe, and you know I know what that feels like. Never in my life would I have ever believed that one could get paid for doing what Santa does, making people happy. I did realize that I was a shill for Frankenstein, and for all I know in the grand scheme of things I may have been the monster's hemorrhoids. Still it was good to get to know each seaman personally and listen to their problems and try to offer a solution. It was especially gratifying to give them their money. I was also selling them the freedom stamps in record numbers and got good at attaching them to their books. In my heart I knew it was selling something that they actually didn't need in the name of "showing support for the union," but in my heart I knew that this was like putting Chicklets under your pillow and still getting money from the good fairy.

Oh the lies we tell ourselves to get through life, and having the illusion of happiness are all amazing. I wanted to think of myself as doing something good, but deep inside I knew Frankenstein didn't have a soul, but my days were good and my nights were better. The three of us, Ronnie, Marcus, and me would go to a bar we found in Harlem called The Regent and raise hell. The Regent was a bar and grill with good food, great women, and fantastic music. This was where the number runners and hustlers would come after milking humanity. There was always a lot of cigarette smoke and Brook Benton and Nat King Cole records on.

Some of the women who came in had bodies that defied gravity. They were attracted to the three of us because I now had Ronnie and Marcus dressing like me, and I only charged them half price. They wore their clothes well. We would sometimes bet on who could take a new lady home first, or who could charm her the best. I would always notice that the pimps and hustlers, never smiled either. I noticed that their laughs were synthetic and labored. I never saw one that looked happy, even when they were given a wad of money from their girls. There was one large gentleman who ran dope, numbers, and women named C.A. He did have an infectious laugh. Whenever a joke was told, his people would always wait until C.A. laughed, and then they would join in. He held court at the bar nightly and had some beautiful women with him. He liked me and once offered me a job on the streets working for him. My two bodyguards would always tell me that I didn't want to see him other than in here; he was one mean bastard on the streets. It was all an education, the kind that white people don't get or even need in their world, but the basics are the same as in any business college.

CA looked like someone straight out of central casting for a ruthless gangster-type appearance. I liked that he looked like the grown-up bully from my neighborhood. C.A. was someone who you could just sit and watch as he interacted with his group. They would meekly approach him and hope that they leave his presence without being yelled at or worse. Watching him with a Nat King Cole song on in the background was like watching a cartoon and hearing an opera. He was not smooth; he was abrupt, crass, corse and gritty, but he liked me and my boys. He would always shower us with drinks, drugs and whatever he had.

Ronnie and Marcus liked to smoke the weed he offered. I tried it once but I hated it. I thought I was shrinking. I literally saw my drink try to run away when I reached for it. I tried it once, and that was two times for me, first and last. It made me put a real stupid smile on my face, which now contradicted my aura. These were good times: my job, my people, my lifestyle. It's amazing how life could put a road in front of you totally different than the one you were traveling yesterday, a road with different scenery and pavement. Dell would always meet me at the bar to bring me my business earnings. He must have really been honest because he was making more than I ever did. I had ladies buying me drinks left and right.

This was amazing because when I was living on the street and drinking cheap wine, I would never have ever thought this could really happen. Every so often I would have to spend time with Adonis from the union, so I could get the inside scoop on what was happening.

She was older but could make love as good as, or even better than, the best young woman. She took making love as a personal challenge to womanhood. It was like a prizefight between man and woman. She would only say two words when she was in passion but would pronounce them about one hundred different ways. It was actually exciting to get a verbal eargasm. I've always been a leg man, and she had enough thighs to last her a lifetime. Her breasts were firm yet soft with a bull's-eye colored nipple on them. She inspired my creative side in ways I never knew existed. When she gave into passion she would sing in my ear and send an encrypted message to my Johnson, who would react accordingly. Yeah, these were good times. Don't think that I became lazy or took things for granted. I would always spend time at my desk behind a newspaper prop, listening to how the pros handled the seamen's problems. I wanted to be the best at it.

The man who I was replacing was still there, and I wasn't told why he was leaving; he never mentioned any health problem to any-one while I was there. He would always conduct his business in private and speak to the seamen who sought his advice or knowledge alone. I never thought much about it. I was collecting dues and selling stamps, but as I stated earlier greed escalates. I was being seduced by the most powerful force around, more powerful than drugs, sex, or vanity. Money was now enticing me to gather more and more. When I was given those suitcases full of money, I started to make believe that it was my money, and I was being paid because I was cute. I never said greed made sense; I said it escalates.

One day a man with one leg came into the office and sat at my desk. He was an older black man on crutches. He reminded me of Solid and Deep

Sea in many ways. He had both character and commitment in his eyes. He looked like a lover of the sea and had big red bloodshot eyes, just like Deep Sea which were kind of sad looking. I didn't know what he wanted so I put my paper down. He said, "Young blood, you carry yourself like a fair man. Are you?"

I answered, "I sincerely hope so."

He then told me a story of being one of the ocean's many lovers who devoted his life to her. He returned from a three-month cruise one day and was leaving the ship after it was docked and tied. After descending the gangplank with his duffel bag, he stopped at the stern to look back at the ship before he realigned himself with his land consciousness. As he turned to leave, the ropes which secured the ship to port snapped and like an unloaded slingshot removed his right leg. He was immediately taken to the hospital. He told me that he had a wife and five children and he was the meal bearer. As he spoke, a group of tears ran down his cheek to validate his sincerity. He said that he tried to work with the shipping line, the H. Jimakraut, who did pay his medicals but never offered him anything for his loss or suffering. He was told that he could no longer work on a ship because he was handicapped. He said that he couldn't even look at a calendar with a picture of the ocean on it now.

I looked around, and every eye and ear in the room was fixed on his tale. I thought that one of the more experienced patrolmen would take over, but they all looked at me. I asked what did he want me to do? He said that the man at the shipping line was a young, educated, hard boy who felt that paying his medicals was more than fair. He wanted this young man's equal from the union to represent him in this mess. He said that the way I carried myself made him think that I was the man for the job. I was flattered but not completely sure that I was the right man for this job, but, then again, as my training had stressed I was indeed the man for this job.

Marty R.

I took his information and told him I would be on it. His name was Trader Horn. I thought that the older pros would counsel me because this was a unique occurrence. But they all just wanted to see how I would handle it, especially Archie Bella. I spoke about it to Adonis, and she said she was already aware of it from the gossip and that the hierarchy was watching me. She assured me that she would back me as long as I didn't yell, curse, threaten, or disrespect the ship-ping line. I was to handle this in a dignified, professional manner. She said that the older boys would butt heads with this shipping line and then look to them for a conservative solution, but a showdown was inevitable. She said that this was my moment to shine and show that I was worthy of this job. The only things they insisted on was that I go alone without my goon guys, and I was not supposed to make any threats I couldn't back up. I thought for days about this situation. I even spent time at the library reading about accidents in law books. One day I asked Adonis to make the appointment with the shipping line so that I may speak with the young man about this. They told her at first that this case was now closed because of the medical bills they paid, but she insisted that it wasn't. I arrived on time and was impeccably dressed, more for business than show. Their office were located in the Brooklyn navy yard. I went there and introduced myself to the receptionist and was told to wait in a small, cold office. I was made to wait about twenty-five minutes until this young, brash, arrogant white gentlemen walked in. I extended my hand to shake his and he just sat and folded his arms.

This was one arrogant boy who looked about twenty. His having this job at his age had to be related to some the kind of inheritance or affirmative-action situation, the kind that America doesn't want to discuss. It's the secret club that presents the golden pass. It reeks of "my father went to this school or held this job or belonged to this club, so I should get it as well." It's remarkable how many rich people's children are given opportunities that other mere mortals aren't privy to by way of their family. These same people would get mad as hell over any such opportunity given to the average American, which would allow them to get from the back to the front of the line. This law has been on the books since time began.

He then said, "Look, I agreed to meet with you, but this is a case-closed issue. It was an accident, and we paid the medicals. He was paid for his work on the ship, and we do not believe that we are obligated to do any more. It was an accident and we didn't cause it." I replied, "I see, so your position is that if this ceiling over my head would suddenly fall and *strike* me dead, as long as it's an accident, you're not liable, and since there would be no medical bills you're not out anything either. This *strikes* me as odd. I then pulled out a pack of Lucky Strike cigarettes from my pocket and placed it in front of him. I said the work *strike* with an unmistakable, vulgar emphasis on the word *strike*. He looked annoyed and short tempered.

He asked, "What do you want?"

I answered, "I only wanted the release from any responsibility signed by your company and our union member that may have been signed. If you do have one, and if it was signed in the hospital when he might have been on medication, understand that it will be nullified."

Trader Horn guaranteed me that he never knowingly signed anything unless they snuck something by while he was under the spell of the pain medication. This arrogant young man who never gave his name or even acknowledged my presence said, "We have lawyers, you know" and then called for one to come into our meeting. He then sat at his desk refusing any eye contact with me.

After another twenty minutes went by, a man who introduced himself as Jewles entered the room and introduced himself as the company's attorney. This was a short Jewish man who looked about eighty. He was the opposite of the younger unfriendly boy; this one very polite yet blunt person.

He asked me what did I want, and I said, "For you to help this man and enable, create, and establish, his new life since the old one died from an accident created by your negligence."

I was told by Jewles in a very polite manner that they could and would fight this, and it would take years to resolve. I said that I had not mentioned the word *fight*, I came to resolve this matter, but that you must be aware of what the union has in their arsenal to fight with. I never mentioned the word *strike*, but it was implied. There was silence as the younger man glared at me, and the older man smiled.

"What do you want, son?"

I replied, "Not an arm and a leg reattached. How 'bout giving Mr. Horn his sea legs and creating a permanent job he could do on board your ship, and a settlement to help his immediate bills?"

Jewles said, "That's impossible. Look, we didn't make the rope." I replied, "OK. As I stated earlier about your ceiling falling and *striking* me, just because you didn't make the ceiling doesn't make

you not partially liable for its condition."

Jewles then said, "Son, you don't understand. You're not a lawyer, are you?"

I replied, "Sir, I have been a liar for a while now."

They both looked at one another with a puzzled look on their faces, they wondered, was I maybe a lawyer with a Southern drawl? They both looked at one another and said, "You're not serious, are you?"

I replied, "Yes, sir, I am. I want this man to get an arm and a leg for this injury, or we all may be crippled by this accident." I was careful not to threaten and added, "morally, of course."

I then said with arrogance, "We must *strike* a deal immediately." The younger man turned red, and the older one got whiter. I continued, "Look gentlemen, we all know that this may take a while in the courts, but we would fill the courtroom with injured seamen sitting next to this man's starving family."

The young man glared and said, "Are you threatening us?" I looked at the older man and said, "You explain it to him."

The younger man said, "No, I've heard enough from you. We did our part, and there is nothing further we can do. I'm sure the union can find him a job at the hall doing something."

The older, wiser man interrupted and said to me, "Son, what do you want?"

I said, "I want him to not have to beg on a corner to feed himself."

I then thought to myself, been there done that.

The older one then said, "Let's all just cool down and agree to meet in one week's time."

The younger man gasped and said, "Are you serious?"

He patted him on his still folded hands and said, "Yes, one week."

As I was leaving, I heard the younger man say, "If we give them one dime I will join their union."

The older man said, "Let me deal with him. It's obvious that they are not taking this seriously, or they wouldn't have sent him."

That hurt, although I was proud of the way I held my own inside the room. I got back to the hall and was immediately called upstairs where I had to report to the people upstairs, as well as the patrolmen what had happened. No one made a sound or even responded to any-thing I said. They all sat and listened. The only question I was asked was, "You never threatened anyone, right?"

I replied no. I then mumbled so no one else heard. I only used the word 'strike' a hundred times. I was told to go back in one week and hear what they had to say, and not to talk, just listen. I was proud that I represented them with some grit but was confused by their lack of questions. I returned to my daily routine with my guys working and drinking. Adonis would call every so often and say to me, "Don't worry, you did well, just keep doing well."

The week shot by, and I was reminded of my appointment at the shipping line. Right before the meeting, Adonis told me that Jewles called and spoke with the president, JC, and was told in no uncertain terms that they would back whatever call I made, 100 per-cent. This time when I arrived I was escorted into a large room with about ten people already seated, the younger man was not there. I was politely told that they thought it over and decided to reopen and settle this matter. They agreed to settle this for fifty thousand dollars, which was considered a large amount. It represented a few years of Traders Horn's pay. I just sat there and swallowed. I was given a check already made out to the union. I was speechless. I looked at it and said "This is all, one week to think it over, and this is all."

They asked, "What else can we do?"

I replied, "Have him mash potatoes or do the laundry on board the ship and guarantee him a job for five years."

They all simultaneously responded and agreed in unison. I just muttered a thank you and got up and left. I was sure that the way I conducted myself the first time made them not want to mess with me, but I knew it was the fact that Frankenstein was totally behind me. I was going back to the hall like I was the monster's master. I went upstairs and told the tale and gave them the check. As I was taught, not all stories start at the beginning, nor end at the end. It was years later that Adonis had too much wine one evening and she was about to drift off and whispered a story in my ear that I would never forget. She told me that a few days after our initial meeting, and a day before the telephone call with JC and Jewles, the younger man at the shipping company went to take his garbage out one night. He lived in a

Robby

house way out in Long Island near the shore. He was grabbed and sedated. When he woke up he was inside of a pine box with his hands tied in front of him and the top open. They dug a hole about four feet, and there were two men with masks on looking down at him. His hands were tied and his mouth was covered. They said to him that they needed a leg to help an old friend, and which one should they take? Right or left?

"Tell us what you think about it and call us on judgment day when you decide. Just remember, this was not our fault. Think of it as an accident as well."

They then closed the cover and threw handfuls of wet sand on top. It sounded like they were burying the box, but there was only a small amount of sand on it. They could hear him screaming with every handful. They left him there. He could have just pushed the top open so no one knew how long he was inside before he tried to push the top open. So coffin open, case closed. I was shocked to hear this but not really surprised. Adonis never mentioned it again and may not have even been aware she even told me. The last thing she said as she was about to drift off was that Trader Horn got the entire twenty-five thousand dollars.

When she went to sleep, I left and I met my crew at the Regent bar. We listened to Nat King Cole sing and I told them about what I heard. Both Ronnie and Marcus laughed and acted somewhat entertained by this tale. They both kept saying "whattttt" in unison. I went to the bathroom after drinking too many beers. As I was coming back to the bar, I saw Marcus take off his expensive shoes and stare at them, saying, "I can't get this damn graveyard mud off still."

After he said that, I thought about it long and hard and settled on, so what if he was commanded by Frankenstein to assist in my negotiations or decided to help me look good? So be it. I tasted and liked both money and power. I was hooked, reeled, and cleaned. I was making money and trying my best to impress Frankenstein. One thing about having and making, it totally made me forget all the things I would ponder while on the streets. I didn't think about what happened to Solid, or if the police were looking for me for either Solid or Joe, or what was going on with my family. All I thought about was tomorrow and how much more I could make. To hell with all the yesterdays.

One day while sitting at my desk. I saw the piper, the always grim reaper who always came to make me pay for the music that I danced to, Mr. Bummy.

Once he appeared, you instantly knew that it was time for a payment. It was like an undertaker coming to your house unannounced to tell you that you owed a payment for your inevitable burial because death was inevitable, so pay up. I was enjoying my new life, and it was all relevant, so I figured what the hell, pay up whatever this payment was for. Bummy gave me another genuine, sincere greeting and spoke as if he was following my success. I only hoped that this visit had nothing to do with any safe. He began a very casual, "So how you been, Young blood? Been hearing good things about you. You've come up in the world, huh?"

That's when I knew I was in trouble. I replied, "Came out my world, and came up in yours."

He flashed a bummy grin. He said, "Let's take a walk outside the office to the hallway."

"You used to hang out in lower Manhattan, right? You know the pulse of the streets, don't you?"

"Yeah, I guess so," I answered.

I could feel Archie Bella looking at me when I said that as if I were crazy. "*You guess?* You stopped guessing when you became a patrolman."

"What do you need?" I asked.

"We need a man who can help our agent get in and get out unseen without incident."

I asked, "Get in and out of what?"

He cracked as close as he could to a smile and answered, "You don't need to know now. Just help this man with whatever he needs done."

"When are we talking about?" I asked, and he replied, "Yesterday." I took a deep breath and reluctantly said, "Tell the powers that be that I'm your man."

Bummy said, "Be here late tomorrow night and dress like you did when you were down there."

I joked and said, "Tattered clothes." And Bummy, he just looked without any expression.

When I walked back inside, Archie Bella tried to smile the best he could, but he never inquired what that was about. Again I spent the night wondering what the hell was this about, knowing that I had to do whatever they needed doing, but why the tattered clothes? I thought maybe bummy didn't know how I dressed when I lived in the shelter. I called Adonis for some info, but she was also in the dark, or just pretended to be. The next evening after work I put on dirty jeans and a dark T-shirt. I waited until late evening to return to the hall. I even tried calling Adonis again, but she couldn't or wouldn't talk each time I called, she kept saying, "I'm sorry, he isn't here."

I was really worried now. I arrived at the office at about 9:00 p.m., and everyone was already gone. I was about to sit at my desk when the phone rang as soon as my ass hit the chair, as if it was wired to alert the powers that be that I had arrived.

"Come upstairs now."

I walked up the stairs, trying to collect my thoughts, and tried to stay calm and collected. The lights were turned down real dim in the hallway. As I reached Adonis's desk, I heard a voice say, "Come in here."

Marty R.

I walked into a dark office; the light was down, and I could barely make out the outline of the figures. One figure belonged to Bummy; damn, I thought, even his shadow is bummy. The other one had a cigarette in his mouth. I could see his hair at the backdrop of the window and it wasn't nappy. It was laying down. This was a white man. Bummy said, "Mack, this is Young blood."

I extended my hand but no one grabbed it. "He just said uh-huh. Young blood knows the territory, the pulse, the flavor. He will get you in and out safe."

I wanted to ask what the mission was but I dared not ask. I knew what my job was, and I guess that was enough. Mack got up, and I noticed that he was a really short man. I couldn't tell what his age was, but he reeked of cigarettes. He said, "I am going to get my car. Be downstairs at the front in five minutes."

He was carrying a case with metal objects in it. I could hear them clang together as he walked. When he left, Bummy came over and whispered, "He's going to send a message, and that's all you need to know."

Send a message? To whom? With what? Why?

He said to Frenchy, the man who I was hired to replace, the one I was told had a secret health issue and would be leaving soon. I was told which bar he was drinking at. I felt a chill run through my body. "Mack is from out of town, so get him in and out and then you leave, understand?"

I went outside and reluctantly waited for the cigarette-reeking grunter. I expected a real fancy Italian car to pull up. I waited about twenty minutes. Then I saw what I thought was a vehicle being driven by someone of very limited means. It looked like it went through a cheap acid-rain carwash about a million times. I looked in the windshield and saw a small man sitting there just staring at me. I never thought that this might have been him. I walked over to the driver's window and asked, "You here for me?

He said, "I got no time for games, get in."

I couldn't believe this car. Inside made outside look like a limo. I opened the passenger's door and brushed off the seat before I sat down. There were still no introductions or anything. He asked, "Where are we going?"

I said, "I was told to take you to downtown Manhattan, to a place on the west side."

He said, "Well, tell me how to get there."

I said, "We have to take the west-side highway."

We started driving, and the only sound was me telling him where and when to make a turn. You could hear a ghost fart in the car. Once we were on the highway, I tried to break the ice with a sarcastic statement. I said, "Nice car."

He looked in my direction and using his peripheral vision, he said in a harsh voice, "You wanna race me to the train station?"

I asked where he was from and he said "Yesterday." I asked, "Can you fill me in on what we are doing?"

"We?" he said. "You pregnant? Your showing me how to get in and how to get out. You can can the small talk, that's all you need to know. Do you know where he would park his car?"

I said, "As far as I know he has no car."

"Are you sure this is the right person?" No comment.

Once we exited the highway he asked me how far we were from our destination, and I answered about ten minutes. He pulled over and just sat and smoked some cigarettes. After about three cigarettes and what I thought was him just wasting time, I asked what we were waiting for.

"Nighttime," he uttered.

I said, "But we left at night."

He said in an upset voice, "No more questions from now on. We're strangers."

Marty R.

I just sat in the car and stared out the window. I remember thinking why am I given all these stupid damn jobs to do. I was getting hungry but had enough sense not to say anything. At about 12:00 a.m. he started the car and drove off very slow. I pointed here and there. He stopped at a gas station and filled the car. I asked if it took regular super or Geritol. We soon arrived at the destination. They had lights and the music were blasting outside. He again turned off the engine and just sat and waited not saying one word. I asked if I could take a short walk. I was thinking sandwich. He said, "We don't leave one another's sight until we finish. I was told to look in the window and see if Frenchy was inside." I looked and there he was. We sat there for an hour. I was confused because I thought Frenchy was a family man. I couldn't believe he was out nightclubbing. We then drove around the block and stopped abruptly. Right then I noticed a real nice new Caddy parked in front of us. I noticed that he was fixated on it. He pulled a small piece of paper out of his pocket and checked the license plates.

We then rode to the corner and made a U-turn and parked across the street near the Caddy. I used to see Frenchy in the morning when I got to work as he got off of the bus when he came to work. Here was a nice shining new Caddy. It made the car we were in look like a rusty nail next to a new hammer. I didn't think this was Frenchy's car, but to tell the truth I really didn't care. I wanted to get the hell out of here and away from Mr. Personality. I was somewhat confused. Why would Frenchy act like a common person when he had a car like this? Other patrolmen had vehicles but not like this. This was new and custom made. Just then a light went off. Again, I heard a voice say, not all stories start at the beginning. It was now nearing 1:30 a.m. Mack asked me to again look in the window and tell me where he was sitting. I looked in and saw Frenchy seated at a booth in the rear of the club with a nice-looking lady next to him. I thought he was a happily married man. All he ever spoke of was his wife and kids. I thought who the hell is this man?

I came back and gave the clunker king the scoop. He immediately got out of this car and went into the trunk. He slowly took out a silver box. He then got back in and started his car and pulled it directly in front of the Caddy as if he was going to give it a jump. He then told me to sit behind his steering where and keep watch, to let him know when someone was coming, either a car or a person. There was sparse traffic in the area; most people were coming to or leaving a bar, and no one was paying attention to us. I thought to myself that we were probably going to rig something to this car to scare the owner. I really didn't think this Caddy had anything to do with Frenchy, so I played along and hoped he would hurry so we can part ways. Maybe he was just going to leave something that made the owner aware of something. Or if by some remote chance it was Frenchy's car, maybe they wanted him to know that Frankenstein knew about this double life he was leading.

The grunter somehow got the Caddy hood open and placed the silver box on the engine. Now it started to make sense. I thought only a gifted mechanic could keep his car running. He moved slow and steady. I couldn't see what he was doing, and to tell you the truth I didn't want to know. He moved deliberately and purposely. Whenever someone would look in our direction, I would motion the grunter to get down. It's amazing that if this was a white neighborhood and a black man was working on a Caddy, the entire police cavalry would have come down on him.

Here in a Black neighborhood a white man working on a Caddy, everyone thought the pimp or pusher must have money. I knew a fat Jamaican pimp who drove a Caddy. I was praying that the car belonged to NoGoSo. He was the biggest pimp in these parts. He was also the biggest liar, hence his name, NoGoSo, because anything he told you, "No go, so." I would have loved to see NoGoSo appear and say, "Mi karrr! Mi karrr!"

and then shove this idiot in his gas tank. In about five minutes he was finished with whatever he was doing. He motioned me to come over to him. I did and was told to put my finger on top of a black wire so he could tie it. I did and he tied it like he was wrapping a special present for someone. I wanted to show him that I was more than a damn watchdog, so I said "Let me wipe my fingerprints off the engine."

He looked at me as if I just told him a joke. He came as close to smiling as I believe he could have. He gently closed the hood, and we both got back into his car. He quickly drove as I directed him to go down the many quiet streets I pointed to. About a mile away he stopped and said good night. I immediately got out, and he peeled out and left. I couldn't tell you what this was all about if I was given a dose of truth serum. I was near the shelter where I used to stay in. My stomach said, "You going to pay some damn attention to me, asshole." I walked to a nearby restaurant. I passed some street people, and they asked me for a handout, which I gladly gave. I remembered the nights I asked for a step to my ladder. I saw a whole new crop of street faces; they were life's new downtrodden recruits.

I hailed a cab and went back uptown. All the time I thought that Frenchy should be leaving that club to get home to his family right about now and how he would react to the surprise if that was indeed his Caddy. I got home and couldn't sleep from all that sitting. I called Adonis and she asked if I was all right. I asked if I could come over, and she said something, which I found strange. She said not tonight. I never got a no from her before. Why tonight? I made something to eat and went to bed. The following morning I arrived at the hall. There was no one in the office. I sat and read yesterday's paper. As I was reading Archie Bella came in and said, "You hear the news this morning, son?" I asked, what news?

He replied, "Frenchy, he's gone."

"Gone where?" I asked, he whispered in a cold tone, probably to the

Robby

damn moon.

"He had an accident in a car last night. It blew up."

I felt the earth sink from under my feet. Blew up. Blew up how? "No one knows what happened. They said that the car he was in blew up. It was in so many pieces, they couldn't identify the cigarette lighter."

I stood up and just needed to walk. I thought we were just there to scare him; they used me. Now everything began to made sense to me. Why Adonis didn't want to associate with me at night, or the look I got asking to wipe off my fingerprints. I was an accessory to murder. I finally did it. You didn't have to be valedictorian of law school to know that stupidity was not a good defense.

That's what crime does. It's like drugs to an addict; you start with something like a beer and then move to alcohol then marijuana then pills then coke then heroin. My progression went from farts in a bottle to stealing money, to selling bootlegged merchandise, to murder. This was what Deep Sea tried to warn me about when he kept asking me if I still had my soul. I didn't know what to do or how to think. I helped a man make a man lose his life. I couldn't even ease the pain by saying that I really didn't know what was actually happening or what the outcome of Mack's actions would have been. I once read that a person being hypnotized would never do anything under hypnosis, if it was not in their true nature to do. If you were to hypnotize a person and place a gun in their hands and instruct the person to kill someone with it, if their true nature was not to inflict harm on another person, they would refuse, wake up, and their con-science mind would take over.

In this case Frankenstein was the hypnotist, and he was smart enough to get around that rule of hypnosis with me. They placed the gun in my hands and said that it wasn't a real gun; it was a water gun. "Now point it at Frenchy and give him a good squirt." I did squirt him and my not knowing

Marty R.

that the gun they gave me was real made me idiot of the year. I felt like the world was closing in on me. Only someone who has taken a human life could understand what it feels like. I couldn't even cry; I was numb. I couldn't even go to Frankenstein the hypnotist and say "You tricked me." I was not a victim, I was a full-fledged volunteer. I felt like what bummy looked like.

I was sick to my stomach. I felt used and dirty, and beyond stupid. I had seen a million movies when someone kills someone else, but they never portray how it makes one feel inside. I couldn't eat or sleep and didn't know whom to trust. I didn't even know the real name of the man I was with that night, so I was rendered helpless to the benevolence of the union. I wondered if anyone could identify me and why Frenchy? What could he have possibly done to deserve this? Did he steal the payroll money? Did he rape Frankenstein's wife? *What?* I thought that this was how doctor Frankenstein cures a health problem; I better never ever get sick. Why Frenchy, and where did he get that car from? And why was it a secret? Why the double life?

As far as it went I was the scapegoat, an accomplice with a motive. They could say that I was hired as temp and wanted his job. Why me? Why not send a goon to help Mack? My mind was reeling. Once again, time answering all questions, I later found out the full story. Frenchy was a family man living well in a house on in Westchester. He had a wife and kids and for all purposes the picture was an all American success story. That was the picture. The X-ray revealed that he was making money on the side sending people to join a competitor's union, hence the fancy car, which he never drove to that hall. Frenchy was playing both ends against the middle; that's why he always whispered to the man he was talking to. When the news spread, there was no outward sympathy for him from any of his coworkers. There wasn't even a collection taken for his family. The men all laughed at the way he

Robby

died. Some joked that he was the only soul who went through the pearly gates wearing a full body cast and a Band-Aid. This was the reason that I was initially hired, to one day replace him.

CHAPTER 10

FALL FROM "HIIIIIIIIGH GRACE"

Had I known at the beginning that I would have to help eliminate Frenchy, I don't believe I would have taken the job, or would I? I sat in the office and listened to the men joke about his death. One would pick up a pencil eraser off the floor and joke that they just found his eardrum. No one expressed any regret, and no one ever mentioned the part that I played. I prayed that they didn't know. This killing had an explosive reaction as far as Frankenstein was concerned. Between Frenchy and the young man from the shipping company in the coffin, the shipping companies were now more cooperative in the negations with the union for the seamen who worked their ships; union dues went up, and work poured in. Frankenstein put fear in the hearts and minds of its affiliates. I was still treated like I had the plague; no one from upstairs approached me. I guess they were waiting to see if anyone from downtown would put things together and identify me. Oh, I was played by a master. Who ever heard of a scholastic monster? Adonis didn't even call me to ask how I was, which was strange. I sat with my two goons at night and just drank at the bar and listened to the music of Nat and Brook Benton. I never even told my boys the part I played. I went from my self-isolation and wandering the streets only to be saved for this lifestyle. I did enjoy the lifestyle and the success and all the glitter, but the truth was as bad as Solid's death. I knew that I contributed to this one firsthand.

All I could think about was Deep Sea's eyes asking me if I had lost my soul yet, and me knowing the answer of the past, which was no. The truth now was that I didn't lose it; I traded it for this new lifestyle. I was only able to control my emotions, thinking about the first time I saw the sea and trying to recapture that moment. I knew that I couldn't show weakness when I showed my face at the hall, so I decided to accept my fate and accept the fact that Frankenstein was my pimp. Like all good whores I was committed to making him money, but I was also now committed to robbing any extra cash I could get my hands on. I felt he owed me all I could get. It was that love/hate feeling that I'm sure a prostitute has for her pimp. I remember one day I was going to pay the men who had just come in from a voyage, and just looking at all the money I had with me from the payroll window, I remember that this time when the suitcase was in my hands, I didn't think of it as the men's money. I thought of it as Frankenstein's money.

My goons were still loyal to me as well as my trainee Dell. My loyalty was a bit confused and mostly directed at me as well. I knew not to mess with Frankenstein, but I had to show myself that his grip and control did not dominate me inwardly. It was my way of showing that I did not kill Frenchy. I was unknowingly used to help kill Frenchy. As time went on, I was finally summoned upstairs, this was about a month after the Frenchy incident. I arrived on time and sat in the front reception area. Adonis, looking as edible as ever, immediately asked, "Where have you been keeping yourself?" As if she never used to initiate contact with me. I told her I was all right and had been working hard. She smiled and said, "Glad to hear that."

I was then beckoned into the back office. Seated was Percy JC, the president, and of course Bummy, who appeared as disheveled as ever in a silk suit. I waited until I was asked to take a seat. I could feel all eyes on me, and I mean all eyes. I sat down and could feel the glare as they examined every part of me from my hands to my eyes to see if they could sense any sign of weakness, regret, or instability. I sat with an expressionless look on my face. I concentrated on my hands, which I had folded on my lap, which I begged not to move with the slightest shake. I was asked how I was doing, and I immediately shot back, fine. They then asked if there was anything I wished to talk about, and I immediately said no, all is well. Silence then filled the room as the eyes tried to peer into my soul. I then knew that this was a visual inquiry to see if I was indeed still a part of Frankenstein.

Bummy then asked if I needed anything, and I took a long breath and looked him dead in the eye and said, "No, sir, you have all given me everything I need."

I could feel the room relax and the air became less dense. Percy said, "We just wanted you to know that you have a bright future here with us and that you will grow as we do. If there is anything you need, anything at all, your Aladdin's lamp is a call away."

JC never spoke, he just looked. I stood up, and they all shook my hand as I slowly turned and walked out. I was sure I played it right, but it wasn't until later that night when Adonis called and invited me over that I was sure that I passed their test. I told her that I was extremely busy but that I would be in touch soon. The fact of the matter was, I didn't trust her the way that I trusted her before. I originally thought that I was going to use her for inside information, and all the time she was on their side, using me.

Frankenstein's reputation and power grew. It got so that they were able to get everything they asked for from the shipping lines pertaining to the workers. The men got better meals, shorter hours, and higher pay. Working on a ship was the place to work at that time. The hall still had its Saturday sales, but now that the men had more money and were able to bring back more expensive items, the sales of high end perfume and liquors filled the hall and my clients' stores. I was still struggling with what I had done. I just knew that if I went into a downward spiral as I did for Solid, I would be dead. Any sign of weakness was my death sentence.

This was my wake-up call. It was now abundantly apparent which part of the monster I was. My head was the giant tumor on the monster's ass. I could never talk about the elections or anything else I may have witnessed. They owned me lock, stock, and barrel. Everything changed and fear was now a union commodity, and the hall now dealt from a position of instilled fear. Membership grew overnight; they rented a large hotel conference room to hold their monthly meetings. They made the members worship and support them and in return promised to make their lives better, and they did. There were no more negotiations with the shipping companies; they demanded what they wanted and got it. Violence was now a business tool. The men in my office showed no pity or concern for what was going on. Every once in a while they would even joke about the violence. I was depressed but couldn't show it; I had to act as if I was the happiest member alive if I wanted to keep breathing regularly. Every once in a while the patrolmen would talk about their outrageous demands, and how they would tie up a ship until their demands were met. Tying up a ship was calling a strike by the shipmates so the ship couldn't leave the dock. It cost the owners a great deal of money. My goons were promoted as well. They became the monster's main muscle. Many times they didn't even want to talk about what they were doing. Ronnie was the arm muscle of the two; he would challenge anyone and render a supreme ass whipping on someone when asked or needed.

I once saw Ronnie tell a man and his friend who bumped him at the bar to say they were sorry, both of them. These were good-sized men. When they refused to apologize Ronnie would stand two inches away from them and say, "If I don't get an apology in two seconds, I'm gonna whip your ass, your friend's ass, and then make you fight each other." "I'm sorry" was immediately given. Marcus changed completely, his walk, talk, and mannerisms. I heard that he was the one who would not hesitate to pull a gun or shoot when needed. We were all once like brothers, but I didn't know these new people. Marcus's eyes were cold and empty. He was in somewhat of a competition with me for women and clothes. We still met and had drinks at the Regent, but it just wasn't the same with Marcus. Ronnie was still the same towards me, he loved me. I saw Marcus change first-hand. He was a man with no fear who didn't speak much as far as small talk. One night we were on our way to a club in Brooklyn, Ronnie was in the back and I was in the passenger's seat, Marcus was driving. There was a long stretch of road, near the public library on the left and Prospect Park on the right. Halfway down the long dark road a police car behind us put their lights on. Marcus pulled over, and a white cop got out alone. He walked over to our vehicle, he said, "License and registration boy." Marcus rolled the window all the way down and took out his license. He held it low by his belly, as if he was shielding a winning hand. The cop looked in then stuck his head inside the window, when suddenly Marcus grabbed him by the shirt. He pulled the cops head in while chocking his collar, he then rolled the window up so the officers shoulders were caught so that he couldn't grab his gun if he wanted to. I thought we were all going to jail that night. Marcus then said in a slow whisper, "If you ever call me boy again, I will kill you, your wife your kids your dog and your entire family." He then locked eyes with the cop for about 20 seconds. Ronnie and I just sat quietly waiting for the cop's reaction. Marcus then rolled the window down, pushed the cop's head back out, and drove off. I said to Ronnie we were in for it now, he will have the whole force on us. Marcus said, "He won't even report it because he will be too embarrassed to mention it." If black men in America really want to solve the civil rights problem. They should do it one by one, and make it personal, not relying on prayer. I don't know how to explain the fact that the cop just let us go I think that whatever he saw in Marcus eyes convinced him that this was not a fight he wanted to have.

I was still paying the seamen returning from sea, but many times I would go alone and just take a taxi straight to the dock with a bag full of money. Ronnie and Marcus were tending to union business somewhere else. The union probably felt that they owned me lock, stock, and bone marrow. I didn't mind. I was coming to terms with my place in this union, but my independence wanted to rebel. Once again, as in any form of rebellion, it may not make sense to anyone but the person rebelling. I would arrive at the ship and open the case of cash I was carrying and nearly cry as I handed it out to the men returning from sea. I thought of it as my pay for being used by Frankenstein. I was trying to once again make sense out of life, and many times life just doesn't make sense, it just is. One day while going back to the hall with an empty suitcase, I mentally devised a plan that put a smile on my face. It was worthy of my father. The more I thought about it, the more I smiled. Understand I was a completely changed man in these times. I became like the monster, and I used anyone who would allow themselves to be used. I would tell the ladies that I loved them and ravage their minds and body with no regard for how they felt or how my lies affected them. As Deep Sea would have worded it, I lost my soul. This time I wasn't feeling sorry for myself and not caring where I ended up. This time I felt that in this game of using people, I was going to match wits with the best of them. I may have been the monster's asshole, but I was going to pick and choose when I crapped on someone.

I was now at a point when I felt somewhat trusted and the eyes of the monster were off of me. Adonis and I spoke, but the sex part was gone on my part. When we did make love she would close her eyes and call the Lord's name as I kept my eyes open as I thought of things to do to her like sticking an umbrella up her twat and opening it. Can you imagine? How dare she use me before I could use her? I felt that everything I did or said to her was reported back to the monster. I just didn't trust her anymore. I was still turning a good profit with my businesses and getting my workers the ships they needed to get in order to get the goods we needed to sell. I looked like a million dollars, but inside I was dead. I was what I became and felt nothing. That is the lowest point in a man's life when God is totally evicted from a man's mind and spirit and replaced with absolutely nothing. I still had my wit and charm, but they were now my web to bring potential victims into my life. At least when I was living on the street before all this union stuff, the only person I was hurting was myself. This person wasn't going to hurt himself anymore for free. It's amazing how in all of the old movies when one would sell their soul to the devil it always involved signing a contract in blood with a man who had horns. I am here to tell you that when you do things for money with no regard for what you're doing, you sold your soul. The actual contractual closing is ultimately unnecessary.

Yes times were a changing after the Frenchy situation. I was still covering the ships, but my two goons were busier than ever and rarely did they speak about what they were doing. Ronnie invested his money in a construction and trucking business, and Marcus started dressing better than me, and he didn't have any agreement with a tailor. He must have spent a fortune on clothes, and they were not mine. Once in a while when we were at the Regent they would talk about having to change a person's opinion, by

Robby

altering their brain's thought path. We would still meet at least three times a week at the Regent. Here was where you either perfected your rap with the ladies or get frustrated and try to just get them alone and just ad an e to your rap, which spelled rape.

I was too smooth to have to force myself on anyone. My rap was like a series of combinations, and the female body was the safe. I would always find the right numbers and didn't care about the after-math of emotions. I would say whatever needed to be said and do whatever needed to be done to add a conquest to my numbers. I would have a woman looking for me the following day with tears in her eyes, and when she found me I would act as if she imagined the entire situation the night before. I was as cold as cold could get. I built this wall around me so that no one could enter. My rap was my bait and my charm was the noose. Once in a while I would meet a woman like the ones on the cruise line, who after sex wanted me to leave as badly as I wanted her to disappear. These women usually became my friends, but many times sooner or later they would give in and allow emotion to set in. I mean, with my pretty ass sitting in front of you looking you square in the eyes and seducing you with my voice, my wit, and my canned lines along with Nat, Brook, or Etta James in the background, it was a no-win scenario. And if your moral police ever got in the way I would render them helpless with the drinks I would buy.

I remember once I met a newbie to the tavern who everyone wanted. She said her boyfriend was in the service and just came in to talk. One night I poured drinks into her and quietly explained how she emitted music. Her voice were the lyrics, her breaths were the tempo, and she inspired my thoughts to sing, and my heart to beat like a bass drum. I could tell the way she breathed every time I whispered in her ear another reason to enjoy the night with me. I told her that our symphony awaited, and all she needed to do was take my hand, and I would be her one-man band. We left together and after the fat lady sang her song, we both went solo that night. I went so low into her pants, and she went on as a single after that, until her Johnny came marching home. I forgot all about her. She came in a few times looking for me, but I never tried to call her, so she stopped coming.

It's amazing how many men never think about the carnage left in a trusting heart. We look at it as the price one pays for being stupid enough to like someone like us. One night I was at the Regent alone Ronnie walked in alone. We sat together and talked. He asked me if I heard about the union organizer from the competitor's union.

I replied, "No, what happened?"

"This was the man from the other union was the one who convinced Frenchy to turn on us."

The monster wanted to pay him back for the disrespect. Ronnie went on to say that one night he had just reached his house when he got out of his car and walked to his front door. As he reached the door he searched for his keys. When he found them he stretched his arms in a yawning manner. Although he was wearing a large overcoat, he was hit in his shoulder by what is called a seasoned bullet. A seasoned bullet is one that a demon would use when they wanted to torture you. It is a bullet coated with paprika, and when shot to a nonlethal area, the paprika got into one's bloodstream, and the victim would literally try to rip their skin off to scratch the itch. It usually results in being blood poisoned, as you're being raped and savaged by pain, or the demon would usually show mercy and finish the job after he ejaculated at the sight and sounds of the agony. Ronnie described the man's screams as a football stadium filled with fingernails and blackboards. Like hearing an elephant caught in quicksand. I wanted to know where Ronnie got so much detail from, what demon would give out that much evidence, but the answer was obvious. When I asked when it happened, he said about an hour ago. I didn't want to ask if he lived or died, or how bad he suffered.

I then asked where was Marcus and he smiled and said "Oh, didn't he tell you? He's working on a ship that left the States last night."

He then gave an insidious smile and said, "Ask anybody." Frankenstein was on a rampage. I may have been a victim, but Marcus was a willing volunteer.

Soon after that, on many occasions, whenever I would cover a ship and take the men's pay to the men, I would leave the ship with a large locked bag, which was to be delivered straight to the upstairs office. I was not to question what it was; I was just to pick up and deliver it. Frankenstein soon moved into a new building, which was designed and constructed just for him. The windows were in the shape of portholes. We ruled the docks as well as New York. I was still bitter that I was used the way I was used, but I sure loved the lifestyle. It was a turbulent time for me. I had to bury these emotions and dare not smile the wrong way whenever I would be in the company of the Frankenstein crew members. We would all go to the convention centers and speak to the members about our love for the hall and their commitment to Frankenstein, and if your smile wasn't wide enough, Doctor Ronnie or one of his many coworkers would adjust your smile, so that the good fairy left you a bundle under your pillow. Remember the idea I told you about, which hatched in the back of the cab and made me smile? I felt that it was time to put it in action.

The union, by making the seasoned bullet statement of the caliber made by Marcus, had a profound effect on the membership, the competition, and the ship owners were all suddenly recruited as pawns. They were all suddenly jolted to the realization that this Frankenstein was armed and extremely dangerous. We were now feared and fear gives a business an unfair advantage over other businesses who just want to peacefully run their business and make a comfortable profit. The forefathers never envisioned the American Dream to include fear as a way of creating wealth, in any other business but slavery. I know that I should have been proud to have been a part of this and just go with the flow and enjoy the fruits of our labor, but I had a hidden anger that took all that I had to conceal. I was used royally by a monster and a bummy gangster. Frenchy was to me a good family man who was enticed by the prospects of being able to amply provide for his family without anyone getting hurt. He just underestimated his allies.

The patrolmen were still joking about him months after the fact, still saying that they could have fit his remains in a thimble. It was time to put my idea into action. The idea of it still brought a smile to my face. It used to hurt my heart to have to turn the money over to the men who earned it whenever I would have to pay them for the trip they just returned from. I now convinced myself that I was owed this money for the Frenchy caper, so I got the brain-child that I would pay these hardworking souls who I knew had their pockets full of money. Some earned so much they had to let the hem out of their pockets just to fit the cash in. I would then offer to buy them a drink at the local bar. After I made them good and drunk, they would just happen to get robbed.

Now how did I know that they would get robbed? Because how else was I supposed to get my money back for the drink and tips? It's amazing how larceny blinds any notion of analytical reasoning one may have. I felt bad because Frenchy didn't hurt anyone, and looked what happened to him. I mourned because Solid never hurt anyone, and looked what happened to him. But I never once thought that these seamen returning home never hurt anyone, and look what will happened to them. As far as I was concerned, they lost their pay for having been associated with Frankenstein; there was always another cruise. I needed a partner whom I could trust, someone who sounded intimating but was not entirely crazy, also someone who would have a spare pocket and not try to hold out on me. That man was Dell. He handled my businesses for me and always seemed to give me my money on time.

Look, everyone steals, but a good businessman finds the people who will steal the least. I also needed someone who would never turn rat and try to get in on Frankenstein's good side. Marcus and Ronnie were too violent and would probably overact the scene and hurt someone. I had to get Dell and dirty him up and invent the right costume. Make him totally unrecognizable. I approached him with my idea and he loved it. As he so eloquently put it upon hearing about it, "My ship finally came in." Lots of people got robbed on the west-side docks. As long as I didn't come back and say that the pay-roll was robbed from me, who cared? I just had to make sure that I appeared to have tried my best to stop it. We rehearsed and rehearsed until I was convinced that he was the real deal. We had signals and code words for who to hit hard and who to take it easy on. Dell was armed of course, with a gun; it was a small funny-looking little item. It was a Saturday night not so special, but when someone has a gun pointed on you, the last thought one has was *I wonder how much he paid for that thing?* We also had to pick a bar that had the least lighting in the area and not many apartment buildings around it.

I immediately thought of a place near where Frenchy was hit; there was not that much pedestrian traffic around and no cops. The plan was that I would pick up a suitcase full of money. Make sure that Marcus and Ronnie wasn't around that day to try to meet and surprise me, and only do this if I wasn't given a suitcase to bring back to the hall. After I dispensed the payroll, I would take the men willing to come out with me for a drink. After spending about a month on a ship, wouldn't you be willing to come? I was to take them to the bar and keep the drinks coming. The bar I choose had songs by Sam Cook, Etta James, and Johnny Mathis playing all night. It was within walking distance of the docks. I took about seventeen volunteers the first trip, to the spot where Dell was waiting nearby. We drank and laughed a lot.

The men kept thanking me for being so generous. The bill came at about midnight. Some of the men even put up some money for the tip and offered to help with the bill. I said no, it's on me. I got patted on my back so much, I felt like a politician.

We all walked out together. These men had no family to meet them at the dock, so they were all bus, subway, or taxi jockeys. As we approached a large area with a parking lot on the left, Dell then jumped out. These men, having just returned from overseas, had to deal with immigrations officials, so we were sure no one had a gun, a knife maybe. He spoke in a raspy voice with his face and hair covered. We rehearsed the scene, so he would say "Now I don't want to kill anyone, but if you decide to give your life for your cash then that's on you." I then said, "They are all broke. I was having a party and I treated everyone," taking responsibility for the money. Dell then marched everyone to the back wall of the parking area and one by one he searched everyone. We never rehearsed or thought to bring a bag for the money, so he had to improvise and place a man's jacket on the ground as he stuffed everything in the jacket. This was after all his pockets were bulging to the rim. He looked like the scarecrow in the Wizard of Oz on steroids. Some of the men protested with me, but this was not a night for heroes. They all complied. Dell would then fold the jacket up and haul ass. The men who wanted to chase him were always discouraged to do so by me, saying, "It isn't worth your life, friend."

This was the easiest money I ever made in my life, I mean real money. The haul was in the tens of thousands. The men who would want to report this to the police were also discouraged by me, saying, "You really think that they are going to spend one minute looking for a junkie to get a brother's money back?"

They all looked like they were all at the racetrack watching their horse have a heart attack and die a foot from the finish line. It's amazing how money quells any thought of repenting when it's rolling in. It wasn't my fault that we got robbed and who was to say it was? The take was huge and as long as we didn't abuse the plan, this was a sweet hustle. Back at the hall the men would talk about how I tried to talk the robber out of doing this even with great risk to myself. The bottom line was that no one at the hall really cared. I was told that the word *sympathy* was in the dictionary between *syphilis* and *sh--*. I thoroughly convinced myself that Frankenstein owed me this and that it was actually his money that I was taking. Hey if by taking crap you could stop your worst headache, wouldn't you take crap? It made my head feel much better. I made twenty-four thousand in one haul. I believe I gave Dell three thousand and told him that he got a third of the haul. Because of his trust and admiration and lack of mathematic skills, he never questioned me.

I figured about three of these hauls a year would put me into another tax-evasion bracket. As I said, I knew never to attempt this when I had a suitcase to bring back to the hall, so Frankenstein wasn't the least bit bothered by this. I never gave one thought to the men who spent months at sea away from their families just so I could extract their reward. I would always give myself a believable lie and tell myself, "Well, at least they got to see the sea." I was totally indifferent to anyone's pain. I figured that a man's life was taken because of me being used and for the part I played, someone owed me every-thing. One night when we all drinking at the bar, Marcus spoke about hearing about the robbery. He said, "Could you imagine being that robber who happened to pick that night and that place to rob that group? I hope he played a number that night because his luck was peaking."

He wished he was there to protect us. He said he would have emptied his gun into the robber then threw the remaining bullets in his pocket at him. I never once got so drunk that I would give anyone any indication that this was the brainchild of mine. I knew bragging could get me killed, so I remained silent and humble. I would just sit and shake my head. I had an unreadable smile on my face, and then said, "Poor souls, I wish there was more." Ronnie immediately looked at me and asked, "More what?" I said, "Choices, friend. Choices."

I never dreamed that I would ever have so much money: my business, my hustles, my job. America is truly the land of opportunity. Inside I may have been dead, but outside I was living the life. I guess the old man on the bus was correct when he so eloquently put it. I was up to my neck in crap, but I was comfortable, so I shut the hell up. Frankenstein was making its play as well. He won every negotiation he was involved in, and with that life got extremely comfortable for the members. No one wanted to piss Frankenstein off, so the opposition caved in no matter what the cost. The suitcases I would sometimes bring back to the hall suddenly got heavier and heavier. My crew and I became very popular at the nightclubs. We drank and partied like no other. Even the pimps and pushers were impressed by us. They all called me "The Robby."

I surpassed my father ten times in success, and I saw no reason to ever look him up to show him. I later learned that my mother and sister married and lived in a nice house in the country. My mother's husband was nearly three times her age, my grandmother went back to Barbados to live with my grandpa. Ronnie and Marcus's reputation also expanded. Ronnie was the bodyguard everyone asked for when they had large sums of money to transport, and Marcus was on the top of everyone's list when they needed someone's puff button pushed. It's amazing how every hustler, every boxer, every actor, every fool always winds up broke. It's because we all never think that we would see old age, so we never prepare for it. Today is the standard bearer of our lifetimes. When you never had money in your life and suddenly get it, by the time you figure out that you should put some-thing away, you're old and broke, and you suddenly find out that your memories are not

Robby

redeemable for jack squat. These are thoughts that don't even invade your mind until you're looking into a mirror and looking back at an unrecognizable fool who followed you into eternity. One you never saw before and certainly never listened to a word he may have tried to mumble about life, health, well-being, old age, or dying. With my pockets, belly, and phone book full, to hell with that.

Well, with that said, months passed, and I was totally monetarily rich along with a wealth of memories. I took some of my cash and put down on a nice brownstone home on Brooklyn, New York. It was right around the corner from Ebbits Fields. I use to love to lay in bed and hear the crowd roar whenever there was a home run hit. The streets were lit up at night by the lights of the games, and with Bonds Bread factory was baking on the corner gave the neighbor-hood an aroma that was beyond words. My business was bringing in money, my hustles were bringing in money, and my lifestyle was flourishing. I was now buying more clothes from different tailors. My silk-suit collection was vast, but my reputation for clothes made me venture outside of my world. I went to a new tailor in the garment district for pants. He wasn't as creative as Ben, but his pants were famous by his signature pocket on the back.

One day as I was leaving after a fitting. I was standing out front hailing a cab when I heard a voice behind me mildly say, "George." I turned, and lo and behold it was Laura's parents. They couldn't believe their eyes nor could I believe mine. Her old man was smiling as if he was actually glad to see me. They complimented me on the way I looked and asked me a dozen questions. How was I doing, where was I working, was I married? I would not answer anything until they told me about the old neighborhood. Once the flood doors were opened, my ears were drowning. Laura had finished college and was working not far from here. She had since married and divorced. They were both just out shopping and having a lunch. They then told me that they had caught Solid's killer; it was a junkie who later tried to rob the barbershop. Solid's wife, Marcie, sold the store and the man with no name took every dime and left her penniless. Laura's mother looked at me like my grandmother sized up my father, like she saw little me's in her life.

I told her that I wasn't married because work was occupying all of my time. I told them of my worldly travels, and they were notice-able impressed. Then the dad who couldn't stand me said, "Laura would love to see you."

It's amazing how garments can change everything. I was now acceptable to him because of the way I looked. I had a bottle of Estée Lauder perfume in my bag, and I reached in and told them to please give it to Laura with my regards. You would have thought that this was a foreign country and I just purchased their daughter. "Please call her, she would love to hear from you. We can't wait to tell her we ran into you. Is there a number she can call you?"

I answered, "No, I may be going away on business but I will call her when I return."

As I motioned at a cab that stopped, I turned before getting in and saw their eyes locked on me. I got in the cab and put my head back. It sunk in what they had told me. Solid's killer was caught. My self-imposed journey into loneliness was all for nothing. Had I not chosen to run, maybe I would have enrolled in that college and had a completely different life, but it was too late. That life got me this life because of the choices I had made, just like Solid's wife Marcie's life changed because of the choices she made. It's a shame that life doesn't come with a manual on how to live it. One wrong choice could affect your entire life as it did mine.

Of course my grandmother would counter argue that the manual for life is the Bible. Well, like the many others, I never read the Bible. I had what little I knew of it divinely delivered like most people do. It came via Grandma, Solid, Deep Sea, and many others who tried to give me positive encouragement my entire life, but like all others, it didn't come exactly when I needed to hear it, hence I ignored it. I paid no attention to it. I heard then forgot it. Hence, subsequently, *me*. Well, so much for the sermon. On the outside I had the life of a star, but the inner turmoil was a large price to pay for the comfort, and the mere thoughts of what could have been extracted a price as well. The only comfort I had was not the money I was making or the house I was in or even the clothes I was wearing. I thought at least I got to see the sea. That was worth the entire price of admission to this life.

I was living large and spending more, It was time to make another big score and collect what I was owed for the part I played in a man's death. Even if my reasoning for stealing was validated by a lie, that's the beauty of a lie. There is no need for truth when another lie will do. Only truth insists on truth; a lie is satisfied with another good-looking lie. Anyway, I wasn't seeking greater comforts, I just wanted more money. Dell was still making a good living handling my import business, he too was dressing like a millionaire, smelling good, and drinking the best liquor in the world. When I called he came running. I was now spending time at the hall looking at the ships that had been out the longest. I was cracking jokes with my coworkers and keeping a calm front. I didn't hear as much as a murmur from Frankenstein concerning the first robbery. The word was that many people got robbed in that neighborhood and that particular thief was just super lucky. The only thing I worried about was when Marcus said he wished he could get him in his sights. I found out from Dell that the MorMcormic freight shipping line had a ship coming in from a really long trip to Africa. I just had to get assigned to it without causing any red flags to go up. A new Patrolman named Clint— an older, gruff Jamaican man who was built like Dumpling, and who looked like someone who thoroughly enjoyed sitting on a Southern porch eating Jerk Pork— was assigned to cover that ship. He would have gladly given me the assignment just so he could remain seated at his desk. I had to get to cover that ship and to make it appear that it was his idea. This was the low tide in life's river for me. I was totally indifferent to anything that wasn't contributing to my lifestyle. Dell wasn't just doing my bidding he was also learning other crafts in the event he ever returned to the ships. I had gotten hold of Dell who enjoyed spending most of his earnings as I did on luxury. Dell was eager to repeat the same script in the same alley stage. His applause for such a performance would be another payday; Dell was someone I totally trusted. I knew that he looked up to me and knew that I was responsible for his lifestyle. A lifestyle that far surpassed his neighborhood buddies. He was wearing hundred-dollar suits; his rep was that he was as lucky a gambler as one could get, and living the life of a high roller. Thanks to me, I trusted him to follow, obey, and keep his mouth shut. The ship was to dock at the end of the week. I had to ensure that Clint wasn't going to cover it. That week I entertained everything from kidnap to murder to be assigned to that ship. I settled for sabotage. The night before the ship docked me and Dell paid a visit to Clint's neighborhood. This was a nice upper lower class neighborhood in Harlem. Finding Clint's car was easy; it was the oldest one on the block. It was amazing how many beautiful cars were parked in Harlem. You walk down any block, and you would think that you were in a car dealers showroom. The residents may have had roaches and mice in their houses, but their rides were pest-free and exquisite. Clint's car looked right at home with the buildings as the backdrop. He didn't have to worry about anyone stealing his chariot. His car looked like something a judge would sentence a pimp to ride in; it was parked three blocks away from his apartment. It was late, so Dell did look out. I was wearing a hat and dark glasses in disguise. It was amazing to see how many men were out that night had on a hat and dark glasses. There was a woman sitting on the steps in front where his car was.

This was an older woman who had on a nice dress and lipstick on. Her

Robby

hair was pinned back and she smelled good even from where we were standing. She just sat and hummed. We waited for her to leave, but she wouldn't leave but she wouldn't leave. I circled the block three times, and each time I got back she was still there. She would look at me and nod her head. I went over to talk with her. I told her that I had a date with a woman I had met who told me that she had a very strict daddy and I should wait outside. She asked me her name and said she knew everyone in the neighborhood. I made up some name and she said, "Oh yeah, I know her. Didn't know her daddy lived there with her."

I said, "Well, it's late, I better go before the night crawlers come out."

She said, "Yeah, they have some bad ones in this neighborhood. Well, good night."

She just stayed there. I asked her if she wanted me to wait until she went inside. She said no. I asked her if she was just getting some air. She said no. She introduced herself as Doh Doh and began to tell me a story which happened about two years ago, she said that she was sitting right here and a night crawler wearing a mask approached her. He made her go inside the building and took her downstairs where he proceeded to rape her. I was shocked. I said, "That's awful, you better go inside now while I'm still here."

She replied, "Hell no, friend, that was the best sex I ever had. Been out here every night since waiting for him to come back. You don't know him, do you?" I nearly bit a hole in my lip from trying not to laugh. I said, "I'm afraid not." I wish I had a picture of Bummy with me to show and tell her it was him to maybe cure her from her obsession. Just show her the picture and whisper, that's him without the mask, "He's out here someplace." We arrived at 11:00 p.m. that night. This lady didn't leave until 2:30 a.m. When she did, we immediately opened Clint's gas tank and pushed twenty sugar cubes into it and left. I now had to get to bed get rested and get to work on time the following day. I got up groggy the following morning, but the thought of returning that night with fifty thousand to sixty thousand was like a double shot of caffeine. I dressed and left for work. Clint never showed. The dispatcher came in and asked for someone to cover the ship that evening, and I jumped up like my ass just snorted pepper. The ship docked at 6:00 p.m. just when it was getting dark.

The phone at the office rang at about three and I answered it. It was Clint with his thick Jamaican-Caribbean accent, and when he was excited his conversation was incoherent. I did understand the words *cerrrr, basterd,* and *rasssss.* He told me that his car wouldn't start. I told him that it was all right, I just told the dispatcher that I would cover for him. I also told him that everyone understood why he was not at work, so he could just tend to his business, and all would be fine. He said "tank que" and hung up. Dell knew where and when to meet. The only thing that changed was the bar we were to go to. I didn't want the exact same pattern. Ronnie's and Marcus's job was to escort me to the dock with the payroll, and I had to get rid of them after I arrived. I told them that I needed them to collect from one of the tailors who owed me five hundred but wasn't paying his debt, and I would meet them at the Regent at midnight. The only thing that could have disrupted this was if I was given a suitcase from the ships' owners to bring back then they may have felt obligated to stay. But usually I am told by upstairs that there will be a pickup, and I wasn't, which made me wonder if maybe I was the only patrolmen who did pickups since this was originally Clint's job. It would make sense since Frankenstein knew that he owned my ass. Ronnie asked if I was going to be all right, and I said of course. Marcus didn't ask me anything; the thought of maybe kicking a tailor's ass was all he needed. I signed out a suitcase full of cash as heavy as the ones I was used to bringing back. My men drove me down to the dock, and I walked up the gangplank like King Crap. I got a sincere welcome from the union men. The

Robby

captain and his senior crew members' welcome were different. Before the union became so powerful; we were all one big happy family. Since they were now paying to play, I represented Robin Hood's brother, Robin Everyone. They resented Frankenstein's greed.

We would take from the rich and screw the poor. I went below to the galley and began shuffling hands of money to this hardworking crew who had just returned from a four-month assignment. I smiled and joked the entire time. Ronnie and Marcus just sat in a corner, looking intimidating. Here you go, friend, this should keep you happy until the next voyage. I handed out cash and sold worth-less freedom stamps. I finished around 8:00 p.m., then told Ronnie and Marcus to go and get the money we talked about. Immigration officials finished their searches to see that no drugs were coming into the country, and more important to me no, illegal weapons. When they left I smiled and said, "C'mon, friends, drinks are on me. Let me show you the many advantages of land. Bars, women, and drinks to wash that salt out of your throat."

I got about twenty-two men to come. I know that this was a lot but greed has no logic. These were seamen who wanted to find the first woman breathing. I would try to get them as well, telling them about the lovely ladies at the bar. Sometimes the female nurses who worked on board the ships would sell themselves on a long voyage to make money and keep the men sane. I thought how that Old Girl on the steps waiting for her rapist would like to find some of these boys who haven't touched a woman in months. They would screw a bald lightbulb into a hairy socket, if they could climax. We arrived at the bar, and I yelled, "Drinks are on me, set them up boys!" It was like watching a free cheese line in my old neighborhood, hands were everywhere. The bartender was inundated with requests. I may have gotten one thank you from them. They drank and told stories of their trips like only seamen could tell. One man called spoke to his family on a pay phone the entire time we were there. He did drink, but you could hear him talk of how much he missed his wife and children. These boys drank twice as much as the first group. At about 12:00 a.m., after being serenaded by white singers like Frank, Dean, Tony and Rosemary, they were well filled with booze and ready to leave.

I got the bill and my eyes nearly popped out; I acted like it was nothing. I felt like those drunks in the movie *Mighty Joe Young* who gave the big ape the liquor, then got mad when he drank it all. The only difference was that I knew I would be reimbursed. This place didn't have any alley, but it did have only one path to the subway and main road. The streets were dark and empty. There was a streetlight out about a block before the train station that was our destiny point. I joked as we walked, and I have to admit I felt a buzz from the drinks and all the toasts I made to make sure they all drank up. I toasted the union, the ships, America, spare ribs, plus the invention of the telephone and condoms, anything to get another drink into these boys. As we approached ground zero, I began to scan the area, looking for Dell. He was well camouflaged. We were now approaching the blown-out light, when I saw this figure walking toward us. I could tell by the walk that it was Dell but he had a different hat on. Once he got closer he began pulling the hat down to cover his face as well as it turned into a small mask.

I thought that this was perfect: no cops, no light, no witnesses. As he walked up in front of us he pulled out his gun and said, "This is a stickup." This crowd was bigger than the first so my eyes kept scanning for any potential hero. I immediately said, "Remain calm, boys, there ain't no reason to die over money." I tried to sound as if there was a remote chance they would be reimbursed by the union, but even a half an idiot knew that was impossible. Dell disguised his voice and made each one hand over their money one by one. I was the first one to empty my pockets. He had a larger pillowcase this time. The men appeared drunk, surprised, and scared. I was coaching them to comply with Dell, I mean the robber. Each man slowly and painfully gave up his money. I said, "Don't worry, friends, it will be all right." I was busy looking at all the money going into the pillow-case and dreaming about good times when suddenly I was awakened when I heard Dell say, "You too, friend, all of it" to one man. This sounded a lot rougher than Dell usually sounds. I looked at his mask into his eyes and they looked like two cherries in the snow. They were both bloodshot red as if he was high on something. I knew this was double the trouble. He pointed the gun at the man. This was the one who couldn't stop taking on the phone to his family. Dell again demanded his money. This stupid, simple seaman said, "No, you're going have to kill me, my family needs this money."

I wanted to just step out of character and yell "Cut!" like some kind of sadistic director. This love-struck idiot was ruining the scene. This was supposed to be an easy take where no one got hurt, and here before me was Super Family Man Seaman. This sobered my buzz up immediately. Dell was high, and this person was ready to die for his cash. I then saw Dell raise the gun to this gentleman's head and say, "Last chance before you commit suicide." My heart started pumping so fast, my blood had to have a beer head on it. The other men said, "Paul, give it to him." They then tried to explain to Dell that his child was very sick, and this money was to pay doctor's bills. Dell responded, "Well, at least this fool won't have any doctor's bills to leave his family." I was now in a state of panic. I knew that Dell's first thought was to impress me and rise to the occasion. I also knew that he was high and irrational. So with everything happening at once, I also got hit with a revelation that I needed to confront, but not at this time, which was the immediate realization that I was not a murderer. I did not want this man to get hurt, let alone die. I now saw that any part I thought I played in Frenchy, or Solid' demise was entirely accidental; I did not have the stomach for murder. Dell slowly cocked the gun when severe reality brought me back to this moment. I tried to telepathically talk to Dell; this was ten times more concentration that I used when I tried to reach Davey on the roof of the projects. My left foot then instinctively said, "You gonna just stand here and watch this murder unfold?"

I stepped in between Dell and the man. I then said, "Please shoot me, take this watch that you overlooked, which was worth more than this poor soul had." I said, "Please, friend, don't shoot him."

You would think that Dell would have gotten it and taken the watch. He looked at me with a confused look as if to ask, "Are you saying this so when I shoot this idiot your hands are clean? Were you adlibbing the scene to show the men you're on their side?" I know that I couldn't grab the gun because the men would have grabbed Dell, and we would both have our asses handed to us. Have you noticed that everything in my life always had to be complicated? Dell looked at me, the watch, the man who refused the money, the other men and his gun. I saw a million things going through his mind all at one time. I also feared that some of the men would detect his weakness to think and try to overpower him. I repeated, "Friend, you have a lot of money in that bag. It's probably the best score you ever had. With this watch you now have enough to retire." I begged please in the most begging whispering voice I could muster. I closed with "Just go."

By the good grace of heaven, Dell got the message and snatched the watch, lowered the gun, took the money, and ran. Some men wanted to go after him, and I grabbed them and said, "Didn't you see his eyes? He's crazy." Now I'm sure you know that when you really want something from God, you usually make every mental deal in the world you can think of. You try to bargain and say, "Lord, just grant me this, and I'll never do that again." Most people make deals until they need to make another one after they broke the last one. I just wanted the men to stay with me and not go after Dell. I wanted this thing to finish with no one getting hurt. You see, the me who watched Dell run was not the same me who led the men to this moment. It may not have been a radical change, but a seed was indeed planted. In their eyes I was a hero, in my eyes I was a zero. The man who refused to give up his money grabbed and hugged me. He squeezed me like I just rescued him from a burning building where he was trapped with gasoline underwear on. The other men also showed me respect. Someone had returned to the bar and called the police who soon arrived and took our statements. When they got to me, they looked deep into my eyes. I knew that I had to be calm and straight. They were white cops who appeared professional. They talked with everyone and radioed the best description of Dell they could put together. I was praying that he was long gone by now. I was also thinking about a thin man walking down the streets of New York with a large sack without a sleigh. They took our names and contact information.

One cop who looked right into my eyes when questioning me said that this was one hell of a coincidence, don't you think? I replied, yes it was, especially if this was the only robbery in the neighborhood tonight, then indeed it was. He just stared at me. Some of the men asked me if the union hall would cover some of their losses. I said I don't see how since they were not responsible. The only one with any money in his pocket was the one who refused. It was amazing how I kept the men from banding together and jumping Dell. We all said our goodbyes and went our separate ways. My mind was traveling a mile a minute. This was nothing like the first one. This was a plan that sprouted other scenarios, all of which were unplanned. I never had a plan B, I never even thought there could be a plan B. You never know exactly just how much you know until you're confronted with how much you don't know. My plan was to meet Dell later that evening at my house. I was now engulfed in paranoia. I felt the men, the police, and even law-abiding space aliens were following me. I just walked and walked. All I needed at this point was to get robbed. I knew that I didn't want to meet Dell, feeling like this and I didn't want him to look for me and come to my house. I also feared that Dell was too high to think rationally. Fear and pain are two teachers who can make their students never forget their lessons.

I found a bench near a bus stop and just sat. I didn't know whether to laugh or cry. There was a bag of money somewhere waiting for me, but it was not something I equated with good times now. I got home that morning at 3:00 a.m. This time I ran every possible scenario through my mind of what to expect. I went through plan a to z and then 1 to 25. I was in a terrible mood; sleep wouldn't even come near me. It was like being on a crooked seesaw. One thought was I hoped Dell was safe and the next was where's that asshole with my money? The time moved like I was back in the safe. I got up at 6:00 a.m. and just sat and stared at nothing, thinking about everything. I began to get dressed for work. At about 8:30, I heard a hard knock on my door. I was somewhat relieved and thought Dell. I opened the door with a "where the hell were you" look on my face. I was confronted by a tall muscular white man in an off-the-rack suit with a "here I am" look on his face. He said, "Robby Robinson?" I said yes. I thought he was going to say New York City Police, but he didn't. He took out a badge and said "Monroe, FBI." I then said to my body, "Relax everyone, and please Mr. Ass, don't crap." Like in the safe, once again my body began its own rebellion; my feet said, "Let's play. Left, jump in front of right then right in front of left for about five miles." I had to take deep breaths and try to discourage them from running. "May I come in?" he said in a stern-toned voice, which meant "Back up, fool." I opened the door and let him in. Now I was back to interviewing thoughts. What if this was about Frenchy? Was this about my business? Suppose Dell now shows up with a pillowcase? What if this was about Frenchie? Could I go to jail for what I did to Dumpling? Suppose I just crap myself in front of him.

Robby

"How may I help you?" I thought the next move was the handcuffs.

"Nice house, boy. You work for the hall, right?" I answered like a kid just learning to talk: "Yeah."

"We have been informed that you personally made pickups from different shipping lines as payment to the hall to prevent strikes."

I took a small sigh of relief although I knew I just escaped the fire and ran on to the shooting range. I did what?

"We are offering you a deal, son. You work with us, and we allow you to breath the air you have become accustomed to breathing, or if you don't work with us you may be nearing your last days of not waking up to a man yelling at you to get out of bed."

I said, "Sir, you caught me at a bad time. I have no idea what you're talking about."

"I'm talking about larceny, graft, and bribes. I'm talking about all the tax free cash that you make with your side businesses jail or freedom. I'm not fluent in stupid, so if you need a real-life illustration, I will be happy to provide one."

He then put his arm on my shoulder and walked me over to the window. There was a car with two men out front and they both were looking up at us. All I needed to see now was Dell to turn the corner, and my heart would have said, "To hell with you friend" as my feet took over this situation.

"This is a limited-time sale, my boy." He then scanned my house and said, "You sure have a lot to lose. Life in prison is much longer for a young man. Here's my card. Should you decide that your life may just be worth something other than jail, you can call me to discuss this in detail."

I asked, "And if I decide not to call?" He smiled and said, "Please don't call. I really don't like you. I'm sure you can prove that this house and all the luxuries in it were purchased with the hall's salary." He smirked turned and left. I stood there with a big crap-eating look on my face. I slumped down in a chair and thought, *And this day just started.* I imagined Frankenstein's big boot being surgically removed from my ass. About fifteen minutes after he left, I then heard a sheepish knock hit my door. I meekly opened the door and saw Dell. He looked pregnant with the sack under his coat. "Where were you?" he asked.

I wasn't smiling. I immediately let him in, and he had an ear-scratching smile on his face. I immediately ran to the window to see if the car was still there; it was gone. "Do you know what we have here?" he asked as he poured the money on the coffee table. Dell may have seen cash; I saw green airline tickets to unnamed countries. Dell asked, "What's the matter, man, you all right? My voice then sounded like a tobacco auction.

"What the hell were you high on? Did anyone follow you here? Were you really going to shoot that poor man? Didn't you under-stand what I was trying to tell you?"

He said, "I'm sorry, man, knowing you like I do, I thought that you wanted the money more than anything. I thought you wanted me to off him, and I was going to, but at the last minute I couldn't squeeze the trigger." Those words hit me, *pow*, right in the kisser. That hurt. The verbal mirror I just looked in was an ugly one. He thought that the money was more important to me than a man's life. He just eulogized my life. I sat there not even wanting to sit next to me. I told him to take the same amount of money as last time, and go, we will count and split later. He acted like he never heard me and asked, how much should I take? I yelled at him to just take what he wanted. He grabbed the money like a starving man who just woke up in a bakery. "I'll see you at the hall later," he said and then he left. I looked at the clock, and it was still morning. What a damn morning. I would bet that not one damn rooster crowed today. I was here but only in body. I felt that I let down everyone who ever saw any good in me. I was a hustler, a fool with a pocket, nothing more. I groomed and left and took a cab to the hall. The news of the night got there before I did. Some called me a hero; some said I had the worst luck in the world having been robbed twice.

The boys in the office just stared, not saying anything. Before I could sit at my desk, I was called upstairs by none other than Bummy. I again took the stairs and slowly walked to the offices. Once again I tried to anticipate the questions but understood that, on this damn morning, I hadn't the slightest idea what was coming. I arrived and Adonis greeted me. She looked stunning and just looked at me with a stony face. I had no idea how to read her or what waited for me. I was beckoned into the office of the president. I went in, all the players were there, all of Frankstein's family.

"Sit down," they said. "What's going on?"
I wanted to ask, "What are you referring to? Which crazy situation in this mixed-up life of mine are you referring to? The robbery, the FBI, my wanting to crap myself? *What?*" They were acting benevolent and asked about the robbery. "We heard that you and the men with you have again been hit. Why didn't Ronnie and Marcus stay with you?" I replied that the men were paid and we thought all was good. Bummy then abruptly asked, "Did the FBI contact you?"

"Yes, they came to my house this morning."

"And what did you tell them?"

"Nothing," I answered.

"What did they ask you?"

"Nothing. They implied that they had all of the answers. They were looking for an asset to collaborate their story."

"What did they say they had?"

"He said that we took payoffs from shipping lines." "Is that all?"

"No, He gave me a card and said to call him soon." "Did you confirm or deny anything?" "No."

"Why didn't you tell us this."

I said, "I just walked in a minute before you called me, I was going to come up and tell you." Bummy said in his usual eloquent way, "Wait outside." Once again a chill went through my body and *BRRRRRRRRRR*, again my mind was racing. Would they sell me out? Did they now fear me talking about the Frenchy murder, did the elections, have anything to do with this? Would they back me? Should I have admitted anything or just covered myself? Adonis walked by and looked at me, she saw that I was in pain. She then walked over and kissed me on the cheek. I said, "Thank you," then after about twenty seconds, I thought, *Bitch.* I looked at the clock and it was now near afternoon. I just sat and waited.

When I was called back in, Bummy said, "So you were again in a robbery with the men?" I answered yes. "I hear you risked your life to help them."

"Yes, I felt it was my duty."

They all just looked at each other. "Go back outside and wait." I made a mental note of this day and promised myself that if I were to live beyond today I would be in a canoe on the ocean, next year on this day. This has got to be my bad-luck day. I was called back in the office a third time and asked, "Who robbed you?" I answered that that was like asking me if all poisonous things are sour. Which meant, how would I know? The next question was why did I take them out and buy them drinks, wasn't that what happened the first time? I swallowed and replied, "Look, I was just trying to make them appreciate us, isn't that my job?" Bummy immediately shot back, at your own expense?

"Go back and sit down," Then they all said in unison, go back outside and sit down. I was ready for this damn day to end. Each time I was called, they only asked one question about the robbery. It was like they wanted me to know that they knew. At 2:00 p.m., I was finally called in for the last time. I was told not to call the FBI. I would be provided a union attorney in about

Robby

a week to go over my answers to everything they needed to know. I asked them what did that mean, and Bummy replied that that was all you needed to know, and, do not to make any call to them whatsoever. I left the room and waited for the elevator. My mind was spinning; they may know about the robbery, and the only reason I was able to still breathe was the fact the FBI was poking around and asking questions. Even if they could prove I masterminded the robbery, they needed me alive for the present time. I understood that it was my ass on the line in spite of the fact they said that I should not worry and that all answers would be given. I didn't understand what that meant. What a position I was in. If this was a board game, I would be checkmated and sent directly to jail without passing go, with the FBI rolling the dice dictating my next move. Or a second outcome was a Frankenstein's season bullet, or his size 86 shoe in my ass if I didn't play ball.

I went downstairs and sat at my desk, trying to act normal. All the men stared at me. I so wanted to ask if the FBI had paid anyone else a visit, or was I the only fool bringing suitcases back? They all looked pretty calm. Why not believe that I was the only one with the suitcases? I was the only one I saw in the safe counting votes, I was the only one who paid Frenchy's car a visit that night, I was the only one robbing payroll. I'm in trouble. Here I was relieved over what Laura's father had told me, and that I never had to leave there and subject myself to that lifestyle that brought me to this lifestyle. And my ass was now in deep hock by the Frankenstein pawnshop. Marcus and Ronnie stopped in and both looked at me and snickered. Too bad you sent us away, huh? I felt that they both knew the truth, or maybe I was just paranoid. Ronnie said, "Let me know what you want us to do." His loyalty was still apparent. One of the patrolmen did break the silence and said, "So you're a hero again, huh?"

I left work early and went home that day. I arrived with the money still on my coffee table. After a while, just sitting and staring got stale. I needed something to do to take my mind off of this entire situation. I called Adonis and asked that she stop by after work. I needed to see what she could tell me. She reluctantly agreed and then abruptly hung up. I gave her my new address, and I immediately cleared the money off the table. I never even counted it. I just threw it in the closet and put a blanket over it. Dell's words about money meaning more to me than life was still wreaking havoc on my mind. When she arrived, she complimented my new home and sat down. I wanted to ask her a million questions; I still didn't completely trust her, but I was happy she came. When she took her coat off, my friend behind my zipper wanted to interrogate her first. She still had the sexist legs I ever saw. I grabbed her hand and led her toward the bedroom, with her repeating in a low, sexy voice, "We better not." I didn't understand why she said that, but making love to her was like this. Was this the last time I was to have a woman before spending the rest of my life in jail?

We both tore each other's clothes off and made passionate, animated love. It was again like the Man vs. Woman Olympics, with each one determined to win. Her legs, her breathing, her body movement, her hair, and the way she smelled made every part of my body take notice. It was as if we were two long lost bodies who just found one another and were thinking of ways to excite each other with every touch, every feel, every breath. I knew some may think that I was just needing information from her and that would be true, but it was much more primal than that, it was a man needing a woman and vice versa. We both feared Frankenstein and did what we had to do to live. Notice that I didn't use the word *survive*. We both lived the good life. While we were making love, she began to cry. When I tasted her tears I was jolted back to when I first saw the sea, how young and impressionable I was. It was a strange way to cry; her crying noise was interrupted by her passion. We never lost a beat; it was actually one of the most sexual moments I ever had. When we reached the moment of sincerity, we held each other tight and embraced at the same time. Her breasts were warm and soft, pressing against my heart, and I could feel my heart beating against them.

At that moment as if a bell was rung; our eyes opened at the same time, and we just stared into one another's soul, and we both held on tight. I didn't want to leave my position between her legs, so we just stayed there slowly stroking one another. The silence was peaceful and we both fell asleep. I really, really needed this rest. I woke up with Adonis staring at me.

"Hello, stranger," she said and whispered, "are you all right?"

I answered, "I don't know. I do know that if I ever have another day like this one, I will immediately fast-forward to when you came over." She smiled.

I asked, "What is happening, lady?"

She placed her head on my chest and began to explain. The union had become rich and successful in every way. Their growth has been exceptional. They won every negotiation and demand with the shipping lines they could come up with. The men were the recipients of that success; they worked shorter hours, ate better food, and made more money than ever before. The owners paid unto Caesar what was Caesar's. It got bigger and bigger. They destroyed anything that got in the way and put fear in the hearts and minds of the victims', and then last week all of it busted. The ship owners got tired of paying graft they organized and called the FBI and reported what was going on and how they had to pay to keep operating and to avoid strikes or risk severe bodily harm. Word of the inevitable investigation came from their connection in Washington, DC. There were meetings being held around the clock, and they were assessing their situation. Everything was backward, it was like an upside-down chess game and all the union heads were afraid that many people knew a little something and should the FBI put them all together, their little became a lot.

"Adonis, am I going to be protected, or like a simple-minded captain, am I to go down with the shipping industry?"

"I really don't know," she answered.

"May I ask you a question?" she whispered. "Please tell me that you have the worst luck in the world, and you didn't have anything to do with robbing those poor men."

"Is that what they think I asked?"

"I don't know what or how they think. I'm asking for me."

I looked her right in the eye, and I heard Dell's voice assessing my life; I didn't want to lie and couldn't tell the truth. I said, "I'm surprised you have to even ask me that." She smiled. We just hugged the entire time. Adonis and I went to sleep again. This was one for the books. If Frankenstein did suspect me of having something to do with the robbery, I guess the FBI may have saved my life by coming to see me. It just wasn't a good time for something to happen to me, but the other side of that logic was, did I know too much for my own good?

I remember being at a wedding when I was younger. When two people got married, the preacher said, "Till death do you part." People always think that it means physical, stop-breathing death. What most people fail to grasp about life is that during a person's life one dies and is reborn about ten times in one lifetime, if they are lucky. Death means change. I died to become Robby, and now I was looking to off this fool to go back to being me. The hardworking, dedicated me who Solid and Deep Sea taught. The boy whom the Old Girl loved was dead. The boy who went to that college with all the wonderment was no more. Here walked Dell's rendition of the me I became. I didn't even want to count the money in my closet; my thoughts were running a mile a minute. Once again I was only sure about one thing, and that was fear could get me killed. I had to look confident and as if I were the best team player on the Frankenstein cheerleader squad. This was supposed to be one more big score for money, not a mind-numbing revelation. As the saying goes, there's *do, don't do,* and *overdo.* I woke up that morning, and it was still dark out. Adonis was getting dressed to leave; I felt that my telephones were tapped. It was only a matter of time before I had to confront the FBI again. I asked Adonis what Frankenstein was doing to prepare for the outcome. She replied that they were taking large sums of money out the country. Had it not been for the series of events that unfolded, I would have probably been the courier. Adonis asked me to walk her to her car. Before she got in, she grabbed me and gave me a kiss that had goodbye, be careful, and run all on the tip of her lips. She said, "I will pray for you. I hope you can find the happiness you deserve." I asked her one more question. Why did they choose me to make a deal with? "Who knows?" she said, "but you have to be careful. It was a blessing as well as a curse." How? With them looking out for you no one could harm you, but they will do whatever they have to do to ensure your silence and cooperation. What should I do? "Leave, disappear now, start over with another name, in another country." How can someone hide from the FBI or Frankenstein? "I have some money to lend you if you need it. Take it and go." I'm supposed to call the FBI, where is there to hide?

She hugged me and said, "You were the best part of my job." "Will you be all right?" I asked.

"As far as they are concerned I don't know anything. Do you want the money?"

"No, I think I can scrape some up should it come to that. They told me their lawyer will help me."

She replied, "Don't trust anyone."

She then drove off as I watched her leave. What to do, where to go. I thought about where I could escape, and the only place I could think of where no one would look was back in a shelter. I got dressed and went to work and acted as if I was immune to all of this. I stayed in the office joking with everyone. Paul came to see me; this was the man who wasn't going to give up his money. He came to again thank me and tell me how much I helped his family. Instead of feeling good, all I heard was Dell's words repeating. I knew that all eyes were on me. After work I met Ronnie and Marcus at the Regent. They asked me what was happening; they were told by the monster's handlers to stay close to me day and night without being told why.

Marcus came right out and asked was the robbery at the dock on the level, and if it wasn't, why didn't I let them in on it? I just flashed a half-baked smile. Ronnie was more the big brother. He said to me that something was wrong, and he didn't know what it was, but he had a really bad feeling about the present atmosphere. His next words were similar to Dell's. He said: "I know all you care about is the money you make, but there is mistrust in the air."

That did it, I hated them. Everyone was convinced they knew and seemed to know better than me. This time in my life was once again similar to being a little boy when my father would promise to get me something. I would go over everything he would say to see if I could flush out a lie or if I was really going to get it. Would Frankenstein really protect me? I was living just to speak with their attorney to see where this would lead. Anytime your life is at the mercy of a stranger that you have to depend on, you're in severe trouble. Time moved like a snail with heels on. I waited for that call to speak with the attorney. I was still a hero to some and a zero to others. I was just going through the motions of life without anyone I could confide to. I couldn't even go back to the church and con-fess. Life had led me here to this point of total confusion. No calls from anyone. I even called Adonis once at her desk and she said in a strange distance voice, "No thank you, I don't read that magazine."

Just think, I still didn't count the money in my closet. About a week went by when I was at the hall and about to leave. Someone called out, "Robby, telephone." I took the phone and heard a voice I never heard before that said in a whisper, "Meet Mr. Gleason at the west-side ship yard at 8:00 pm." I asked who exactly was Mr. Gleason and they replied, the attorney. I then asked, "Who is this?"

And they replied, "Your guardian angel."

I asked Archie Bella who answered the phone who that was, and he said, "How the hell should I know? I'm not your damn secretary." Why would the attorney want to meet me at night at the docks?

I called Ronnie and Marcus, who were instructed to stay close to me and asked, if they had gotten any word about tonight. Ronnie told me he just received a special assignment in Long Island, straight from upstairs. Now I was really scared. Everyone at the hall was either going home or getting ready to go home. I shot upstairs in the elevator but everyone was already gone. The only thing there was the smell of Adonis's perfume. *Should I go tonight?* I thought. If they wanted to hit me, they could hit me anywhere. I really have nothing to lose. Any way I turn I was a doomed man. I will go to the docks but I will be dressed. That meant I will have a pistol with me.

I called Dell and got his pistol, you know the one that was like putting a bullet in a slingshot. He asked me if I needed any help, and I said no, I'm just taking this gun with me in case I needed to shoot myself first. I was so nervous I couldn't even cut my steak at dinner tonight. I went home and changed and gave in to logic: I'm either going to get or need help tonight. What's the difference? Either way, I was living in crap but I wasn't comfortable. I thought about counting the money but then decided that the last thing I needed was some-thing new on my mind. I didn't want to hurt anyone, that was the last thing I wanted, but I didn't feel right just giving someone my life. They would have to take it. Maybe I was just paranoid, maybe Mr. Gleason would be my salvation, and make everything right.

It was about 7:00 p.m., and I took a cab to the west-side docks. There were no ships in port, so it wasn't very well lit. I was met at the gate by an old security guard named Jasper. He was shocked to see me. I asked, "Didn't anyone tell you I was coming?" and he said no.

"What are ya doing here?"

"I'm supposed to meet someone."

"Where?" he asked.

I said, "Here at 8:00 p.m. Is anyone else here?"

"Just some more guards inside."

"Why are there more guards inside?" He told me it was old Moe who looked like Jasper's father and another man. I was somewhat relieved that there were other people here. If this was a setup, there would be no witnesses. Jasper said that the cargo area was full from ship's cargo which they have been unloading all week, but for some reason the union workers wasn't picking the cargo up and the ship-ping owners were very concerned about their ships being unloaded, and no one allowed to pick up the cargo.

"Is there a strike or sumting?"

I walked inside the cargo bay area and saw boxes on top of boxes. *Holy crap*, I thought, *this is a huge backup.*

"I didn't hear of any strike. When I get back to work, I will inform the hall what is happening."

He asked me, "Who you s'pose to meet tonight?"

I said a delegate. He then picked up his flashlight to do his rounds. It was dark and lonely in here, and the only noise was my heart beating and the sounds of the police sirens in the street I sat and waited. Now the only noise were the police sirens. I remember thinking that at the pace Jasper walked, it must take him an entire shift to scan the yard. I just sat and waited and let my mind wonder about the situation I was in. What will this lawyer tell me? How can he help me? What was wrong with me to keep reacting to whatever life threw me and not having a positive cohesive plan? The life of a hustler is a lonely existence. Anytime you have to depend on some-one else to do well, you're going to do bad. I sat and waited until my mind interrupted and said to me, "Hey, stupid, you trying to hatch that chair? At what point will you realize that no one is coming? What was I doing here? I didn't even know who it was I spoke to on the telephone about this appointment. Jasper still did not return, so I just left it was now about 10 pm, I walked.

I walked by the dock, heading downtown. The smell of the Hudson River was like an ocean fart. You could tell it was, water but the aroma sucked. I got tired and flagged a cab and went home. I was even more confused than when I left the house. What was this all about? Why didn't the attorney show? Tomorrow was Saturday, so I had to wait all weekend to get an answer. I got home, and the first thing I did was throw the pistol into the closet with the money. I sat back on my couch, staring at the air. I was lost, confused, and in pain. I had money, I had clothes, I had a position, but I did not have peace or happiness. I fell asleep right there with my clothes on.

I woke up early and made some coffee. I turned on my television and waited for the picture to arrive. I sat and sipped my coffee. When the picture finally turned on, I thought I had a bad reception; it was a foggy screen. I waited for it to clear up. It never did, then all of a sudden I got the wakeup call of my life. Standing on the screen in the fog was a man who I recognized as *Jasper*. I went up to the screen and knelt before it. I didn't have to wait until Monday to find out what was happening. My mind was now wide awake. It wasn't fog I was looking at, it was smoke. The reporter then described the scene as one of the biggest fires ever to hit New York. The dock where I had been the night before was burning. One need not have be valedictorian from detective school to understand the situation. I was set up by a damn monster. Frankenstein had no more use for me, and I was being fed to the wolves.

I dropped my coffee and immediately changed my clothes. I got my suitcase and placed all of the money in it. I washed my fingerprints off the gun and took one last look at my clothes, my house, and my life. I had some other money that Dell had given me from my businesses in the bedroom. I got that as well and walked out. I don't even know if I locked the door behind me. I remember saying, "Goodbye, Robby" as I left. I heard the telephone ring but I didn't dare answer it. I remember feeling bad that no one in my family or neighborhood would ever see what I accomplished or how I lived. Would they even believe me if I spoke about it? Life was once again kicking me in the nuts. As soon as I got outside, I dropped the pistol in the garbage can. As I walked it all became clear to me; it was a genius setup. I was the only one from the hall at the docks last night. They saw me arrive but no one saw me leave. I had been used and kicked aside by a Frankenstein pimp. I heard my father laughing at me for being so stupid. I heard Deep Sea asking me, did I lose my soul. I heard Solid asking me, did I give my best? I was a fool's fool. The only thing that partially consoled me was that fact I had a bag full of money, except when I thought about Dell and Ronnie's opinion of me.

This union set up wasn't about the robbery. It was about the FBI inquiry. Frankenstein said a mouthful to the shipping owners about squealing to the FBI without opening his mouth or using one curse word. He said with one match to kiss my huge monster sized, sewed on, crap dispensing butt. Suppose I didn't go for that last score? I would still be in this situation having to survive on the money I made. It's like I was supposed to take the money

Robby

for this moment in time. Remember what I told you about a lie being better than the truth when you really need comfort? I knew that I had to get away and get away fast. The only identification I had said Robby Robinson. I decided to first stop in lower Manhattan and get a copy of my birth certificate. I arrived at the Department of Records and realized that today was Saturday. There was a building across the street, which had a sign that read FBI. Once again I forgot it was Saturday and hauled my sorry butt away fast. I stopped on the corner and took one last look at New York. A tear ran down my face, and then a homeless man standing next to me stuck his hand out. I gave him the roll of money in my pocket. He smiled at me and said, "Bless you."

I replied, "Thanks, I need it."

It then hit me that once again I was running, and once again I didn't do anything to have to run. I had enough money in my suit-case to make a good start somewhere. The trick would be getting somewhere.

I hailed a cab to take me to the train station. You know you're in trouble when you have to take a cab to the train station instead of taking the cab all the way. I then caught the downtown train. I looked over my shoulder so much I had a pain in my neck. When I got downtown, I caught the first Greyhound leaving New York City, heading in any direction the long way. I had a bag full of money and a fast beating heart. At each layover stop I would eat then grab another bus, and in some cases I was doubling back and covering my so-called tracks. I fell asleep and I woke up, changed buses, and repeated the drill. I stopped in a hotel in Georgia. Amazing how here I was with a suitcase full of money, and no one thought to rob me. I kept my suitcase on my lap the entire bus ride. Once I began to feel somewhat safe I began to formulate a plan.

My plan was to get to Miami Florida and then to take the first ship going far, far away to Barbados or Jamaica. I arrived in Florida and went to a really nice hotel, a place where I could leave my bag and expect it to still here when I got back. I then took a cab to the closest us, meaning black community. I asked around and found a local black-owned barbershop. This is where one such as myself would go to get things they needed in another state. Black people all knew the drill. If you need a place to stay or eat, you would go to a church; if you need something to feel good, go to the local bar. For what I needed it was a barbershop. I still needed identification. I was told to see an older man named name Pody. He was to be at the shop later that evening, so I had dinner and waited. We met, and he said he could get what I still needed new identification, and a phony birth certificate. He wanted three hundred dollars. One fifty up front and one fifty on delivery. I paid his price and didn't try to bargain. The fact was I needed it. The ironic part was that the information I gave him was all true. He would have charged me double had he known that all the information I gave was actually thoroughly true. The name on the identification I needed was George Robinson. It also was to have the actual hospital I was born in, and my parents' real names. As he was writing down the information he asked what he could call me, and I said Ishkabibble Wehawkin. Pody said, "He would have it to me as soon as he could." Yes, Robby Robinson was to be laid to rest, I want back to the hotel, and my next move was to get to Florida and either get a ship or charter a boat. If it was a ship, it would have to be one with registry from another country.

One thing was certain. even though I paid cash at the hotel, I was aware that I was no longer respected and looked up to. I was treated like any other black man in a nice hotel. Once when walking down to dinner, some guests was putting their shoes outside of their rooms to get shined. They looked at me as they were about to place them on the floor by their door, and quickly grabbed them back. I started singing, "I got shoes, you got shoes, all God's children got shoes." The door slammed with direct intention. Two days passed and I tried to get some news about the fire in New York but there was nothing here about it. I picked up my birth certificate and immediately caught a train to Miami. Once there I went down to a few marinas and spoke with several boat owners and some arriving voyagers. I told one man who worked there that I was looking to go Deep Sea fishing (no pun intended) with a group of people. I said that these were show-business folks and needed a good boat at a fair price. He asked me who was the star involved. I told him it was for my brother Buck Wheat; I was his half-brother, Kareema Wheat.

He said, "Wow, I know him, seen all his movies." I was still looking over my shoulder, reading everything I could get my hands on. I still wanted to get whatever information I could get about the fire in New York. Once again, I was on the run for something I didn't do; the difference this time was I wasn't going to internalize it and punish myself. This time I was ready to try to move on. I knew I had to kill all aspects of Robby and purge his greed and need to get over out of my system. I knew better, but I now had to try to live better. I also thought that the FBI couldn't be that stupid to think I would go to the dock and wait with Jasper then set the place on fire. I also was aware that being stupid wasn't a good defense in any situation. It hit me that this logic was just another lie to help me feel good. Then it hit me like a lightning bolt, the fact that I was just like my father, much more successful but the same mind-set.

Later I secured passage on a sightseeing cruise ship, which was not part of the unions ships; this was an illegal gambling junket leaving the next morning, going to Nassau. It was a two-day cruise leaving the following day. My plan was to get there and then hire a private boat to Jamaica, Barbados, or Cuba. I just wanted to be alone that night and leave without any fanfare. I was in bed watching television. As I was about to drift off, all I thought of was the fire and the setup. This was Frankenstein's answer to the ship owners and the FBI. The monster was going down with a bang. I felt an odd kind of pride; I must admit that I belonged to one of the most powerful unions the world had ever seen. I remember when I was younger I saw an old Abbot and Costello movie called *Abbot and Costello Meets Frankenstein*, and at the end they set the monster on fire on a dock. The monster was still defiant and threw a wooden bench at the fire as it trapped and engulfed him. I felt that this was what I was living in my reality now. Frankenstein throwing wood at the fire and saying, "If I die it will be my way." The fire was magnificent. I sat there thinking that I was lucky I left New York. I also thought that the fire was probably Marcus's work.

Yeah, I was pissed that I was set up and trying to come up with the best believable lie to validate my present predicament. There is an analogy about two men in a basement with a gas leak, and one man strikes a match to burn the other. Frankenstein used and discarded me, but I was happy to have been in the basement when the match that destroyed both of us was finally lit, I was happy the union would be paid back by the FIB for how I was used in the Frenchy caper. I dozed off, and the following day dressed in a bad disguise and got my dumb ass self on the ship. I remember the first day there. I wasn't doing any gambling or drinking; I nursed my suitcase. When night fell I walked to the top deck and began looking over the side at the dark, hearing the sound of the waves hitting the bow.

I may have had the golden touch but I felt like King MidAss; everything I touched turned to crap. Slowly the tempo of the waves synchronized with my heartbeat. Then suddenly on my cheek appeared the misty kiss that welcomed me home. When the clouds parted and the moon shone through, I looked up and saw the mistress. She remembered me, and I felt another sincere spray kiss on my cheek. I stood there asking myself, "Did I dream all that has happened, or did I really live the way I had?" In my twenties I thought I knew it all, I thought that all people were stupid. In my thirties I still thought that all people were stupid, but I now understood that you have to try to get along with some of them. I was approaching my mid thirties and realized that I didn't know anything. Everything I thought I knew was wrong. Life was about family. The boys in my neighborhood who migrated toward gangs and crime did so for a sense of family. I belonged to a family that was all about caring and sharing and in their way they protected me, yet I pushed them all away. The price I paid for the gang I joined, the union hall's protection, was a piece of my soul, but I thought for a still relatively young man the price that I paid to belong was still a nominal cover charge was a small price to pay in order to belong, as long as the FBI didn't catch me. I stood there looking over the side, and my most dominant thought with my world crumbling around me was, I was more thankful than hurt. Thank God Dell didn't kill that man. The worst thing that a hustler could be endowed with was analytical reasoning.

I thought about how, in spite of it all, God sent messengers to me, maybe not at the time I was most receptive to what they were trying to tell me, but I was thankful for the messenger farmers who brought the seeds to plant in my mind. I felt some growing as I looked out at the ocean. I thought that if I could make it to Jamaica, Barbados, or Cuba I would open a bar and try to live a sincere life like the many farmers God had sent to plant their truths in my mind. Maybe even reconnect with my family.

I wasn't sure if there was a real tear on my face, or if I was being abundantly romanced by Deep Seas mistress for the newly found realization that there are no shortcuts in life. A successful, happy life requires hard work and routine consistency. I looked out and thought, suppose everlasting life is all absolutely true, and millions of years from now the earth is gone, don't you think one of the most commonly blessed memories of the spirits will be the ocean? If a soul does indeed dream when it rests, would not the ocean be the most dominant? I used to think that seamen by the way they carried themselves all knew a sacred secret that one can only learn from the ocean. I now understood the secret, by now understanding myself. The secret is the patience learned and developed by the long voyages. It somehow manifested itself in one's aura. Patience with one's self while life's truths are unraveling because of age and life's experiences are indeed a blessing. I never got to fulfill my dream and go to college, but the self-education I received on the ships from my continued reading were indeed my salvation.

EPILOGUE

The Hierarchy of the Union in New York City was dissolved in the late '60s. Although they were intensely investigated by the FBI, no one was ever indicted. There has not been a United States registered passenger ship in the United States since.

Robby made it and retired to Jamaica where he remained loyal to his reading and quest for knowledge until his death in 1999.

ABOUT THE AUTHOR

Born and raised in New York City. Growing up in Manhattan he became an authority on the best ways of not wasting one's life and taking full advantage of every opportunity afforded. Marty R. is a master of analytical reasoning. He has worked as a professional actor singer and model. He wanted to "write something that means something" so that the reader will care about and understand the character and how intelligence faith and a positive attitude is the only way out of most bad situations.

www.ingramcontent.com/pod-product-compliance
Lightning Source LLC
LaVergne TN
LVHW041756060526
838201LV00046B/1021